IAN HAMILTON has had a range of careers over the span of his life, from journalist to diplomat, but it wasn't until a health scare that he sat down to write his first novel. Ava Lee was the heroine that came to him and so the series was born. But before Ava, Hamilton's journalism was featured in *Maclean's, Boston* magazine, *Saturday Night Magazine,* the *Leader-Post* (Regina, Canada), the *Calgary Albertan,* and the *Calgary Herald.* He has traveled the world as an international businessman, exposing him to many of the exotic locations that feature vividly in the Ava Lee series. He lives in Burlington, Ontario, with his wife, Lorraine. He has four children and seven grandchildren.

www.ianhamiltonbooks.com

Also by Ian Hamilton

The Disciple of Las Vegas

THE WILD BEASTS OF WUHAN

AN AVA LEE NOVEL

IAN HAMILTON

Picador

———

New York

THE WILD BEASTS OF WUHAN. Copyright © 2012 by Ian Hamilton. All rights reserved. Printed in the United States of America. For information, address Picador, 175 Fifth Avenue, New York, N.Y. 10010.

www.picadorusa.com
www.twitter.com/picadorusa • www.facebook.com/picadorusa
picadorbookroom.tumblr.com

Picador® is a U.S. registered trademark and is used by St. Martin's Press under license from Pan Books Limited.

Design by Alysia Shewchuk

For book club information, please visit www.facebook.com/picadorbookclub or e-mail marketing@picadorusa.com.

Library of Congress Cataloging-in-Publication Data

Hamilton, Ian, 1946–
    The wild beasts of Wuhan : an Ava Lee novel / Ian Hamilton.—First U.S. edition.
        pages cm
    Originally published in Canada by Spiderline, 2012.
    ISBN 978-1-250-03515-8 (paper over board)
    ISBN 978-1-250-03229-4 (paperback)
    ISBN 978-1-250-03230-0 (e-book)
    1. Lee, Ava (Fictitious character)—Fiction.   2. Women accountants—Fiction.
3. Forensic accounting—Fiction.   4. Elite (Social sciences)—China—Fiction.
5. Painting—Forgeries—Fiction.   6. Art dealers—Fiction.   I. Title.
    PR9199.4.H3564W55 2013
    813'.6—dc23

                                                                                                2012043257

Picador books may be purchased for educational, business, or promotional use. For information on bulk purchases, please contact Macmillan Corporate and Premium Sales Department at 1-800-221-7945 extension 5442 or write specialmarkets@macmillan.com.

Originally published in Canada by Spiderline, an imprint of House of Anansi Press, Inc. Reprinted by arrangement of House of Anansi Press, Inc., www.houseofanansi.com.

First U.S. Edition: July 2013

10   9   8   7   6   5   4   3   2   1

For Jill, Ian, Stephanie, and Alexis

THE
WILD BEASTS
OF
WUHAN

AVA LEE SAT ON A BENCH ON THE OTROBANDA SIDE of Willemstad, the capital city of Curaçao, watching ships from China, Indonesia, Panama, and the Netherlands come and go. The crews stood by the railings, waving down at the onlookers as their vessels moved almost rhythmically in and out of St. Anna Bay. Ava waved back.

It was mid-afternoon. She had arrived that morning on a cruise ship that was moored about a kilometre away, at a fort that had once guarded the entrance to the harbour. The fort had been converted into a tourist spot with restaurants, shops, a hotel, and a casino.

She was on vacation with her family: her father, her mother, and her older sister, Marian, who had also brought her husband, Bruce, and their two daughters. They were eight days into the trip, with six to go. Ava wondered if they would survive the long journey back to Miami.

The Lees were not a traditional family by Western standards. Ava's mother, Jennie, was the second wife of Marcus. Following tradition, he had married her without divorcing his first wife. They had lived in Hong Kong until Ava was two and Marian four, when Marcus had taken on a third wife. The new family dynamic had caused friction between Marcus and Jennie, so she and her daughters had been relocated to Canada. It was an arrangement that suited them both. He looked after all his families financially, spoke to Jennie every day by phone, and visited her for two weeks every year. Although Ava and Marian had grown up without the physical presence of their father, they knew that Marcus loved them. So, traditional or not, their time together was enjoyed, if only because everyone knew the rules and had the appropriate expectations.

This cruise, though, was a first. Marcus's visits usually consisted of a stay at Jennie's house north of Toronto, lunches and dinners with her and Ava, and a two-day trip to Ottawa to see Marian and the girls. The extended holiday had been Marcus's idea; the cruise, Marian's. In hindsight, Ava thought they should have known better. It hadn't taken long for discord to surface.

The main combatants were Jennie and Bruce. Bruce was a *gweilo*, a Westerner, and a senior civil servant with the Canadian government. But the fact that he wasn't Chinese wasn't the issue; it was the kind of *gweilo* he was — uptight and anal. The kind of person who got up early to secure deck chairs for the day. The kind who pre-organized a full day of activities at every port of call. The kind who made sure to use every facility and perk offered by the cruise. The kind who had to be in line at five forty-five for a six-o'clock dinner.

Marian and the girls were used to Bruce's ways and didn't think twice about it. Marcus and Ava had rolled with the punches for the first few days before politely begging off some of the group activities. But from the moment she stepped on the ship, Jennie Lee had refused to fall in line. She declined to go on any of Bruce's planned excursions, and she arrived later and later for every lunch and dinner. She never came to breakfast, being too tired from late nights at the gaming tables.

By day three, Bruce and Jennie had stopped talking. He had taken to glaring at her and she pretended he didn't exist. It was hard on Marian, and Ava felt sorry for her. Marian had always had a more difficult relationship with their mother than Ava did.

"Why did she come?" Marian demanded.

"What choice did she have? Daddy wanted to take us on a family holiday and you talked him into booking the cruise without discussing it with her first. Did you expect her to stay in Toronto for the two weeks of the year she has with her husband?"

"I thought it would be different."

"It's never different with her, or with Bruce," Ava said. "So don't make it one-sided. Neither of them is easy."

When they berthed at Willemstad, Bruce had organized a tour of Curaçao; a driver was waiting for them at the dock. Jennie didn't show. Marcus went on the tour, grudgingly. Ava had said she wanted to spend a quiet day in town.

She shifted on the bench and gazed at the Queen Emma Bridge, which connected the Otrobanda and Punda quarters of the city. Willemstad was a busy commercial port — Curaçao was a major oil refiner and exporter — and the bridge was in constant motion, opening and closing for vessels coming in and out of the harbour. She looked across the bay, admiring the rows of two- and three-storey stucco buildings painted in pastel blues, greens, and yellows, all of them topped with red tile roofs. The tiles had originally served as ballast on the ships that had brought Dutch settlers to the Caribbean in the seventeenth century. Ava felt as if she were in Amsterdam, in one of the old neighbourhoods built on the canals.

The cruise had come after a two-month break from chasing bad debts halfway around the world. Chasing bad debts was what Ava, a forensic accountant, did for a living, and after back-to-back jobs that had taxed her both physically and emotionally, she had needed some time off. She had spent time with friends, danced at salsa clubs, eaten more than she should, burned off the extra calories by running, eaten some more, and gone to her regular bak mei workouts. She had also been exploring a growing relationship with a Colombian woman named Maria Gonzalez.

Maria was an assistant trade commissioner at the Colombian consulate in Toronto, a newcomer to the city. Ava's best friend, Mimi, had met her at a function and done some matchmaking via email. The two women had connected while Ava was travelling, and when she flew home, Maria was waiting for her at the airport. The physical attraction had been instantaneous. Emotionally, Ava was still feeling tentative. She and Maria had vacationed in Thailand for two glorious weeks, and they had managed to end every day wanting to see each other the next. When they got back to Toronto, Maria had begun to hint that they move in together. Ava was relieved that the cruise would give her some breathing space.

The sun was higher in the sky now and the pastel buildings glistened in its light. She got up and walked towards

Kura Hulanda, a hotel, conference centre, and museum complex that Dutch businessman and philanthropist Jacob Gelt Dekker had created out of what were originally the city's slums. The original street layout, including the cobblestones, had been kept intact. The old housing had been demolished, and colourful new stucco and wooden houses had been built that now functioned as stand-alone hotel units.

Ava headed for the Kura Hulanda Museum, which was famous for a collection that described the history of the slave trade. The museum was made up of several low-lying buildings linked in an L shape; its dark painted walls and small windows made the edifice look gloomy.

She walked through the galleries, admiring the sculptures, masks, weapons, and descriptions of the societies and cultures of West Africa. All the exhibits were drawn from Dekker's private collection. The final section of the museum presented the two-hundred-year history of the Dutch slave trade. Curaçao had been an auction centre for slaves sold into the Caribbean and all of South America. *Kura hulanda* was a Papiamentu term meaning "Dutch courtyard." As Ava walked out the front door of the museum, she found herself standing in just such a courtyard, on the very spot where hundreds of thousands of enslaved people had been bought and sold. She shuddered.

She walked back into the bright sunlight and crossed the Queen Emma Bridge over the harbour to Punda. There she found an outdoor Italian restaurant and ordered a glass of Pinot Grigio and a plate of spaghetti *aglio e olio*.

She recognized an elderly couple from the cruise sitting at the next table. The woman kept looking at her until Ava finally said hello. They introduced themselves as Henry and Bella from Singer Island, Florida, via New York. "I've seen you on the ship with your family. So attractive, all of you," Bella said.

Ava smiled. "Thank you."

"Your mother's name is Jennie, right?"

"It is."

"I thought so. Such a pistol! She and I close the casino most nights," Bella said. "What are you doing this afternoon?"

"I don't have any plans," Ava said, digging into her spaghetti, which had just arrived.

"Henry and I are going to the Snoga Synagogue. It's the oldest synagogue in the western hemisphere." She turned to her husband. "Henry, when was it built?"

"Sixteen something."

"In the sixteen hundreds. Crazy, huh?"

"Sephardic Jews from Amsterdam," Henry said. "They modelled it after the Esnoga Synagogue there."

"It's not far from here," Bella said. "Would you like to join us? It'll be interesting."

Ava was in theory a Roman Catholic. She had been raised in the Church and her mother and sister were still devout. But in her mind the Church had rejected her with its views on homosexuality. She now preferred to think of herself as a Buddhist — live and let live. But she couldn't explain why she still prayed to St. Jude in times of crisis and wore a gold crucifix around her neck.

"Sure, why not?" Ava said.

They paid their bills and left the restaurant. After walking past stores, cafés, and small office buildings, they stopped outside a bright gold stucco building. It was three storeys high, with a red tile roof; the windows and double doors were painted white. Henry and Bella led her into an inner courtyard, where they were greeted by a woman seated at a table.

"The synagogue is there to the right," the woman said. "It was built in 1692, and some additions were made in 1732."

Henry and Bella walked tentatively towards the entrance, Ava trailing behind them. As they stepped inside, she heard them gasp. Ava peered over Bella's shoulder and saw an almost perfect jewel box of a building. A straight line from the doorway led to a wooden pulpit at the opposite end; along either side of the aisle were rows of dark wooden benches. Just above, balconies ran down both sides, and four marble columns extended upwards to an arched ceiling from which hung three huge chandeliers.

They took several steps into the synagogue. As she entered, Ava noticed that Henry and Bella's eyes were transfixed by the floor. She looked down and saw that it was covered entirely in thick white sand.

She watched as Bella and Henry pressed their feet into the sand. Then Bella began to cry. Henry put his arm around her shoulders and started to sob as well. Ava didn't know why they were crying, but she felt their emotion all the same.

"The sand is the Sinai Desert," Henry said. "They brought it here to remind them of Sinai." He kneeled, picked up a handful, and pressed it to his lips.

"This isn't common?" Ava asked softly.

"There's maybe one other synagogue in the world with a floor like this," he said.

Ava was about to follow Henry and Bella farther into the synagogue when her phone rang. She apologized and excused herself, stepping outside. "Ava Lee," she answered.

"Ava, it is Uncle."

Uncle was her partner and mentor; they had been in the debt collection business together for more than ten years. He was in his seventies, but he showed no signs of slowing down and still maintained a massive network of contacts that provided them with business and support. It was a common rumour that in his past life he had ties to the triads. Ava didn't know for certain; she had only the deepest respect for the man she knew.

"Uncle," she said, glancing at her watch. It was two a.m. in Hong Kong, and he was usually asleep well before that. "You're up late."

"Am I disturbing you?"

"I'm in Curaçao. I'm sightseeing."

"Still on that cruise?"

"Yes."

"Can you talk?"

"Sure."

"Are you ready to come back to work?"

She took a deep breath. "That depends on what you have. I have no interest in chasing after some scumbag from General Santos City who cheated people with tuna sashimi that's been gas-flushed twenty times."

"So you are ready."

"What do you have?"

"How soon can you get to Hong Kong?"

"Uncle, is it that important?" she asked, knowing already that it probably was.

"Wong Changxing."

"The Emperor of Hubei?"

"He hates being called that. Even if it is said respectfully, he worries that it is offensive to the government and military officials whose support he needs."

"I'm sorry. Do you know him from Wuhan?"

Uncle had been born in Wuhan, the capital of Hubei province. He had escaped the Communist regime and fled to Hong Kong when he was a young man, but he still maintained close ties there and had built a big enough reputation that his Wuhan roots were a source of pride to many people who lived there. "He knows me from Wuhan," Uncle said.

"Ah."

"He has a problem."

"What is it?"

"I am not sure, but he sounded distressed."

"Something personal?"

"Certainly pressing, if I read his manner correctly."

"So it's urgent?"

"He asked us to come to Wuhan to talk. He offered to pay our expenses and a fee of fifty thousand dollars for our time."

"I'm still on the cruise for another week."

"He said he needs to see us as soon as possible."

"You mean, Uncle, that he needs to see you."

"No, Ava. He was very specific that you come with me."

"How does he know —"

"That does not matter. He does."

"The cruise —"

"When he says as soon as possible, he does not mean a week from now."

Ava paused. The idea of working for Wong Changxing intrigued her, and if her father hadn't been on the cruise she wouldn't have hesitated to leave for Hong Kong. But she couldn't abandon him so easily. "I'll have to talk to my father," she said.

"He is a man who has always understood the demands of business," Uncle said.

"Perhaps, but I still need to talk to him, and I can't assume he'll be that understanding. So let me call you back."

"I will wait up."

She called her father's cellphone, which he answered on the first ring. She could hear kids shouting and water splashing in the background.

"Can you talk?" she asked.

"I'm at a dolphin sanctuary, or show, or something. Bruce paid several hundred dollars so that he, Marian, and the girls could swim with the dolphins. They're in the water now. I'm supposed to be taking pictures."

"Something has come up," she said.

"Business?"

"Yes, I just got a call from Uncle. He wants me to go to Hong Kong right away."

Her father had heard the rumours about Uncle's past and was quietly disapproving about her association with him. "Is it that important?"

"Wong Changxing."

"The Emperor of Hubei."

"I'm told we shouldn't refer to him as that."

"It doesn't change the fact that he's the most powerful man in the province."

"No matter, he's asked us to go to Wuhan for a meeting.

I asked if Uncle could go alone, and he said Wong specifi-cally requested that I accompany him."

"And you're calling me to ask for permission."

"Yes."

"You don't have to."

"Yes, I do. This is your holiday, and if you think that my absence will cause any disruption I won't go."

"This holiday was the worst idea —"

"I've spoken to Marian about Bruce."

"And I've spoken to your mother."

"Two immovable forces."

"Bruce is a bureaucrat, professionally and personally. Your mother is every bureaucrat's nightmare. He wants a plan for everything and your mother can't think past her next meal."

"So do you need me? Do you want me to stay?"

"No, you go," he said quickly. "I'll try to spend as much time as I can with Marian and the girls and hope time flies."

"I love you."

"Me too. Be careful."

Ava went inside the synagogue to say goodbye to Henry and Bella. They were sitting on one of the benches, their eyes closed. She left as quietly as she could and made her way back to the ship to look for Jennie Lee.

She found her mother in the casino, sitting at the baccarat table with a stack of twenty-five-dollar chips in front of her.

"I have to leave," Ava said. "Uncle just called. We have a client in Wuhan who needs us."

"No."

"Yes."

"Your father won't be happy."

"I spoke to him first and asked his permission. He told me to go."

Her mother shook her head. "You can't leave me alone with them."

"Marian and the girls love you to death. And Daddy is still here."

"You are the only one who understands me."

You mean who tolerates you, Ava thought. "That's not true," she said.

"Stay until we get back to Miami."

"I can't. It's a crisis."

Her mother stared at her. When Ava didn't capitulate, she said, "I think Bruce may try to throw me into the sea somewhere between here and Miami."

"He probably thinks the same of you."

Her mother continued playing while she talked to Ava, her stack growing larger as she doubled her bet on the banker. When she won, she doubled her bet again, with success. "I suppose I can't stop you from leaving, can I?"

"No."

"Well, have a safe trip and call me whenever you can."

"I need you to do something for me," Ava said.

"What?"

"My clothes — I brought this ridiculous suitcase with me and I have all these clothes that I can't wear anywhere else. Can you take them back to Toronto for me?"

"What will you wear?"

"I'll take my running gear, some T-shirts, my toiletries, and some jewellery. I'll throw everything in my carry-on. I can buy some business clothes when I get to Hong Kong. I need some new things anyway."

Her mother sighed and passed her room key to Ava. "Leave your case in my room."

Ava leaned over to kiss her mother on the forehead.

"Be careful," Jennie said.

Ava went to her room and turned on her laptop. She found a flight that landed at eight a.m. in Hong Kong with a stop in Newark. She booked it and then called Uncle. He didn't react when she told him she was coming, and she knew he had probably expected nothing less.

"There is an early Dragonair flight from Hong Kong to Wuhan," he said.

"No, Uncle, I'm sorry. I have no business clothes with me and I need to shop. See if you can book something for later in the day."

"Where do you want to shop?"

"There's a Brooks Brothers store in Tsim Sha Tsui," she said, knowing that his Kowloon apartment was no more than ten minutes from the popular shopping district and tourist destination.

"I will send Sonny to meet you at the airport. He will take you wherever you need to go. Wong will have to wait." Uncle paused. "I hear that his wife is very attractive and a real power in their business. They should know that we have the whole package too."

THERE WAS NO WI-FI AT CURAÇAO'S HATO AIRPORT
but there was an Internet café, where Ava bought fifteen
minutes of time. She emailed Mimi to let her know about
her change in plans. The two women had been friends since
meeting at Havergal College, a private girls' high school in
Toronto, and there wasn't much they didn't know about
each other.

In recent months Ava had had some worries about their
friendship. Mimi had fallen in love with Derek Liang, Ava's
best male friend and at times associate, when she needed
the extra muscle. Like her, he practised bak mei, an ancient
and lethal martial art that was taught strictly one on one.
Their teacher, Grandmaster Tang, had introduced them
to each other; they were his only two students in the discipline. Derek joked that the Grandmaster had dreamed
they would one day produce a baby he could turn into the
perfect fighting machine. Instead they had become friends,
and occasionally employer and employee.

Ava had inadvertently brought Mimi and Derek
together, not anticipating that the two would fall so hard

for each other. Within days of meeting they had moved in together. As it turned out, Ava's concerns about how their relationship would affect her friendship with Mimi had been unfounded. Mimi was as available and open as she had ever been. The only negatives were that Ava had to listen to Mimi's graphic descriptions of their sex life, and so long as they were together, she didn't feel she could ask Derek to work with her. Over the years they had confronted knives and guns and chains and even been outnumbered by three or four men. Now she didn't see how she could put Derek at risk, knowing how devastated Mimi would be if anything happened to him. *I can't*, she thought, and she closed her email by writing and give Derek a big kiss for me.

Ava thought about phoning Maria but sent an email instead. For someone who was so beautiful and intelligent, there was something almost heartbreakingly simple about the girl. When they were together, Maria was unfailingly buoyant, but the second that Ava left her side she was overwhelmed by waves of self-doubt.

"You need to have more trust," Ava told her.

"You don't understand," Maria said, her voice quivering. "I lived at home in Bogotá before I came here to Toronto. I have never been apart from my family, and my very Catholic family — especially my mother — would never have accepted my sexuality. So I led a life of secrets. I hid my true self. It's only now, living in a city where I'm anonymous, that I've finally been able to be open."

When Ava told this to Mimi, her friend said, "You need to give her more time. She's still learning how to be in a relationship."

"What scares me is her intensity. I'm not ready to commit to being a life partner."

"Has she asked you to be one?"

"No."

"Then enjoy her. Let things develop. There's so much to love about that girl."

Yes, there is, Ava thought as she sat at her computer and wrote:

> I have to go to Hong Kong and then China on busi-
> ness. I've been forced to cut short the cruise. I'm
> not sure when I'll be back. I'll email when I can.
> Don't worry, everything is fine. Love, Ava.

She left the café and walked to the departures gate to catch her flight to Newark. As a rule, Ava avoided American airlines, but there was no way to get out of Curaçao that made sense other than flying on Continental. She thought business class might be passable. It was — barely.

The flight at least landed on time, and once she had cleared Customs she boarded a Qantas flight that would take her directly to Hong Kong. Business class was only a third occupied and Ava had no one sitting next to her. She declined dinner, drank three glasses of Pinot Grigio, and then slept for the next eight hours. When she awoke, she ate a bowl of noodles and then debated whether to go online to research Wong Changxing or watch a Gong Li film. She opted for Gong Li.

The airline was screening both *Raise the Red Lantern* and *To Live*. She watched *To Live* first, quietly weeping three or four times during the movie. It was a powerful film, set in China during the tumultuous decades of the Cultural Revolution, that followed a land-owning couple and their descent into poverty. Li was at its core, her life a continuing tragedy that she bore with courage and tenacity. Ava couldn't help but think of Wuhan as she watched. It wasn't that long ago that it had been at the epicentre of the Cultural Revolution and women like Gong Li were going through hell.

Ava had never seen a Chinese actress as good as Gong Li, and *Raise the Red Lantern* only confirmed her opinion. Set in the 1920s, the film told the story of a young woman who becomes the fourth wife of a wealthy Chinese man at the head of a powerful family. In Ava's mind the story was timeless, and she never watched it without thinking about her mother. Her father didn't house all his families in a compound, but not much else had changed in terms of the essential relationship between the man and the women.

As the film ended, the plane began its slow descent over the South China Sea to Chek Lap Kok, the man-made island where Hong Kong's airport was located. It was an overcast day and Ava couldn't see the water below until they cleared the cloud cover. By then they were nearing land, and the ocean traffic was thick with fishing boats heading in and out, sampans that doubled as homes for families and their import/export businesses, and hundreds of ocean freighters sitting patiently offshore, waiting to be towed into Hong Kong Harbour to load or unload the containers stacked three and four high on deck. Kwai Chung Container Terminal was the largest port in Asia, and one of the largest in the world.

Ava was fifteenth in line at Hong Kong Customs and Immigration, and she knew that meant she'd be cleared in

fifteen minutes. One minute per arrival, that was the standard. Anyone who needed to be questioned was promptly
shuffled off so the line wouldn't be delayed.

On most of her trips to Hong Kong, Uncle met her in the
Kit Kat Koffee House, a Chinese newspaper or the racing
form open in front of him, an unlit cigarette dangling from
his lips. This time she walked into the cavernous arrivals
hall to see Sonny, Uncle's driver and bodyguard, standing
directly under a sign that read MEETING PLACE. She imagined he had been there for a while.

He was six foot two and weighed about two hundred and
fifty pounds, with a layer of body fat that made him look a
bit soft. Nothing could have been more deceptive. She had
never seen anyone who could move more quickly or be
as vicious as Sonny. Of all the men she had encountered
he was one of the three whom she doubted she could best
physically — the other two being Derek and Grandmaster
Tang. Ava had once remarked to Uncle that Sonny seemed
to lack imagination. Uncle said, "Imagination is the last
thing you want in a man like Sonny. He is reliable and does
exactly what he is told to do. That is all you should expect
and ask for."

Sonny wasn't accustomed to seeing Ava without Uncle,
and he smiled shyly when he caught sight of her. Ava blinked.
Seeing Sonny smile was a rarity. His dark brown eyes were
normally watchful, alert, full of menace, and his brow was
locked in a permanent scowl. She nodded at him and then
watched in surprise as he put his hands together in front
of his chest, bowed his head, and moved his hands up and
down. It was a sign of respect, a greeting to a superior. Ava
felt a surge of pride, and then slightly embarrassed.

The Mercedes S-Class was parked directly outside the terminal in a no-parking zone. The only other vehicles there were police cars. Sonny waved at two policemen as Ava got into the car, and she heard him yell thanks to them for looking after it.

She sat in the back, in Uncle's usual spot. "Where are we going?" Sonny asked.

"Ocean Terminal, Tsim Sha Tsui."

Sonny's phone rang just as they started across the Tsing Ma Bridge, which linked Ma Wan Island to Tsing Yi, the northwest corner of urban Hong Kong. The bridge had been built to move cars and trains from the city to the airport. It was almost a kilometre and a half long, and double-decked. The top deck had six lanes for cars, while underneath were two sets of railway tracks. Ava looked down on Ma Wan Channel, which connected the South China Sea to Hong Kong's harbour. It was a more than two-hundred-metre drop from the bridge to the water; the vessels that had looked so small from the plane didn't look much bigger from the bridge.

Sonny listened to the phone for a moment and then passed it to her. She didn't have to guess who was calling.

"How was your flight?"

"Good. I slept a lot, and then I watched Gong Li." Ava doubted that Uncle knew who she was.

"We are leaving tonight at five thirty on Cathay. That will get us into Wuhan at seven thirty. Wong Changxing said there is some kind of formal dinner, so do not eat too much today."

"Dinner?"

"It was already scheduled and we have been added to the guest list. I tried to beg off but I am finding he is a hard man to reason with."

What wealthy Chinese isn't? she thought.

"I had also booked us into a hotel and he cancelled the reservations when he found out. We are going to be guests at his house."

"Uncle, is that really a good —"

"I agreed," he said, cutting short her protest. "It is a very large house — more than eighty rooms, I am told, more like a hotel. Besides, he said the reason for our visit is in the house."

"Do you have any idea what he's talking about?"

"No."

And you didn't ask, she thought, knowing that he respected the old-fashioned courtship that went with establishing new business. "What time do we need to leave for the airport?"

"I told Sonny to pick me up here at three. You can come earlier if you want."

"Meet me for dim sum?"

"I have a meeting."

"Okay, but I don't need Sonny to wait for me while I shop. I'll send him away. I'll take a taxi to the airport when I'm done here."

"If you prefer, I can meet you in the Wing business lounge."

Hearing that name startled Ava. The last time she had been in the lounge, a former colleague of Uncle's had informed him that a contract had been put out on Ava's life. She was superstitious by nature. Still, it did remind her that the job had its peculiar challenges.

THE BROOKS BROTHERS STORE WAS ON THE THIRD
floor of the Ocean Terminal. It was early and the shop was
quiet. Two salesgirls began to fuss over Ava the second she
stepped inside. Over the past few years the level of service
in Hong Kong stores had transformed remarkably. In the
not-so-recent past it seemed that sales associates were hired
for their ability to ignore customers, and they were sometimes surly when asked for help. The Hong Kong–based
Giordano clothing chain had changed things by insisting
that the staff smile and welcome people into their stores.
The trend — and Ava thought Hong Kong had to be the
trendiest city in the world — caught on, and now you
couldn't walk into a brand-name boutique without being
smothered with attention.

Ava had been dressing in Brooks Brothers for years. The
crisp, tailored look fit the image she wanted to project as
an accountant, as a serious professional. At five foot three
and a hundred and fifteen pounds, she was lean and toned,
but her breasts were large for a Chinese woman — she was
among the small percentage who didn't need to wear a

padded bra. Her legs and bum were muscular from years of running and practising bak mei. She was almost perfectly proportioned, something she was grateful for. She had a particular aversion — even admitting it was odd — to women with long waists.

Ava hated the idea of being thought of as a sex object. So while she was working she dressed as conservatively as she could. And when she wasn't working, she wore Adidas training pants and Giordano T-shirts. Mimi often teased Ava, calling her preference for Brooks Brothers her "butch look." But there was nothing remotely butch about Ava. When she put on a bit of makeup, let her black, silky hair hang loose or wore it swept up with one of her collection of clasps and hairpins, and slipped on a slim-fitting skirt with a pair of black leather Cole Haan heels, she turned heads — male and female.

There were four Brooks Brothers stores in Hong Kong, but Ava knew from previous trips that this one was the largest and had the best selection of women's clothing. She bought three button-down, no-iron tailored shirts with modified Italian collars and French cuffs, in pink, black, and white with blue pinstripes. She also purchased two pairs of black slacks, one cotton, the other linen. The slacks came in three styles; she opted for the Lucia fit, a clean look without pleats or cuffs.

She was about to pay for the items when she spotted a pair of black alligator high heels. They were gorgeous: soft, supple, classic. Ava turned a shoe over to look at the price tag. They cost more than eight thousand Hong Kong dollars, over a thousand U.S. *What the hell*, she thought, *I'll expense them.*

It was almost noon when she walked out of the Ocean Terminal with her Brooks Brothers bags and another from Cole Haan with a pair of black leather pumps. She had two more shops to visit, but they were on Hong Kong Island, directly across Victoria Harbour from where she stood in Kowloon.

Ava walked to the Tsim Sha Tsui terminal and boarded the Star Ferry. The passenger load was light and she was able to find a seat near the front. Kowloon was the primary entertainment and shopping district in the Territory, but Central District on Hong Kong Island was where its financial and business heart beat, and its skyline reflected that powerfully. Directly ahead of Ava was Hong Kong's southern shoreline, a virtual wall of modern buildings and skyscrapers that ran for more than five kilometres. She could pick out the two International Commerce Centres, both over 450 metres high and among the ten tallest buildings in the world; the triangular peak of Central Plaza; the steel and glass angles of the Bank of China Tower; and The Center, sheathed entirely in steel and lit up at night in a varying spectrum of neon colours.

The two shops she wanted to visit were a stationery store a few blocks north of the Mandarin Oriental Hotel, and the Shanghai Tang flagship store on Pedder Street, only a few hundred metres farther. But as she exited the ferry, she felt hunger pangs. The Mandarin Oriental had a wonderful dim sum restaurant, Man Wah, on its twenty-fifth and top floor. It wasn't quite noon, so she decided to eat now and beat the lunchtime mob.

Man Wah was just getting busy and she managed to get a table near the back. Within ten minutes of her arrival there was a lineup out the door and down the hall. She ordered hot and sour soup, chicken feet, har gow, and baby bok choy in oyster sauce.

As she poured herself a cup of jasmine tea, Ava noticed out of the corner of her eye a man several tables away staring at her. When she looked up at him, he turned away. There were four men at the table, all in their thirties and dressed in expensive suits, two of them wearing designer glasses. The one who had been staring at her looked vaguely familiar.

Her soup arrived. She was picking up her spoon when she caught him staring at her again. For the next fifteen minutes they played what she thought was a ridiculous game of cat and mouse. She was about to walk over to his table when he stood up and walked towards her.

"You're Ava, aren't you?" he asked.

She looked up at him. "I may be."

"I'm Michael."

Ava looked into his face. It finally struck her. Beads of sweat began forming on her brow and her upper lip. She dabbed her forehead with her napkin as she tried to think of what to say.

"Dad called me this morning from the ship. He said you had left and were coming through Hong Kong to Hubei. I just never thought I'd see you here."

"How did you know it was me?" she asked, still dazed.

"Pictures. I've seen many pictures of you and Marian. You have very particular looks."

"Daddy has shown you pictures of us?"

"For years."

"I never knew."

"I'm the oldest son, so if anything happened to our father then I would become head of the family. He wants me to take that responsibility seriously, and that means acknowledging and accepting half-sisters and half-brothers and aunties."

"He talks to you about us?"

"Has he never spoken to you about us?"

"Actually, he has. And to my mother. But he's never shown me any pictures."

"Well, here I am."

Michael hovered by her table. He shared their father's distinctive thick head of hair, which he wore slicked back. His face was lean and fine-boned, and his eyes were slightly rounder than Marcus's — Jennie had told Ava once that Marcus's first wife, Elizabeth, had some *gweilo* genes — but they had their father's darkness, depth, and warmth. Michael wasn't as tall as Marcus, but he had the same lean physique.

"You look so much like him that I want to cry," Ava said. "It makes me jealous."

He smiled, the same easy smile her father used to win her over. "You look like him as well. Have you never been told that?"

"Now and then, I guess."

"And as for being jealous — well, my father thinks you can do no wrong."

"Nonsense," she said, blushing. "Michael, do you want to sit?"

"I can't. I'm with three colleagues and we have to head back to the office," he said. "But here, take my business card. My cellphone number and email address are on it. Call me the next time you're in Hong Kong. We can have dinner or something. You can meet my girlfriend."

"I'd like that, I think," Ava said, pulling out her own card. "You can call me anytime too."

As Ava watched Michael leave the restaurant, she noticed that he walked like her father too, erect, relaxed, confident. He turned at the door and waved to her.

Ava looked down at Michael's business card before slipping it into her purse. Despite what she had said, she could never imagine actually calling him. It was one thing to know and accept her father's other families; it was another to meet them.

Ava thought about her father. She knew that he talked about his various children with her mother all the time, and that Jennie Lee took almost as much pride in their accomplishments as she did in those of Ava and Marian. And lately Marcus had become more open with Ava, especially about her older half-brothers. On her last trip to Hong Kong he had spoken about them quite freely. She hadn't liked it at first but gradually began to realize he was trying to bring his families closer together. *Is he feeling his mortality?* She pushed the thought aside. She couldn't contemplate the passing of Marcus Lee.

Her phone rang. Ava saw it was an incoming Hong Kong number and for a second she thought it might be Michael. But when she answered she heard Sonny's deep bass. "Uncle told me to call you," he said, almost apologetically.

"I'm just finishing dim sum, and then I have two more shops to visit. Tell Uncle that I'm on schedule and that I'll meet him at the airport."

"Are you sure you don't want a ride? It isn't any bother."

"I'm in Central now and I'd rather not feel pressured to finish my shopping. I'll take a taxi."

"I'm picking him up at three."

"I know. I'll co-ordinate as best as I can."

"I have your bag in the trunk of the car. I'll wait for you at the check-in counter."

"Perfect."

She hung up and waved down the waiter for the bill. She paid, then walked out of Man Wah to finish her shopping.

It was three o'clock by the time Ava left Shanghai Tang with a new purse and a pair of deep blue enamel cufflinks with the words "good fortune" carved in gold Chinese script. When she left the store, she flagged a taxi, then sat quietly in the back looking at the city as the cab retraced the route Sonny had taken that morning. As they were crossing Tsing Ma Bridge, Ava took out the Moleskine notebook she had just purchased — something she used for every job she had ever taken, filling it with facts, figures, addresses, phone numbers, and a history of the job's progression. She opened it to the front page and wrote *Changxing Wong* in large letters across the top.

4

AVA ARRIVED AT HONG KONG INTERNATIONAL JUST after 3:30 p.m. to find Sonny standing by the Dragonair check-in counter, with her bag in one hand and an envelope in the other.

"Uncle has checked in and gone to the lounge," he said. "Here is your ticket."

She took the envelope. "You aren't coming with us?"

"I'm not needed."

Ava nodded, then went to a public washroom with her shopping bags and carry-on. She was still dressed in the training pants and black T-shirt she had worn from Curaçao. She knew she'd have to change but wanted to wait until she was in the lounge, where she could shower and have some measure of privacy. She removed her laptop and some T-shirts and underwear from her carry-on and placed them in the new computer bag. She then pulled the tags off her new clothes and shoes and packed them neatly into her Shanghai Tang "Double Happiness" carry-on.

Twenty minutes later, Ava was checked in, through security, and walking into the Wing lounge. There was no sign of Uncle. She sat in one of the large chairs dotted around the lounge and opened her laptop. She punched "Wong Changxing" into the search engine and found multiple entries that described the man almost as a folk hero. Wong was the son of factory workers, had virtually no education, yet had built an enormous empire through a combination of unrelenting hard work, determination, foresight, and smarts — or so the official line went. The government held him up as an example of the unlimited possibilities and success available to every Chinese citizen. Ava wondered what Uncle would have to say about him.

She looked up and saw Uncle at the entrance of the lounge. He was standing at the sign-in desk, his head barely visible above the counter. Uncle was, she assumed, in his seventies or early eighties, but he had the skin and hair of a younger man. He was about the same height as she was and weighed maybe ten pounds more. He was dressed in his usual uniform: a black suit and crisp white shirt buttoned to the collar, with no tie.

She walked to the lounge entrance to greet him. He smiled when he saw her, and then frowned when he saw how she was dressed. "You need to change," he said. "There is the dinner when we arrive."

"Hello to you too," she said, as she leaned forward and kissed him on the forehead. "I have my change of clothes with me. I was waiting until you arrived before going to the washroom."

"I just finished talking to Wuhan and it was on my mind," he said. He reached for her hand. "It has been too long between visits. I am very happy to see you, as beautiful as ever."

"Hardly," she said. "But give me a few minutes and I'll see if I can do better."

"And I will find us a place to sit."

In a private cubicle the size of the bathroom in her condo in Yorkville, one of Toronto's ritziest neighbourhoods, Ava showered, put on a clean bra and underwear, and then laid out her new clothes. It was her experience that most Chinese businessmen preferred the women they employed or did business with to dress conservatively. Ava chose the black cotton slacks and the more modest Cole Haan pumps, and offset the dark palette with her new pink Brooks Brothers shirt. It was bright but plainly cut and, buttoned close to the neck, it would look professional enough. Besides, given Uncle's monochromatic look she felt they needed a little colour. The Shanghai Tang cufflinks completed the outfit and contrasted nicely with her shirt.

Ava applied a light touch of red lipstick and black mascara and then sprayed some Annick Goutal perfume behind her ears and on both wrists. She freed her shoulder-length glossy black hair from the rubber band, brushed it, and then pinned it up with her favourite hair piece: an ivory chignon pin. The pin had come from the pouch where she kept her jewellery; Ava also took from it a simple gold crucifix, which she slipped around her neck, and a Cartier Tank Française watch. The watch was the most expensive piece of jewellery she owned; she liked the way it spoke to success and professionalism.

When she strolled back into the lounge, she could feel all eyes following her. She walked slowly, her head held high, her shoulders back — a woman full of self-confidence.

Uncle sat at the back of the lounge, sipping tea. Ava took

the seat next to him. He glanced at her and smiled. "I was going to have a beer, but I think it is best to save myself for dinner," he said.

Ava could see in his eyes how pleased he was with her appearance. She loved his eyes: lively, curious, probing. Ava had learned early on that Uncle's world was defined through his eyes and not through his words. "I was reading about Wong before you arrived," she said, a question more than a statement.

"I met him once, about fifteen years ago, when Uncle Chang and Tommy Ordonez wanted to build a cigarette factory in Wuhan," Uncle said. Tommy Ordonez was the richest man in the Philippines and Chang Wang was his long-time business partner and an old friend of Uncle's. He and Ava had just finished a job for them, recovering $50 million from a gambling swindle that had taken Ava from Vancouver to San Francisco, Las Vegas, and finally London, where she had found herself confronting a prominent U.K. cabinet minister and his daughter. "There were problems getting the right location, and then more problems with building permits and licences. I went to Wuhan to straighten it out and found myself dealing with Wong. His *guanxi* was impressive then. It must be stronger now."

"And what was he like?"

"For someone with his connections, he was friendly enough, and easy to do business with if you understood what his requirements were and complied with them. Of course, many people are friendly if you are doing what they want you to do. What was different about Wong was that he was not arrogant or boastful. Most of the new-rich Chinese, especially those from humble backgrounds, are vain and selfish. They have so much and everyone else has so little, and they cannot seem to help rubbing it in. Wong never took that path. He prides himself on being loyal to everyone who helped him along the way. I did hear, of course, that he is not a man to mislead, and that if you do, he never forgives and is relentless in getting revenge."

"The government?"

"He was respectful. He obeyed the law as much as was necessary. He did not embarrass officials with his wealth and power, and he did not, as far as I know, bribe them excessively. He exchanged favours, of course, but where he was clever was that his door was open to them and their children if they chose to join one of his companies. That was the carrot, rather than an envelope filled with cash, though I am sure from time to time that was needed too. So he has never been associated with any overt corruption, and the officials who have worked with him over the years have not had to worry about getting shot."

"Why does a man with such *guanxi* need us?"

"I do not know, but I am curious, and not many things make me curious these days."

"He seems to have his fingers in many pies."

"More than we could know."

"Toys, plastics, garments, computer parts, cigarettes."

"It is difficult to do anything in Wuhan without his assistance, and his assistance always comes at the cost of a piece of the business."

"What if you refuse?"

"Then maybe your plant does not get built or it takes longer than you thought and costs more. And then you might have problems with warehousing and transportation, because he controls much of that too."

"So Uncle Chang made him a partner in the cigarette business?"

"Of course, but as Wong explained — and he was right — making him a partner opened many doors. Chang got the land he wanted at a reduced price. Instead of waiting two years for a building permit, he had one in two weeks. The equipment he was bringing over from the Philippines cleared Customs, without a bribe, in half the scheduled time. And when the plant was running, Wong spoke to his friend the governor of Hubei, who spoke to his friend the mayor of Shanghai, and the cigarettes had an instant new market. And so on and so on. Wong is the kind of partner everyone needs in China."

"*Guanxi*," she said.

Uncle sipped his tea. "A man in business in China is nothing without family and *guanxi*."

"What kind of family does he have?"

"I was going to speak to you about that," he said slowly. "As I told you, we will be staying at his house, so you will undoubtedly meet part of the family there, and at dinner. He works from home and entertains there as well."

"I see."

"And he has surrounded himself with his family."

"How large is the family?"

"When I met him, he had a first wife with one daughter. She had been a teenage sweetheart, a factory worker. And he had just taken a second wife, the child of a business associate, a very smart woman who handled his money, and from what I have been told she still does. They have no children. I am told he took a third wife about eight years ago and they have two sons."

"They live under one roof?"

"They do, on separate floors."

"How difficult is that?"

"We will find out," Uncle said, as the lounge P.A. announced that their flight was boarding.

There was a long, winding line at the gate, a smattering of businesspeople, but the majority of the passengers were tourists being herded by guides waving umbrellas with coloured flags attached to them. Ava wasn't sure what the attraction was in Wuhan. She had been to China more times than she could count, but always for work. Her only trip to Wuhan had been a two-day blur of meetings in hotel lobbies and boardrooms as she tried, successfully, to convince a meat importer that the fact he had lodged a quality complaint about four containers of chicken feet didn't mean he could avoid paying for them, especially when he had managed to sell them all. It had been one of her first assignments for Uncle.

Her memories of Wuhan were as blurred as the meetings had seemed. The city was surprisingly big — more than nine million people — and like all major Chinese cities it was awash in construction cranes. Her most vivid memory was the shroud of dirt and dust from the building sites that melded with bus fumes and industrial smog. Many of the people she saw on the streets wore masks, which she had thought was unnecessary until she went jogging one morning. When she got back to the hotel, her lungs were sore, and when she blew her nose, black mucus coated the tissue.

She and Uncle bypassed the boarding lines and went directly through the first-class entrance. Wuhan was in Hubei province, almost in the centre of eastern China and a two-hour flight from Hong Kong. As soon as they had settled into their seats Uncle pulled out a racing form and began studying the Sha Tin race card. Ava closed her eyes and napped.

When she woke, they were over a large body of water and starting to make their descent into Wuhan.

"Lake Dongting," Uncle said. "When I was a boy, we would go there in the summer to swim and to watch the dragon-boat races. That is where dragon-boat racing began."

She knew that *Hubei* meant "north of the lake" and that the name of the neighbouring province, *Hunan*, meant "south of the lake," but she had never associated the names with an actual body of water.

Like virtually every city in China, Wuhan had a relatively new airport, and Tianhe International was one of the busiest in the country, serving the nine million people in Wuhan and the sixty million who lived in Hubei. It reflected the province's central position in China's economic life.

Ava and Uncle were met at the arrivals gate by a middle-aged man who was about the same size as Sonny. His large belly pushed out a blue Lacoste shirt to what Ava thought had to be its breaking point, and what little hair he had was worn long in the back and braided. Ava couldn't help but notice the tattoos that covered both his bare arms and peeked out around his collarbones. He bowed to Uncle and nodded at her.

"This is Tam," Uncle said to Ava.

Tam took their carry-on bags and walked them to a door that had POLICE written on it. He opened it and led them through a cavernous office to another door that led them outside. A Mercedes-Benz sat at the curb. The driver, who looked as if he doubled as a bodyguard, rushed to open the car's back door. He bowed so low that his chin almost hit his knees. "Don't make such a fuss," Uncle said as he slid into the back seat.

Ava sat in the back with Uncle. Tam was in the front, his body turned towards them so he could look at Uncle while he spoke.

"I have not been here since they built the new airport. How far are we from the city?" Uncle asked in Mandarin.

"About thirty kilometres, but Wong Changxing's house is only twenty kilometres away."

Ava's Mandarin was not quite as good as her Cantonese. She understood the nuances of what she heard, but her ability to speak the language was more rudimentary.

"Did Wong's people object when you told them you were coming to meet me?"

"Hmmm . . . they went on and on about how it shamed them."

"What did you find out about his problem?"

"Nothing."

"How can that be?" Although Uncle had asked the question gently, Ava saw that it stung Tam.

"We spoke to everyone we know, including some of his own people. No one can explain."

Uncle shifted his attention to the countryside that flanked the superhighway. "I remember when there were no highways here," he said to Ava. "Now Wuhan has more than Hong Kong, and dozens of railroads."

Tam nodded in agreement, looking relieved that the topic of conversation had changed.

Uncle turned back to him. "Explain to Ava about Wong's family situation. I am not sure I understand it completely myself."

"He has three wives," Tam began.

"We know the numbers. Explain the relationships, with him, among themselves," Uncle said.

"The first wife is from Wuhan. She was a factory worker and they married when they were teenagers, before Wong started to succeed. She is a simple woman, not very bright, and he soon surpassed her. They have one child, a daughter, who now goes to university in Australia. The second wife, May Ling, is also from Wuhan. Her father was an important man in the Party and she went to university in Beijing. When Wong married her, May Ling began to work in the business. She has a reputation for being shrewd and tough. People say she has as much, if not more, to do with the business's growth as he does."

"So she is still involved?" Uncle asked.

"Side by side. He does nothing without May Ling."

"I did not meet her when I was here."

"If you had, you would have remembered her. She looks like a slightly older version of —" Tam motioned his head in Ava's direction.

"Then why the third wife?" Ava asked.

"May Ling couldn't have children."

"He had a child."

"No son."

"So he went looking for a brood mare?" Ava said.

"People say it was May Ling's idea, that she found the girl working in Shanghai, had her tested, and brought her back here. Luckily she gave him sons."

"Do you believe that? What woman —"

"I believe," Tam said, "that the third wife was just for children. It is May Ling whom he still lives with. She is the real wife."

"All of them in the same house?" Ava asked.

"When he married May Ling, both wives had their own houses, but he found it impractical to run back and forth. So he built a house for the two of them, and then when the third wife came, he built a new one for all of them. The first wife lives on the second floor with her mother and father and some aunties. The third wife lives on the third floor with the two sons, her mother, a sister, and the amah. May Ling and Wong Changxing have the eighth floor."

"A house with eight floors?" Ava said.

"It is like a castle," Tam said.

"What's on the other floors?"

"I'm told the ground floor has a banquet hall, a theatre, and kitchens."

"And on the floors between the third and the eighth?"

"Offices? Rooms for visitors? I really don't know."

As natural as Ava found her own mother's relationship with her father, and her father's relationship with her and Marian, the idea of all Marcus Lee's wives and children living in harmony under one roof seemed impossible to her.

"I wonder what they want from us," Uncle murmured.

Dusk was settling as they drew near the city. The overhead highway lights cast a refracted glow, and it looked as if tiny fireflies were dancing in it. Ava looked more closely and saw that the light was playing on dense smog. Not even in the countryside could you get away from the industrial invasion. "Is the air always this bad?" she asked.

"It's worse in the summer," Tam said.

The driver turned off the highway before they reached the city limits. He drove down a two-lane road flanked on either side by factories. Ava saw the workers' residences and shuddered at their gloominess. Four identical twelve-storey buildings with grey concrete walls, no trace of colour, and rows of tiny windows designed for peering out rather than letting in light. All that was missing for them to look like a prison was a fence topped with razor wire. Outside, in the floodlit factory courtyards, life looked more pleasant. She saw people playing volleyball and badminton, groups of women chatting, makeshift barbershops, and of course ballroom dancing. Such dancing was the most pleasant and lasting image Ava had of Chinese cities. In the mornings, couples could be found dancing to a tune being coaxed out of an old phonograph in every park and factory courtyard.

"Wong's factories, most of them," Tam said.

They saw the lights of Wong's property some distance down the road. As they got closer, Ava could see that the mansion was set about a hundred metres back from the entrance, which was guarded by a tall, spiked wrought-iron fence. The car paused in front of the solid metal gate while the security cameras identified them. When it swung open, Ava gasped. She found herself looking at a replica of the gate of Tiananmen Square, the Gate of Heavenly Peace.

"It is an exact reproduction," Tam said.

"Let's hope the house is not a reproduction of the Forbidden City," Uncle said. "The plumbing there is not up to par."

Ava laughed. Tam looked as if he wasn't sure whether Uncle was joking.

As they passed under the gate, the Wong castle loomed in front of them. It was a traditional Chinese design, constructed with red brick and a sweeping green tiled roof. There were eight floors, each with eight large picture windows across the front façade, ten metres below those on the next floor. The scale and breadth of the magnificent structure conjured up images of the Louvre.

The Mercedes stopped in front of a wide stone stairway. Ava and Uncle climbed out of the car and found themselves looking up twenty steps, towards a set of red double doors flanked by enormous stone lions. The staircase was almost as wide as it was high. They started to climb, Tam two steps behind carrying their luggage.

The doors swung open. A man and a woman appeared and walked to the top of the staircase. Ava could feel their eyes following her and Uncle. When they reached the landing, the man took a step forward.

"Welcome to my home, Uncle," Wong Changxing said.

5

EVERYTHING ABOUT WONG CHANGXING IS NONDESCRIPT, Ava thought. Medium height, medium build, clean-shaven, hair neatly trimmed, and clear, inquisitive eyes. Take away the Armani suit and the Gucci loafers and he could have been any small businessman.

Wong May Ling was not quite so neutral. She was slightly taller than her husband, and striking in a pink and white wool Chanel suit. Her hair was pulled back tightly, exposing fine cheekbones and smooth, delicate skin. She had a small, pert nose and thin lips. Ava noticed that she was wearing hardly any makeup. She also wasn't wearing any jewellery, and Ava made a note to leave hers in the room.

The most striking thing about May Ling was her eyes. They were a deep, dark brown, almost black, an effect heightened by a touch of mascara. In Ava's world, Chinese women were, if not deferential, then often reserved on a first meeting, avoiding direct eye contact. But May Ling's eyes bore into Uncle's, and then they turned to Ava. She did a quick appraisal of Ava's clothes and then moved to her face. Ava stared back. May Ling didn't turn away, but Ava saw her eyes flicker and wondered what she was thinking.

"We'll have dinner in about half an hour. Unfortunately we have company tonight. It is an arrangement that was made some time ago and we couldn't cancel. You will meet some interesting people, though," Wong Changxing said. "Would you like to go to your rooms first?"

"Yes," Uncle said for both of them.

May Ling nodded in their direction, then wordlessly turned and left. "She needs to check on dinner," Wong said with a slight sweep of his hand, inviting them into the house. "My man will bring your bags. Your man can leave them here at the door."

Wong walked them to an elevator. "You will be staying on the seventh floor. Staff are there waiting for you. If you need anything, just ask. Dinner will be served on the ground floor."

When the elevator doors opened onto the seventh floor, two maids greeted Ava and Uncle and led them to their suites. Ava looked around the room, admiring the teak floors, the walls lined in soft, iridescent white silk tinged with pink. The bamboo furniture had plush cushions that matched the silk on the walls, and in the centre of the room was a solid oak four-poster bed that led Ava to assume the suite was intended for Westerners. She went to the window and looked out on a beautifully manicured back garden and land that seemed to stretch for about a hundred metres.

She turned away from the window and walked into the four-piece marble bathroom to freshen up for dinner, and to take off her watch. She was thinking about lying down on the bed when she heard a knock on the door. Uncle walked in and said, "Come to my room."

Ava followed him to his room. Uncle motioned for her to join him at the window, which looked out on the front of the Wong property. "Look," he said. "Those two are military cars. Generals, I would think. And those other two are government cars."

"I hope the evening doesn't turn into a food-and-drink binge."

Uncle shrugged. "What did you think of the Wongs?"

"He seems more passive than I would have thought. She seems the opposite."

"We will see."

The other guests were already in the dining room when Uncle and Ava arrived. There were seven other couples. All of the men were dressed in business suits while the women were dressed more elaborately, in evening gowns. Ava took in the cavernous room with its six-metre ceiling, white marble floors, and dark wood-panelled walls decorated with Chinese landscapes of the countryside.

Wong stood with his male guests at one end of an immense bar in a corner of the room. He waved at them and introduced them to two generals dressed in plain military uniforms, the mayor of Wuhan, an assistant to the governor of Hubei, and two executives from Wong's business.

Ava gravitated towards the women at the other end of the bar. The youngest looked to be in her forties. Aside from May Ling, they were all wearing floor-length designer dresses and dripping with platinum, gold, diamonds, and jade. The other women eyed Ava, in her pink Brooks

Brothers shirt and black slacks, with either suspicion or disdain.

"This is Ms. Ava Lee," May Ling said. "She is here to help us with a project."

A few of the women nodded at her while the others continued their conversations. Ava could feel May Ling's eyes on her again and was about to say something when their hostess said, "It's time to sit, ladies."

May Ling lightly touched Ava's elbow, guiding her to the enormous dining room table, and whispered, "It is General Pan's birthday that we are here to celebrate."

The general sat to the right of Wong, and Uncle to the left. Ava was directly across from them, sandwiched between two wives. At each place setting was a gold-plated Dupont lighter and a pack of Dunhill cigarettes. The women on either side of her lit cigarettes, and Uncle and most of the other men did the same. He looked at her across the table, a tiny smile tugging at his lips. *You are in China now*, he mouthed.

The meal was served with almost military precision; each dish was brought out to a side table and served at the exact moment when the previous dish was finished. It was a meal designed to show respect, a parade of the most expensive, top-quality food. Shark fin soup. Whole abalone. Jumbo prawns in chili sauce. Slivers of filet mignon. Crispy pigeon. Fukin rice. A live fish that must have weighed two kilograms was brought to Wong before being prepared. He tapped the fish on its chin with a chopstick. The mouth flapped up and down. *That redefines fresh*, Ava thought. To end the meal, long boiled noodles were served with sesame paste.

Four glasses were placed in front of each guest. One held cognac, another beer, the third wine, and the fourth *maotai*, a Chinese liquor made from fermented sorghum. Two servers with a bottle in each hand were in constant circulation behind the diners. *This is sophisticated China*, Ava thought.

Once all the courses had been served, one of the servers brought out a huge mango cake with one lit candle. A magnum of Dom Pérignon was opened and the group sang "Happy Birthday." Red pockets — small envelopes filled with cash — were passed to the general.

The Wongs invited their guests to retreat to the karaoke room. Ava sat quietly for an hour as the guests became increasingly drunk and more adventuresome in their song choices. Out went the Chinese revolutionary marching songs and in came Rod Stewart, Elton John, and Céline Dion. In the midst of a murderous rendition of a Joe Cocker–Jennifer Warnes duet, May Ling slipped into the seat next to her. "Come upstairs with me," she said, her hand sliding into Ava's.

Wong and Uncle had already left without Ava noticing.

They rode the elevator in silence to the eighth floor. "Over here," May Ling said to Ava when the elevator doors opened, directing her to the right.

Wong and Uncle were standing in the middle of a huge foyer, looking at a large glass case that showcased some of the most beautiful Chinese ceramics Ava had ever seen. Wong looked over at her, and Ava saw a tension in him that she hadn't noticed before.

"We started collecting these about fifteen years ago," May Ling said. "The paintings came a little later."

The other cases in the room were in small lit alcoves. They housed more ceramics, some earthenware vessels, and several small statues, many of Buddha.

"I don't see any paintings," Ava said.

"Come with me," May Ling said.

They walked through a door at the far end of the foyer and into a cauldron of intense colour.

Twenty paintings hung on the walls of a tiny room not more than six metres across. Its diminutive size seemed to add to the intensity of the colours in the paintings, none of which were Chinese. Ava felt as if her senses were under attack.

"Wong Changxing was in London as part of a trade mission and they were taken on a tour of the Tate Gallery. You've heard of the Tate?"

"I've been there."

"Well, he went and he fell in love."

"I don't understand."

May Ling pulled her towards one wall. "Have you heard of the Fauves?"

"No."

"It means 'wild beasts.' It was a French art movement at the beginning of the twentieth century. As you can see, the artists were in love with colour and were famous for their bold brushwork."

Ava walked up to one of the paintings and looked down at the signature. "Matisse?"

"Yes, these are all supposedly by Matisse," May Ling said. She turned and pointed to another wall. "And over there, André Derain, Georges Braque, Raoul Dufy, Maurice de Vlaminck, and, of course, our Monet."

"This is spectacular."

Uncle and Wong Changxing entered the room. Ava saw surprise register on her boss's face, while the tension she had detected in Wong's was now ripping across his.

"When my husband came back to Wuhan," May Ling continued, "he told me about the paintings he had seen and how much he loved them. He bought some art books, and though he couldn't read them because they were in English or French, he used to stay up at night, poring over them as if he was looking at pictures of his children. I started looking into the movement myself, and I began to share his passion for the Fauvists. It was the colour and the simplicity of the paintings that attracted him, and then me.

"I bought the first one — that Derain painting of the Tower Bridge in London — for his birthday. He was upset with me for spending so much money, but after I explained what a good investment I thought it would be, we decided to buy more. Our little gallery here became the largest private Fauvist collection outside of Europe.

"Our Chinese friends never saw the sense in it and didn't appreciate them. Among the Westerners, though, it changed their perception of Wong Changxing. He was no longer just another newly rich Chinese businessman, a man with no education, no breeding, no manners."

"This is such a beautiful collection," Ava said. "It does speak well of its owners."

May Ling exhaled and then seemed to struggle to catch her breath. "Except — many of these paintings are fakes."

Ava turned to look at Uncle. His face was impassive.

"Fakes?" Ava said.

"Yes, forgeries."

Wong Changxing opened his mouth as if to speak, but nothing came out. He waved an arm at the paintings. "Fakes!" he finally yelled, his arm rotating like a windmill, his eyes squeezed shut in rage.

"Can we go somewhere to sit and talk?" Uncle said.

May Ling looped her arm through Wong Changxing's. "Calm," she said.

They walked through the living quarters and entered a kitchen. It was a Chinese kitchen that could have been found in a hundred million homes: a small round table with four chairs, a standard fridge and oven, and on the counter a rice cooker and hot water Thermos.

"Your guests?" Ava asked.

"They'll sing and drink for another four hours," May Ling said.

"What happened with the paintings?" Uncle asked.

Wong Changxing banged his fist on the table.

"Calm," May Ling said again to her husband, resting her hand on his arm. She turned to Uncle and Ava. "It began when I bought the first one. I was ignorant about how to proceed, so I went to the art dealer in Hong Kong who helped us acquire our ceramics — they are genuine, by the way. I talked to him about the Fauvists and asked him to find me one. He called me in two months, saying he had located the Derain in a private collection in Switzerland and that it was ours if we wanted to pay the price. I did. When it got here, we loved it and we decided to buy more. I commissioned the dealer to do exactly that."

"*We* commissioned," Wong Changxing said.

"Yes, sorry, we did make the decision together. His name — the dealer — was Kwong Kan and his gallery was

near Lan Kwai Fong. We told him to call us whenever a
Fauvist painting came on the market. Over the following
years we bought the twenty you just saw. Braque. Dufy.
Matisse. More Derain. Vlaminck. And the Monet, which
cost fifteen million dollars. Then two years ago our dealer
died — cancer — and we took a break.

"Our collection was already impressive and, more
important, we loved it. My husband started every day
with tea, hot and dry noodles, and time alone in the
room with the paintings. But he was never really comfortable with the Monet *Water Lilies* because it was
clearly Impressionist. About six weeks ago we decided to
sell it. We had no idea how to go about this, so I called
Harrington's auction house in Hong Kong and told them
what we wanted to do. They sent an appraiser here to look
at it."

"A tall *gweilo* with no manners and bad teeth," Wong
Changxing said.

"He was just doing his job," May Ling said. "He spent
more than two hours with the painting and then he spent
another two hours on his laptop. When he was finished, he
told us he thought the Monet was a fake."

"How did he know?" Uncle asked.

"There was no record of it. It had never been catalogued
anywhere. And when he checked the provenance, it was fic-
titious," she said.

"Do you understand this?" Uncle said to Ava.

"Some of it."

"What did you do?" Uncle asked May Ling.

"I asked him to look at our other paintings."

"He did?"

"He spent close to a week here. I never knew just how much detail they go into, and how much detail is available."

"What was the outcome?"

"He was certain that ten other paintings were fakes, three were probably genuine, and the rest were problematic."

"What did you do?"

"We gave him a cheque for eighty thousand Hong Kong dollars and asked him not to say anything to anyone until we had a chance to investigate."

"He agreed?"

"He did, and so far he has kept his word."

"So where does this leave us?"

"We apparently have seventeen fake paintings that cost us more than eighty million U.S. dollars," she said.

"And a dealer who is dead," Ava added.

"And whose shop was closed when he died and whose records were destroyed by his family. I spoke to Kwong's brother last week, and he told me he didn't see the point of keeping all that paperwork when there was no more business."

"What do you want us to do?" Uncle asked, the difficulty implied.

"Find the people who cheated us," Wong said.

Uncle glanced at Ava. "Wong Changxing, you must understand how complicated this could be."

"Find them."

"Find who? The dealer is dead."

"He wasn't smart enough to do this on his own. He had help. He worked with someone who knew his stuff, some-one who orchestrated this."

May Ling said, "Actually, he may not have known they

were fakes either. Looking back, we made a mistake going to him. He was an expert in ceramics, not paintings. We — I just assumed he would apply the same degree of due diligence. Now it is obvious that he didn't."

"Who did you pay?" Ava asked.

"His company, but that means nothing."

"There are a lot of paintings. What if he was dealing with a lot of people?" Ava said.

"Then find them all," Wong said.

"Let's suppose I do, then what? How do I get your money back? They sold to the dealer and he sold to you."

"I don't need the money."

"What are you saying?" Ava asked.

Wong stared at Uncle. "You can make them pay in some other way."

"I'm an accountant," Ava said carefully. "My job is to find and recover funds that have been stolen. I'm not in the revenge business."

"I have heard that, from time to time, you employ unconventional methods," said May Ling.

"Not with any pleasure, only when necessary, and always as a means to an end, not as the end itself."

Wong turned to Uncle. "Is this your view?"

"Ava and I need to talk," Uncle said.

"We'll wait," Wong said.

"No, this is a very complicated business and it could take some time. And I have to tell you, I am not sure it is right for us."

"You are our best hope," May Ling said.

"We do not perform miracles," Uncle said, standing up. "So, if you will forgive me, we will go to our rooms and let you return to your guests. We can meet again in the morning."

Ava saw that Uncle's remarks did not sit well with Wong, but before he could speak, Uncle was already halfway out of the kitchen. She followed, feeling two sets of eyes boring into her back.

"Could you find the person — the people who did this?" Uncle asked when they were in the elevator.

"Maybe. But it's messy, old."

"Did Wong's request for retribution bother you as much as it seemed to?"

"Yes."

"He is no different than many of our other clients. They all feel the same; they just can't bring themselves to say it."

"Is that why he brought us here? Because he thinks that's what we do?"

"He probably had nowhere else to turn," Uncle said, side-stepping her question.

The elevator doors opened on the seventh floor and they stepped out into the hallway. "Do we really need to talk about this anymore?" Ava said.

"No. I will tell them in the morning that we have to turn down their project."

"He's a very powerful man. It isn't my intention to cause him offence."

Uncle shrugged. "Even powerful men need to be reminded now and again that there are things in this world they cannot control or command."

6

AVA CRAWLED INTO BED AND LAY ON HER BACK, HER hands folded on her chest. She found herself thinking about Michael Lee, and fell asleep with her mind full of brothers and sisters she had never met.

She woke with a start, a ripple of fear running through her belly.

"I'm sorry to come into your room like this, but I knocked and you didn't answer," May Ling said. She was standing about six feet from the bed.

"My God." Ava sat up. "What are you doing here?"

"I want to talk to you."

"Uncle said we'd talk in the morning."

"No, I want to talk to *you*. I don't want the men involved."

"I'm not sure —"

"It will take five minutes," May Ling said. "You've come all this way; give me five minutes."

Ava turned on the bedside lamp. May Ling had changed from the Chanel suit into black silk pyjamas. Ava looked at the clock on the nightstand; it was almost four a.m. She sat up, ready to move to a chair, but May Ling walked over and sat on the edge of the bed.

"I couldn't sleep."

In the glare of the lamp, Ava could see faint worry lines on her face. "Your husband?"

"He drank so much with the guests that he could barely get his clothes off before he passed out."

"What do you want?" Ava said.

"Are you always this direct?"

"I try to be."

"Good, me too. It saves time."

"So, what do you want?"

"You're going to turn us down, aren't you."

"Yes."

"I thought so. My husband was foolish to talk about revenge. It was disrespectful to you. But this affair has affected him in a way that I can scarcely believe."

"Such anger is common."

"No, no, this goes well beyond anger. I don't know where to begin . . . You know — I'm sure you know — he comes from very humble roots. He has virtually no formal education, his reading and writing skills are basic, and when it comes to the financial complications of our business, well, he is strictly a micromanager."

"Leaving the macroeconomics to you?"

"We are a team."

"You weren't always."

"No, he started without me and he did very well. He worked twenty hours a day, seven days a week, building a distribution business. It wasn't big but it brought him in contact with a wide range of people, and he had a talent for making clients like him and trust him. And because he never betrayed a trust, because his word was better than any contract, he became someone who people went to when they wanted to broker a deal but didn't want to be directly implicated."

"Like the military?"

"Yes, and Customs, and provincial government officials, and city officials. All of them used him, and they still do."

"The Emperor of Hubei."

"Yes, he is in many ways the line connecting all the dots."

"So what does it matter if he bought some fake paintings? No one will think any less of him."

"First of all, I am the one who bought them. I did it with his knowledge and approval, but I am the one who hired the dealer, negotiated the terms, and convinced him they were a good investment."

"I see."

"But they were his paintings, you can be certain of that. He was a bit embarrassed at the beginning, the idea of someone like him collecting fine art and specializing in something as abstract as the Fauvists. He never talked about it with our Chinese friends."

"What about the ceramics?"

"Those? That's what every successful Chinese businessman or official buys. Old Chinese plates, paintings, sculptures. Those people who were here last night, they all have houses full of them. No, the paintings were different. He was the one who first saw them, and he was the one — on his own — fell in love with them. They symbolized in his mind what he had become: a man of taste, of culture, a worldly man. They gave him a sense of self-worth that money alone could never do. And let me tell you, others began to look upon him in that way as well. I can't begin to guess how many Western diplomats, politicians, and businessmen have been to our house. Every visit starts the same: they expect us to ply them with liquor and food and then — their idea of our culture — sing karaoke with them. Well, we are always good hosts when it comes to food and liquor, but karaoke is for the Japanese and Chinese visitors. Instead we would take the Westerners upstairs to see our collection. Their reaction was always the same: they would be dumbfounded, and then impressed. And whatever opinion they had of my husband would never be the same again. What he especially liked was that many of these people stayed in touch with him because of the art, not the business."

"I think I understand a bit better," Ava said.

"A bit?"

"Yes."

May's eyes became more focused. "That's such a little word. I would have thought my husband's pain would be clearer to you."

"I have had less than fifteen minutes of actual contact with him."

"I have tried to explain."

"And I haven't spent that much more time with you."

May lowered her head. "It is still a little word," she said.

"I'm sorry. I meant no disrespect."

May Ling nodded. "I know I'm going on too much. The thing is, you need to understand how he felt about the paintings so you can understand how devastated he was when he found out about the fakes."

"So tell me more."

May Ling shifted and then looked up at the ceiling. "He said to me that it was like falling in love with a beautiful woman, courting her for years, falling more and more in love with her every year, until she finally agrees to marry you. Then, on your wedding night, she climbs into bed and you find out she's a man." She moved closer to Ava, then reached out and grasped her knee. "All I want you to do is try to find out who did this to him."

"For what purpose?"

"I could tell you it's because I want our money back, and maybe that is part of it, but mainly I need you to do it so I can help my husband get some of his pride back. He hasn't actually said it to me, but I know he equates those pictures with the image he has of himself. If the paintings are shams, then so is he."

"What if no one knows? What if you don't say a word?"

"He would know, and that's all that matters. He's the kind of man who could never show them to anyone again, because if he lied about them, he would be as fake as they are."

"Then let them be."

"He won't have any peace. Someone, some people some- where have made a fool of him. They took his dream and they mocked him. He is convinced that they talk about him, laugh at him — the Chinese ignoramus in backwater Wuhan spending millions of dollars on fake art."

"What if I find someone, or some people, who might be responsible?"

"Then get back as much money as you can. Let us pros- ecute them in a proper legal manner and expose them so they can't do this to anyone again."

"Are you just telling me what you think I need to hear?"

"No, I'm being sincere."

"But what about your husband?"

"We won't tell him."

"What do you mean?"

"You'll do the work for me. I'll pay you. He doesn't have to know. If you're successful, then I'll tell him."

"That's not how —"

"Please," May Ling said, squeezing Ava's knee again. "I feel responsible for this calamity that's fallen on my husband. I found the dealer. I encouraged my husband. I even pushed him at times to buy paintings he thought we should hold off on."

"But, Auntie, even if I do this I have to tell Uncle."

"I know he's a man who can keep a secret."

"And truthfully, I wouldn't even know where to start. This is so far out of my area of expertise —"

"You can find a way, I know you can. Will you do it?"

"I'm not sure."

"Ava, please, I need to absolve myself of the blame for this. Every time I look at my husband I want to cry," May Ling said, her eyes filling with tears. "Do this for me, please."

Ava looked into her face, searching for any hint of insincerity. All she saw was grief. "I still don't know where to start," she said.

"The man from Harrington's — go and see him. See if he can point you in some direction. I'll give you everything I have on the art dealer Kwong, his business, his family, his friends. Just spend a few days in Hong Kong and then decide. Do that for me. Just that."

Ava sighed. "Okay, I'll tell you what: I will go to Hong

Kong. But that doesn't mean I'm taking the job."

"I'll pay you anyway."

"No, I don't want anything from you unless we have an actual agreement in place. If I decide to take this job, then you can work out the financial details with Uncle."

"Thank you," she whispered.

"You can't say anything to your husband."

"I won't."

"And I'm not making any promises past Hong Kong."

"I understand."

"I shouldn't be doing this," Ava said softly. "You should know that I'm not hopeful."

May Ling touched Ava's hand. "My husband was the one who insisted on calling Uncle. When I found out, I was nervous. Uncle hasn't lived in Wuhan for many years, but people here know all about him. They take pride in a home-town boy doing well, even if his chosen profession doesn't always sit well with the authorities. I made some phone calls and was told that he had retired from the old business to start a new one, and that there was a young woman working with him whom he admired, a young woman who had special talents. So I told my husband he could invite Uncle here only if you came with him."

Ava nodded.

"They told me you were extraordinarily pretty. I admit I was surprised when I saw you, so plainly dressed, hardly any makeup, simple hair. Not what I expected, but very pretty all the same. When my husband saw you, he said that you reminded him of me when I was younger. I know he meant it as compliment, but no woman likes to be told that she's aged."

"Auntie, you're beautiful and very elegant."

"Stop calling me Auntie. It really does make me feel old."

"What should I call you?"

"May."

"May, you are very beautiful and very elegant."

She shrugged as if it was something she had heard countless times. "Ava, I would give up everything — *everything* — if I thought I could undo the harm that has been caused my husband."

7

AVA HAD DIFFICULTY GETTING BACK TO SLEEP AFTER May Ling left. Changing her mind wasn't something she did often, and she couldn't help but feel she had been manipulated at some level. The woman was shrewd, coming to Ava in the middle of the night to share confidences, appealing to her as a woman living in a man's world. *Well, what's done is done*, Ava thought. She had given her word and she would honour it. She'd spend two days in Hong Kong, and if nothing came of it she'd move on.

Uncle was an early riser, and the door to his room was open when Ava went to see him.

"Wong Changxing was here an hour ago," Uncle said. "I told him that we are not going to take the job. Tam is outside waiting to take us to the airport."

"May Ling came to my room last night," Ava said.

Uncle looked surprised, an infrequent reaction.

"She begged me to talk to some people in Hong Kong. I said I would."

"You want to take the job?"

"No, I would never agree to anything like that without

talking to you first. I just said I would do some investigating for a couple of days, no commitment beyond that. She was very persistent. It was hard to turn her down."

"Wong did not mention this to me."

"He doesn't know, and that's part of the arrangement. I don't want him to know; I only want to talk to May Ling. Uncle, if after Hong Kong I think there is something in this, some way to recover money, then you can negotiate our fee with her."

"Are you sure she won't tell him?"

"If she does, I'm gone. I refuse to be a party to some triad vigilante action." She regretted the words the moment she had said them.

"He was emotional," Uncle said.

"Still truthful, I think," she said.

"Perhaps."

"Uncle, I didn't mean to imply —"

"No bother," he said.

They rode the elevator to the ground floor, bags in hand. Ava was dying for a coffee but was even more eager to get away from the Wongs. There was no sign of either of them, just staff scurrying back and forth. "Is the mistress here?" Ava asked one of the servers.

"No, but she left this for you," he said, handing her a large brown envelope.

She opened it. Three pages of notes, names, phone numbers, a cheque for fifty thousand dollars, and May Ling's business card. On the back she had written her mobile number, her direct business line, and her private email. The word *private* was underlined. So were the words *Thank you. Love, May.*

She handed the cheque to Uncle, and everything else went into her Double Happiness computer bag.

They caught a Dragonair flight back to Hong Kong. Uncle returned to his racing form while Ava pulled May Ling's papers and her notebook from her bag. She scanned the documentation. Every painting they had bought was listed, along with the date and price and its supposed origins. The ones that the appraiser thought were genuine were marked with a black asterisk, fakes with a red one, and those in doubt with blue. Many of them had been plucked from private collections, others from galleries, none acquired at auction. *That should have raised some questions*, Ava thought. She did some quick math. The Wongs had spent more than a hundred million dollars on their collection, the Monet the most expensive, at fifteen million.

The appraiser they had worked with at Harrington's was Brian Torrence. May Ling had included his cellphone and office number. The office was on the Hong Kong side, in the Langley Tower on Queen's Road Central. That made her hotel choice easy.

Kwong's business was called Great Wall Antiques and Fine Art. He had been the sole owner and the business had been shuttered when he died. His brother had inherited everything. He had sold off the inventory, shredded the records, and made Great Wall history. *That doesn't mean there aren't records somewhere*, she thought. The Hong Kong Department of Inland Revenue would certainly have tax returns.

The flight was uneventful, and Uncle and Ava breezed through Hong Kong Immigration. She called the Mandarin

Oriental Hotel as they were walking out of the arrivals hall to meet Sonny, booking a room for three nights. As she did she saw Uncle glancing sideways at her.

"I have been thinking you need to be careful with this woman," he said.

"A couple of days, that's all. If I don't find anything, then that's it."

"She will have expectations."

"I made no promises."

"You know how selective some people's memories are. I do not want you to be the subject of recriminations."

"I'll be careful what I say."

"I would be happier if her husband knew," he said.

"Let me try it my way for a few days. That's all — a few days."

She knew Uncle wasn't arguing with her and that he wasn't about to tell her to change her decision. He just needed to let her know that he was concerned.

"*Momentai*," he said.

They saw Sonny leaning against the Mercedes, talking to a couple of policemen. He rushed to Uncle as soon as he saw him, grabbing the carry-on. The policemen lowered their heads in Uncle's direction.

"I'm staying at the Mandarin Oriental in Central," she said to Sonny as the car pulled away from the curb. "But drop me off at the Star Ferry terminal in Kowloon. I'll take the boat over to Central. That way you won't have to fight the Harbour Tunnel traffic."

"Hot pot tonight?" Uncle asked.

Ava hesitated. "I may work late. The sooner I start on this case, the sooner I'll get it behind us."

"That is sensible," Uncle said.

"I'll keep in touch," she said, kissing him on the forehead as Sonny eased the car up to the terminal entrance.

At just past one o'clock she boarded the ferry. It was a gorgeous day. Spring was the only season she had ever enjoyed in Hong Kong. The summers were oppressively hot and the fall was too often cold and rainy. The winters were perpetually damp, with temperatures low enough to make the chill seep into the bones. She was able to get a seat near the front but she moved back from the rail to avoid the odours wafting off the water. As the ferry churned its way across Victoria Harbour towards the Hong Kong shoreline, Ava watched the sun flicker off the skyscrapers, the light shimmering on black, silver, and gold glass. *What a marvel it is*, she thought for the second time in two days. People raved about the view of the harbour from Victoria Peak, but for Ava there was no better way to see it than from the ferry on a beautiful day.

When the boat docked, she walked across Connaught Road to the Mandarin Oriental Hotel. Entering through its front doors was like coming home for her. She was a frequent guest, and within five minutes she was checked in and had been escorted by one of the front desk associates to her room.

Ava quickly unpacked. She put her laptop on the desk, turned it on, and then opened her notebook, where she had copied the notes May Ling had given her. She found the phone number for Brian Torrence and dialled it.

"Torrence," he answered.

He can't be senior, she thought, *if he's answering his own phone.* "Hello, my name is Ava Lee. May Ling Wong gave me your number."

"I spoke with her this morning."

"Good. So you're free to talk to me?"

"Whenever you want."

"How about right now? I'm staying at the Mandarin Oriental. Your office is no more than a five-minute walk."

"Have you had lunch?"

"No."

"Me neither. There's an Italian restaurant on the ground floor of my building. Why don't you meet me there in about ten minutes? Ask for me, or just look for me. I'm tall, skinny, blond hair, and I'm wearing a navy-blue suit today."

"Mr. Torrence, did May Ling tell you why I want to talk to you?"

"There's only one thing it could be about," he said. "Truthfully, I found it a puzzling request."

"Why is that?"

"I've never heard of you, and in my field there aren't that many strangers."

"Well, I guess we'll have to remedy that."

8

AVA WALKED INTO THE ITALIAN RESTAURANT AND quickly found Brian Torrence. Even seated he seemed taller than the waiter who was attending to him, and his bushy mop of blond hair was hard to miss.

"Mr. Torrence," she said.

He looked up and smiled. *He's young, probably in his mid-thirties*, she thought.

"Call me Brian," he said, without getting up.

"And I'm Ava."

"Your accent — I can't place it. Certainly not Hong Kong English."

"I'm Canadian."

"The Wongs reach out to a young Canadian woman? The mystery deepens."

"I'm hardly mysterious."

"But you are here to talk about the paintings?"

"Exactly."

"Quite a problem."

"So it seems."

The waiter interrupted them. "I've ordered sparkling

water, unless you want something stronger," Torrence said.

"That's perfect."

"I recommend the antipasto, and they make a damn fine Caesar. And the brick-oven pizza isn't half bad."

"Then why don't you order for both of us," she said.

After the waiter had taken their order, Torrence turned back to Ava and said, "The first thing you have to tell me, Ava, is what do you know about this apparent mess we've unearthed?"

"Virtually nothing."

"So you aren't you in the art business?"

"No, I'm an accountant."

"I don't mean to sound rude, but why would the Wongs hire an accountant to help out with this problem? Do you have extra qualifications in the art field?"

"None whatsoever. I barely know anything at all about art."

He chewed on a breadstick. "I don't understand."

"The Wongs have been defrauded of many millions of dollars. My company specializes in finding out who did it and where the money is. We then do what we can to recover as much money as possible. It doesn't make any difference to us if we're dealing with computer parts, shrimp, textiles, or paintings."

"But if you know nothing about the art world, how do you even know where to begin?"

"That's why I'm here. You're my beginning."

"Ah, silly me."

"Do you have plans for this afternoon?" she asked.

"If I did, I imagine they've just changed."

"I like perceptive men," she said.

Their food came all at once and the conversation dwindled. Ava waited until the pizza was almost gone before taking out her notebook. "Can we stay here to talk?"

"I don't see why not. But if we do, I expect you to buy me something stronger than sparkling water."

"Whatever you want."

"They have a brilliant Chianti."

"Order away."

She passed on the wine, which didn't seem to bother Torrence. He downed one glass quickly and was halfway through a second by the time the table was cleared.

"I need to understand how it's possible for the Wongs to end up with all of those fakes. Wong isn't a stupid man. He isn't an art expert but he does seem to know a lot about the Fauvists. And then there's that man Kwong. They seem to think he may have had nothing to do with it, that he was as much a dupe as they were. So explain to me, how does something like this happen?"

"Something like this, as you say, happens all the time. Art galleries and museums throughout the world are filled with forgeries and fakes of all kinds — pictures, sculptures, antiquities — but not many people want to talk about it. No one wants to look stupid. No one wants to devalue their collection."

"Let's stick to the paintings. Wong Changxing wanted to sell the Monet, so let's concentrate specifically on that piece. When he bought it, why wouldn't he have known it was a copy? Surely there has to be a record of it somewhere."

"It wasn't a copy," Torrence said.

"What do you mean?"

"It was an original painting."

"I don't understand."

"Someone painted water lilies in the style of Monet. There is absolutely nothing wrong with that unless you try to pass it off as a Monet. Until it's signed *Monet* the painting is actually paying homage to the original artist; after it's signed, it's a fake and a criminal offence."

"In the style of?"

"Yes, like most of the rest of the Wongs' pictures."

"But when you say 'in the style of,' how many water lilies paintings are there?"

"That's where it gets a bit tricky. Many of these artists fell in love with a subject and painted and repainted it from different perspectives, different angles, in different light conditions. The artist Derain, for example, whom your Mr. Wong adores, painted the Tower Bridge and the other major London bridges ad nauseam. Monet did hundreds of variations on water lilies. So, what your clever forger does is find a subject that an artist has done several versions of and then adds one more. So it isn't a copy, it's just another interpretation of a familiar subject. Which he does well, mind you. A good forger gets into the head of the original artist. The colours, the kind of paint, the technique, the brushstrokes, the canvas — they are almost as one. And the Wongs, I have to say, have some absolutely top-class fakes."

"So no actual copies?"

"No. It wouldn't do to sell someone a painting that is already hanging in an art gallery. I mean, even the dullest of us would be able to figure out that a con was on."

"Okay, but if the Wong pieces are so good, how did you determine they're fakes?"

"This should quicken your accountant's heart: due diligence. Or, as we prefer to say, provenance."

"I understand that from a financial viewpoint."

"It's much the same when you're talking about a painting. There's its creation, duly noted by the artist; the assignment or sale to a gallery, an agent, or a patron, duly noted as a commercial transaction; then usually another sale or two — all of them recorded. And most times when there is a sale, you can expect to find authentication by a curator, an insurance appraisal, a condition report. They even look at the back of the painting to make sure the stretchers and nails are of the period. So no painting travels the world alone. They're all accompanied by bits of paper that attest to what they are and where they've been. It may not have always been like that, but I can tell you that in the past few hundred years it has been absolutely the norm."

"And Wong's paintings — what about their paperwork?"

"It was there. It was just bogus."

"How?"

"Your good forger is an intelligent person. He understands that the provenance means almost as much, if not more, than the painting, so he spends considerable time and effort creating facsimiles. Bills of sale, shipping documents, condition reports, authentication documents, letters between dealer and customer — he does them all."

"And what process do you go through to discredit it?"

"I should make it sound more difficult than it is, but in this computer day and age — and given that we're dealing with paintings that are hardly a hundred years old — it wasn't all that hard. I started with a catalogue of the artist's known works, a complete list, with pictures. As I said, there are hundreds of water lilies, but none that matched the one Mr. Wong owned. Now, it is possible — unlikely, but possible — that one slipped through the cracks. Maybe Monsieur Monet gave one to a chum as a gift and neglected to make a note of it; it does happen. So I burrowed into the paperwork.

"It said that this particular painting was consigned to a gallery in Zurich. There is no record of Monet's ever working with any Zurich gallery. No matter; the painting was supposedly sent to Switzerland. When I checked into the Swiss gallery, it turned out that it had existed but went out of business thirty years ago. Convenient, no? The gallery sells the painting two months later to a Herr Bauer, a Zurich resident. There's an address on the bill of sale, and it turned out to be the address of a bakery. Well, maybe Herr Bauer was a baker. So I kept ploughing on. Just before the Second World War, Herr Bauer sells the painting back to the gallery where he bought it originally. The gallery sells it again, this time to a Norwegian named Andersen, who takes it off to Oslo. Again the bill of sale is informative, but when I check on Mr. Andersen, I discover he doesn't exist or he gave the gallery the wrong address. And finally we have Mr. Andersen selling it through an agent to Mr. Kwong. I can't locate the agent.

"Aside from the consistency in discrepancies — and consistency is what I look for, mind you; anyone can make a bookkeeping error, but when they pile up, the notion of error disappears — I did a search to see if the painting had ever been exhibited anywhere. It hadn't. Now, we're talking about a Monet, not your brother Harry's watercolour that you might hang on the living room wall, and there's nothing more that art collectors love than showing off their collection. There isn't a museum or art gallery in the world that can stay fresh without loans from private collections. So unless Herr Bauer and Mr. Andersen were complete recluses, the odds are that the picture would have surfaced somewhere, sometime — Is this helpful?"

"Tremendously," Ava said. "Tell me, though, wouldn't it be quicker and easier just to send the painting to a lab for an analysis?"

"That is the last thing to rely on," Torrence said. His face was getting flushed, the Chianti taking its toll. "Your good forger knows his paints and, more important, knows his artists' paints. Paint can be aged, and canvases too. It isn't difficult."

"This is really quite interesting," Ava said.

"These are clever men."

"That leads me to Mr. Kwong. I know very little about him other than that he was a dealer whom the Wongs trusted."

"He was a ceramics dealer, and not half bad at it. He wasn't big time but he knew his stuff and had a decent enough clientele, nearly all Chinese, of course."

"So how did he get into paintings?"

"The Wongs asked him."

"He knew how much about the area?"

"From what I can gather, hardly anything. The Wongs seem to have been his only clients for paintings."

"So how could he locate and buy all those works?"

"Now that is the question, isn't it?" Torrence said, emptying the bottle into his wineglass. "How did he indeed?"

"Have you given it any thought?"

"A bit, and it seems to me he probably just tapped into associates here who referred him to some people in Europe or the U.S. It isn't that big a world, our art world. All he had to do was contact some of the major dealers and galleries, tell them he had a client who was interested in buying Fauvist works, and ask them to let him know if something came on the market. There's always someone interested in selling."

"How would he finance those purchases?"

"He didn't, I would imagine. He probably had some kind of commission arrangement."

"But he did the invoicing."

"He wasn't dumb. The last thing he would want to do is let his client know who he was buying from, and vice versa. You can be sure, though, that no painting arrived in Wuhan until it had been paid for."

"How did the real paintings get mixed in?"

"Kwong was obviously buying from a number of people, some of whom just happened to be honest. There's no way he was dealing with just one group or gallery."

"Could he have somehow orchestrated the fakes himself?"

"I don't think so."

"Why not?"

"There's the matter of the real paintings, and the questionable ones — I haven't ruled them out as real too. If he was reasonably certain he could cheat the Wongs without their figuring it out, why would he bother to send them a genuine Matisse and Dufy? It doesn't make sense to me. No, I think your man Kwong got in over his head. He was only too happy to be a scout for the Wongs and to take a commission from the other end. I'm sure he looked at the provenances supplied with the paintings, but that's about all he did. I'd also bet that he was doing business with some supposedly reputable companies, and that he was prepared to take their assurance at face value."

"Like which companies?"

"The real paintings were bought from three separate galleries, two in France and one in New York. First-rate firms. The questionable ones are more of a mixed bag. I recognize some of the names attached to them, but not all."

"The fakes?"

"Nearly all of them bought from individual collectors, sometimes through agents and some through galleries. The paperwork was always complete and always bogus."

"How would he have been able to contact all those people, or they him?"

Torrence threw his head back and then shook it as if it needed to be cleared. "My guess — actually, my opinion — is that none of it was random. There's no way that all those fakes could have found their way to Wuhan without some orchestration. I think you'll find that Kwong was working with an agent. So rather than hunting down Fauvist works himself, Kwong entrusted that job to the agent. You find that agent and you'll be on your way to finding your perpetrator."

"You make it sound simple."

"It isn't. There's nothing in the paperwork I saw that hints at one person. All the bills of sale are from a myriad of individuals and galleries and addressed to Kwong."

"You do know that all the records from his business have been destroyed?"

"Yes. It doesn't leave you much to go on, does it."

"I have a few ideas," she said.

"Like what?"

She shook her head. "They're not important," she said. "Let me go back to the fakes for a minute. If someone was going to organize this kind of fraud, they would need a painter, or painters, yes?"

"They would indeed, unless they scoured the world looking for fakes that already existed. But given the consistency in the quality of work I saw, though, I would think most of them could have been done by one person."

"One, or more?"

"Given the time frame over which it took place, it could have been one. It would have been more secure that way. And they were all Fauvist works, and these forgers do tend to specialize."

"So this agent, he just contacts an artist and says, 'Paint me a Monet'?"

"Something like that."

"And in this case you think an agent commissioned an entire range of Fauvist paintings from a forger or forgers and then passed them along to Kwong with dummy paperwork?"

"I think that's probably the case."

"What would the artist get paid?"

"I have no idea. It might depend on whether or not he had to sign it. Remember what I told you earlier: if the painting isn't signed, it isn't a forgery. So I imagine there would be a premium attached for a signature."

"These forgers, how easy are they to locate?"

"Well, they don't have a union or anything, but within the art world there are certainly some who are known.

Elmyr de Hory was one — he did Monets, by the way. Then there was John Myatt, who did versions of Matisse and Dufy. David Stein did Picasso and Chagall. And then there was Hans van Meegeren, who managed to do more than a passable imitation of Vermeer."

"You're using the past tense."

"They're all dead."

"How about current artists?"

"Not my field."

"Who could I talk to?"

"We have a chap in London, Frederick Locke, who's very good at this kind of thing. He's the one I referred the Wongs' questionable paintings to."

"Would he speak to me?"

Torrence said, "I don't see why not. I'll make a call for you."

"Thank you."

He looked at his watch. "We seem to have talked away a lot of the afternoon. Is there any way I can interest you in extending your stay to dinner?"

"I'd love to, but it will have to be another time," she said. "I have some other business I need to attend to." She took out her business card and passed it to him. "My cellphone number is on the back, my email address on the front. Could you call me after you've contacted Frederick Locke? It's just about the start of the workday in London, so you might be able to reach him in the next hour or so."

"You move quickly."

"I have a definite time frame."

"Have the Wongs decided what to do with their paintings? They seemed quite upset when I left, him in particular.

You know, we would still be very happy to sell the genuine paintings for them. Would you let them know that?"

"Sure, but I don't think they have a clue about what they want to do," Ava said. "When will you know about the questionable paintings?"

"It could take a little while. Frederick is meticulous."

9

AVA GRABBED A CAB AND ASKED THE DRIVER TO TAKE her to the office of the Hong Kong Inland Revenue Service on Gloucester Road, at the far end of Wanchai.

Hong Kong arguably had the world's most efficient tax system, imposing a flat corporate rate of 17.5 percent and a flat personal rate of 16 percent. When the Chinese took over and turned Hong Kong into a Special Administrative Region, they were smart enough to leave the tax system in place. The few people Ava knew of who had tried to avoid paying were soon brought to heel and severely punished by a system that was rigorous, incorruptible, and invasive.

Ava paid the driver and walked into the building. She presented her business card to a woman in uniform at the information desk in the front lobby. "My name is Ava Lee. I'm an accountant representing a Canadian firm that has done business in Hong Kong with a company called Great Wall Antiques and Fine Art. My client has become embroiled in a tax dispute with the Canadian government involving several transactions with Great Wall. We unsuccessfully tried to contact someone at that business, and now

I've discovered that it's closed, the owner is deceased, and its records have been destroyed. So I was hoping someone here could help access the company's tax records so we can clear up this problem."

The woman was reading Ava's card while she spoke. She looked up and said, "You came all the way to Hong Kong to do this?"

"I was here on other business and decided to kill two birds with one stone."

"Wait a minute," the woman said, picking up the phone.

"You can go to fourth-floor reception," she said when she hung up. "Ask for Mr. Po. Sign in here and take a visitor's badge."

Ava rode the elevator to the fourth floor. When she approached the receptionist's desk, she was told that Mr. Po would be with her shortly. No more than five minutes later, a small, trim man in his sixties came through a door behind the desk with a file folder in his hand. Ava gave him her finest smile. "I'm so sorry to bother you with this, and thank you for being so efficient," she said.

"It isn't a bother," he said, "but there isn't much I can do for you."

"You don't have their tax records?"

"Where was the company located?" Po asked.

Ava took out her notebook. "Kau U Fong Road, in Lan Kwai Fong."

"Yes, that's the one," he said, looking at the computer printout in the file folder.

"So you have their tax records?"

"Of course, but as I said, there isn't anything I can do for you. The records are confidential."

"My client in Canada is having a terrible time with the tax department there. We believe that Great Wall's tax records will help to resolve those problems. Even if I could just spend ten minutes with them, in your presence, it might help. I'm not asking to take copies of any documents." She saw that he was considering her suggestion, and she pressed. "I would sign any confidentiality agreement or any other form you think necessary."

"No, it just won't work," he said. "Our rules are quite strict and I won't bend them."

"Well, could you at least help us, and the Canadian tax department, by telling me who filed the returns for Great Wall? I'm sure they used an accounting firm here in Hong Kong. If I could get the name of the company I could contact them directly and see if they retained copies. We wouldn't be doing all this if Mr. Kwong's heirs hadn't so stupidly destroyed the company records after the business was closed."

Po opened his file again. "They should have kept the records for seven years," he said.

"I know."

"There's a name here."

"Please."

He hesitated, and she knew he was searching his mind for the rules. "I'm not asking you to breach any confidence," Ava said. "You aren't telling me anything that would compromise the integrity of Inland Revenue."

"Miss, you cannot tell them that we provided you with this information."

"Most certainly not," she said.

"Great Wall used Landmark Accounting. They have their offices in Landmark Plaza," he said.

She called Uncle on her way out of the building. "It's Ava. Could you please make some calls for me and see if you can get someone at Landmark Accounting in Landmark Plaza to co-operate with us? They were the accounting firm for the dealer who worked with the Wongs. I need access to some of his old tax records."

"I think we do have a contact there. How is it going?"

"I'm learning a lot about art forgeries but not much else."

She took a taxi back to the Mandarin Oriental. It was late afternoon and jet lag was beginning to get to her. She decided she needed a run, and the day was so pleasant that going outdoors seemed ideal. When she got to her room, she put on her running gear and headed back out, walking to the MTR station at Central. It wasn't rush hour yet so she managed to get on the first train that arrived. Ava got off at the Causeway Bay station, right across from the park.

Ava loved urban parks, and Victoria was one of her favourites. Only nineteen hectares — less than one-twentieth the size of New York's Central Park — it was the sole piece of green space she knew of in Hong Kong. In a city of seven million people, where space was at such a premium and ninety-nine percent of the population lived in apartments, Victoria Park was a sanctuary. She had tried running there some mornings but found it tough. The jogging trail was only six hundred metres long and not that wide, and there were so many people that she couldn't run fast enough to break a sweat. Weekends were worse. In addition to the weekday morning mix of tai chi practitioners, people with their caged birds, ballroom dancers, walkers, joggers, lawn bowlers, and tennis and badminton players, there were various protest groups, public forums, exhibits, and a large

Indonesian nanny population that congregated there every Sunday, leaving Statue Square in Central to the Filipino *yaya*s.

Ava's guess was that a weekday late afternoon might work, and when she got to the park there was hardly a soul using the trail. She ripped off six quick laps, the jet lag receding as her adrenalin surged. She found herself gazing at the apartment buildings and office towers that surrounded the park on three sides and the web of highway overpasses on the fourth. She knew that beyond the overpasses was Causeway Bay, where sampans bobbed at the pier. She couldn't see it but she could smell exhaust fumes from the late-afternoon traffic.

The MTR was getting busy as she returned to the station. She was sweating profusely when she boarded the train, and the other passengers gave her some space.

When she got back to the hotel she showered and changed into a clean bra and underwear, a clean black T-shirt, and a pair of training pants. She turned on her laptop for the first time that day. Nothing from the Caribbean cruisers — that was good. Not much to do with business — also good. An email from Maria that was almost too full of love. The days are too long. This past week has felt like a month. My bed is cold and too large for me alone. Hurry home, she wrote. While Ava liked the fact that she was being missed, she was troubled that Maria seemed so needy. She clicked on an email from Mimi that was even more unsettling. Thought I'd let you know that things are moving more quickly with Derek than I could have imagined. Love the man. Just love him to death. I'm going to sell my condo, I think. We're talking about buying a place together. In fact, we've started looking. *What next?* Ava wondered. *A wedding? Children?* Her thoughts were interrupted by her cellphone. "Ava Lee."

"Brian Torrence."

"Thanks for calling so promptly."

"I spoke with Locke. Write down this number: it's his direct line. He said you can call anytime."

"I appreciate it."

"Enough to have dinner with me?"

"I told you, I can't make it this evening."

"Tomorrow?"

"I'm not sure I'm going to be here."

"How about tentatively?"

"Okay, tell you what, if I'm here I'll call you," she said.

"Brilliant."

Ava hung up and checked the time. It was mid-morning in London. She dialled Frederick Locke's number.

"This is Frederick Locke."

"Thank you for taking my call," she said. "This is Ava Lee. Brian Torrence gave me your number."

"Brian tells me you're poking into this fake painting mess he's uncovered."

"*Poking* is probably the right word. I don't know enough to manage it intelligently."

"Well, it does get a bit complicated, and I don't pretend to know everything myself."

"Brian explained to me how the forgers work and said that you're familiar with some of them. I was wondering if you had any idea who might have done these paintings."

Locke chuckled. "I don't have the foggiest."

"No idea at all?"

"They don't exactly advertise their services. Those that are known usually pack it in after they're identified."

"Brian thought it was probably one person who painted all the fakes."

"I would agree with that."

"How does that work from a business viewpoint?"

"What do you mean?"

"The painter obviously wasn't selling directly to my clients," she said.

"Of course not. He or she would have worked through a gallery or an agent."

"And produced the works to order?"

"Probably not specifically, I would think. I mean, I can't imagine the agent saying, 'Give me a Monet *Water Lilies*.' He might say, 'Give me a Monet, two Derains, and a Matisse,' and then let the artist sort it out."

"For a fee?"

"Absolutely."

"A large fee?"

"No, I can't imagine it would be for a huge sum of money. Most of these people are anxious for work, any kind of work, normally to subsidize their own art. At least, that's the way it was for men like de Hory and Myatt."

"What kind of people were they?"

"Talented. Amazingly talented, most of them, but for some reason their own art just never took hold, never gripped the public's imagination. So to make a living and to be able to afford to keep painting their own work, they would knock off a Chagall and have someone flog it for them."

"Knock off?"

"Wrong choice of words, actually, a bit of a disservice to them. How about they would create a work in the style of Chagall?"

"But you think in this case the fakes were actually commissioned?"

"Yes, as I said, in this case that makes sense."

"Are the galleries and agents that unscrupulous?"

"My God, that hardly begins to describe them."

"I wouldn't have thought —"

"Ms. Lee, beneath the suave veneer of most art agents is a twisted, demented soul willing to sell his crippled mother into whoredom if the price is right."

"I was going to ask if you had a list of galleries and agents who might do this kind of thing."

"Open the New York phone book, find the heading 'Art Galleries,' and use every name on it as your initial list. Then get a Paris phone book, a London phone book —"

"I get it."

"Sorry. I wish I could be more helpful in that regard."

"No, that's okay. I'm not sure what I was expecting."

"So what's next?"

"I don't know. Maybe not much of anything," Ava said. "Those paintings you're examining, when will you be done?"

"Not sure. I have a heavy workload and they aren't at the top of my list right now."

"That's honest."

"I try."

"Me too."

"Look, you can call me anytime if you have questions, but frankly I think this is a bit of a wild goose chase."

"So it seems. Well, thanks anyway."

She hung up and looked at the clock on the nightstand. It was going on six o'clock. *I should check in with Uncle*, she thought.

"*Wei.*"

"Hi, Uncle, it's Ava."

"Ava, about that accounting firm — I have a name and phone number for you," Uncle said. "The woman's name is Grace Chan, she works for Landmark, and she did the books for Great Wall Antiques for ten years," he said, then recited the number.

"I'll call her now."

"Someone will have told her your name."

"Thank you, Uncle." Ava hung up and then dialled the number Uncle had given her.

Grace Chan answered the phone with a brisker "*Wei*" than Uncle's. "Ms. Chan, my name is Ava Lee."

"My boss said you'd be calling."

"Thanks for taking my call. Ms. Chan, I'm told you did the books for Great Wall Antiques for at least ten years."

"I did, until Mr. Kwong died."

"I'm looking for some information that might help me resolve a problem. It doesn't involve Landmark in any way, and I don't think it actually involves Mr. Kwong either," Ava said. "Some years ago, Kwong broadened his business to include paintings, specifically paintings for the Wong family in Wuhan."

"He did."

"Could you go through the records you have and pull out everything associated with those transactions?"

"There aren't many of them."

"Then that shouldn't be difficult."

"The files are in our Hong Kong office. I live in Tai Wai Village and work mainly from home."

"Tai Wai in the New Territories?"

"Yes, past Sha Tin, on the way to the Chinese border."

"Can you get to the office tomorrow?"

There was a long pause.

"I have been authorized by my clients to pay consulting fees," Ava said. "Would two thousand dollars make it easier for you?"

"The office doesn't open until nine, and it will take me a while to find the files and go through them," she said quickly.

"So what time?"

"Eleven."

"See you then."

10

AVA GOT TO THE LANDMARK OFFICE AN HOUR EARLY, hoping Grace Chan had already located the files she needed. The receptionist asked her to take a seat while she called Ms. Chan. A minute later a diminutive Chinese woman in a plain white dress buttoned to the collar and falling below her knees walked into the area. Her grey hair was cut in a pageboy. Ava thought the hairstyle a curious choice for a woman who looked as if she was in her fifties.

"Ava?"

"Yes. I'm sorry if I'm a little early. I was rather anxious to see what you have."

"Not to worry, your timing is actually quite good. Come with me."

Ava followed Chan to the boardroom, where three files were laid out side by side on the table. "Those are his annual financial statements and tax returns," Chan said, pointing to the stack. "I separated the paintings transactions into these three files to make it easier for you."

"Three files. Three transactions?"

"No, five. Two each in two years and one in another year."

"There were twenty transactions."

"I have records for five, that's all."

"Let's look at them," Ava said, knowing there was no point in arguing.

She sat next to Chan, who opened the first file. "Kwong paid $1.5 million for this painting from a gallery in Paris. Actually, he didn't technically pay. He negotiated a price, invoiced the Wongs, took their payment, deducted a commission of five percent, and then forwarded the balance of the money to the seller. The seller then sent the painting to Kwong. He used the same procedure for all five of the paintings I have records for."

"That was trusting of the Wongs," Ava said.

"Kwong wasn't a fool," Chan said. "Why would he risk making an enemy of one of the most powerful men in China?"

Ava leafed through the paperwork. Chan had grouped it in chronological order, making it easy to follow. The procedure she had described for the first painting had been repeated four more times. Each had a different seller. "So he was acting as a broker, a middle man. He never had actual possession of any of these paintings."

"That's the case."

Ava worked through the files again, noting the dates, the artists, the paintings. Then she opened her notebook and compared them against her list. Chan's files documented three of the five paintings Torrence judged to be genuine; the other two were on his questionable list. She guessed those two were going to pass muster.

"I have a problem," Ava said to Chan. "Our records show that the Wongs bought twenty paintings from Great Wall, not five."

"This is all I have."

"Could you leave me alone with these other files for a little while?" Ava asked, pointing to the stack.

"Certainly. I'm borrowing an office two doors down. Come and get me when you're done."

Grace Chan was a good accountant. Ava found it easy to go through a year of business at Great Wall. The income statements and balance sheets were clear and concise, the backup was referenced. It wasn't much of a business, not in ceramics anyway. The first year she examined had sales of less than HK$2 million — about US$300,000 — and after a myriad of expenses the company was US$20,000 in the red. It was only with the commission on the Wong sale that the company had made any profit.

The next year was more of the same, except this time Grace Chan had recorded four commission payments. *Four?* Ava thought. *Two paintings were sold to the Wongs that year, not four. Where did the other two commissions come from?*

She left the boardroom, the file under her arm, and found Grace Chan. "These two commissions," she said, pointing to the entries. "Were they invoiced?"

"Yes. I only pulled out the copies of invoices and paperwork relating to the five paintings, but yes, those entries were invoiced. The paperwork is in the back storeroom."

"Could you get them for me, please?" Ava asked. "And Grace, how many other large commissions were there over that period — commissions not directly related to Kwong and Wong?"

"Quite a few. They were making him wealthy. He could have retired in style if not for the cancer."

"What were the commissions for?"

"I was never sure. The invoices just say, 'For consulting services rendered.' When I asked him what that meant, he said he was doing provenance work on Chinese ceramics for a European company."

"And you believed him?"

"Ava, as long as the paperwork and the money matched, and as long as he was properly declaring his income and paying his taxes, it wasn't up to me to question him."

"I think we should look at all the files and put dates and amounts to these commissions."

"I'll get the files."

It took them more than two hours to go through each file and find the appropriate copies of invoices. Ava recorded everything in her notebook. When they were done, she compared dates and amounts. There were exactly fifteen invoices, each issued shortly after the Wongs had bought a painting from Great Wall. But the commission invoices weren't made out to the Wongs; they were made out to a numbered company with a Liechtenstein address. The invoice amount was exactly three percent of the Wongs' purchase price.

"Is it possible for me to make a private phone call?" Ava asked Grace.

"Certainly. I'll be in my office if you need me."

Ava tried May Ling's office line first and got voicemail. She didn't leave a message. She tried May Ling's cellphone, which she answered on the first ring. "Ava, I was hoping you would call."

"I'm in a meeting but I need you to answer a couple of simple questions for me. First, the paintings you bought, how did you pay for them?"

"By cheque or by wire transfer, a bit of both."

"You paid against an invoice, correct?"

"Yes, of course."

"Always?"

"No invoice, no payment."

"I need you to do something for me. Get one of your financial people to go back through the twenty transactions. Dig out the invoices and then tell me who, when, and how you paid. It's probably best to email everything to me. I'd like copies of the invoices and any wire transfers, and copies of the returned cheques — back and front."

"What have you found?"

Ava heard the eagerness in her voice and knew she was going to have to be cautious about how often and in how much detail she spoke to May Ling. "Nothing yet. I'm just trying to be thorough about recreating the transactions."

"I'll have someone do it right away."

"Thanks."

"Please call me later."

"If I have something to report."

Ava hung up and then used the boardroom phone to call reception. She asked to be connected to Grace Chan. "How was Mr. Kwong paid these commissions, the ones for the supposed ceramic provenance consultations?" she asked.

"By cheque."

"Do you have the bank deposit slips, the cheques?"

"Not the original cheques; they stayed with Mr. Kwong. I have copies."

"They will do just fine."

Ten minutes later she had copies of the fifteen cheques the numbered company had sent to Kwong for commissions.

The company's bank was the Liechtenstein Private Estate Bank. Ava knew what her chances were of getting any information from the bank: zero. She wrote down the address anyway and double-checked the numbered company. If it wasn't registered in Liechtenstein she might be able to find out something about it.

"You've been really helpful," Ava said to Grace, passing her a sealed envelope with HK$2,000 in it. Grace looked at it but didn't open it. *The lady has some class*, Ava thought. "If this works out well, I'll see if I can find an additional bonus for you."

"To be honest, the money doesn't mean that much to me," Grace said, not raising her eyes from the envelope.

"Pardon?"

"I'm more interested in knowing whether Mr. Kwong was involved in something improper and if I've been a party to it. I've found all this quite unusual, and upsetting."

"I don't know what he was actually involved in, but whatever it was it won't be any reflection on how well you did your job. I found your work completely professional and beyond reproach. You have nothing to fear."

Grace looked at Ava. "And I guess Mr. Kwong has nothing to fear now either."

AVA WENT ONLINE AS SOON AS SHE RETURNED TO THE Mandarin. There was nothing yet from Wuhan. Still, she pushed aside any idea of returning that day to Toronto. There was something odd enough about Great Wall's accounts to compel her to stay at least until she had figured it out. Wherever it led, she would have fulfilled her commitment to May Ling and could head home knowing she had done all she could.

The thought of home brought her father to mind. How was he surviving the cruise from hell? It was late in the evening wherever at sea he was, but she knew he was a night owl. She punched his number into her cellphone. It rang once and went immediately to voicemail. "It's Ava. I'm in Hong Kong. The job in Wuhan may not turn into anything worth pursuing, and if it doesn't I'll be back in Toronto before you. Give my love to everyone, and tell Mummy I said she's to behave."

She hung up and went back to the computer. An email from May Ling with attachments was now in her inbox. When she clicked on it, the email simply said, Here is everything you requested. There were twenty invoices, all from Great Wall Antiques and Fine Art. Five had no payment instructions other than a net ten-day term request; cheques were mailed to the Kau U Fong Road address. The other fifteen specifically requested that the cheques be sent to Great Wall Antiques and Fine Art, care of the Kowloon Light Industrial Bank. An address was provided for the bank, along with Great Wall's account number.

She checked her notes. The five cheques sent directly to the street address of Great Wall were for paintings Brian Torrence deemed genuine or possibly genuine. The fifteen cheques sent to the account at the Kowloon bank were for those Torrence was sure were forgeries. What was stranger was that the five cheques had been deposited into an account at the Hong Kong Shanghai Bank, which was where Kwong banked, according to Grace Chan's audit records.

Was Kwong running two accounts? And if he was, why? Grace Chan had made it clear that she wouldn't have tolerated it if he'd been trying to avoid taxes.

Ava phoned Uncle. "Do we know anyone at the Kowloon Light Industrial Bank?"

"Friends own most of the Kowloon Light Industrial Bank."

"Then I need you to talk to them."

"What do you want to know?"

"Great Wall Antiques and Fine Art. Who controlled the account? I need copies of all the activity going through the account over the past ten years."

"I will see what I can do."

"Thank you, Uncle."

"You have that tone in your voice, the one you get when you have found something."

"I'm easily excited," she said.

"I will pretend I believe you," he said. "What are you doing for dinner?"

"No plans."

"There is a new Shanghai restaurant near the Peninsula that they say has the best stewed sea cucumber in Hong Kong."

"My mother would be happy."

"*Momentai.*"

Ava was lying on the bed, closing her eyes for a few moments, when her cellphone rang. "Ava Lee."

"Ms. Lee, I'm Henry Chew from Kowloon Light Industrial Bank." Uncle's *guanxi* never failed to impress her.

"Thank you for calling."

"My pleasure," he said. Ava could hear the nervousness in his voice. "I have an assistant trying to locate the documentation you want. We'll send it to the hotel by courier when we have it. In the meantime, I've taken a look at the account. What do you want to know?"

"It was in the name of Great Wall Antiques and Fine Art?"

"Actually no, it was a DBA account. The account holder was a numbered company doing business as Great Wall."

"Where was the company registered?"

"Liechtenstein."

Shit, she thought. "A bit unusual, isn't it, for a company registered there to open a Hong Kong bank account?"

"There was less scrutiny then, fewer concerns about money laundering and that kind of thing. As long as the company was a legal entity and as long as it was obeying Hong Kong law, opening a bank account wasn't that difficult."

"Who was the signing authority?"

"A Georges Brun."

"Just one?"

"It appears that way."

"What information do you have on him?"

"He has the same address as the numbered company, a phone number that I would guess is in Liechtenstein. The copies of his photo ID all have a Liechtenstein address."

"Can you give me the phone number now and send copies of the photo ID with the other information?"

"Sure," he said, and recited the phone number.

"The account is closed now?" Ava prodded.

"Dormant. It still has a minimum balance."

"When was the last transaction?"

"More than two years ago."

"How active an account was it?"

"Not very, although a lot of money certainly went through it."

"Put a number to *not very*."

"After the initial opening deposit, there were fifteen more. As for withdrawals, there were fifteen large wire transfers and two smaller ones."

"You're sending me copies of all those transactions?"

"We're searching for them as we speak."

"Who did the small wires go to?"

"I won't know where any of them went until we see the wires."

"I want to thank you for this," Ava said. "You've been helpful."

"Not a problem, except — can I assume you'll try to contact Georges Brun and maybe the overseas bank?"

"You can."

"You can't mention that we gave you this information."

"I won't. And look, send the information to me as soon as you have it. Don't wait until tomorrow."

"Will do."

She stared at the Liechtenstein phone number. Everything she knew about Liechtenstein told her that the number was probably the bank's and that Brun was probably a bank employee. Assuming that was true, she tried to come up with a plausible excuse for calling that would get Georges Brun or whoever else was at the other end of the line to speak to her. She came up dry.

Frustrated with herself, she went online and began to research Liechtenstein banking and company registration regulations. *Maybe I'm overthinking this*, Ava thought. *Maybe the country's reputation as a haven for offshore accounts has been overstated.*

Half an hour later she gave up. Incorporating a company in Liechtenstein was as easy as buying milk at a corner store in Canada. There were officially more than seventy thousand registered holding companies in a country with a population of thirty-five thousand. And there were more than two hundred private banks to service those companies. Their reputation for secrecy was second to none, although they frowned on money laundering and were prepared to work with foreign government authorities if any fraudulent activity was suspected. Ava had no government credentials she could wave at them, and there was no hint of money laundering.

She then began considering the idea that the phone number was an actual company's, not the bank's. If it was, there would be a real name attached to the number she had. *What the hell,* she thought, *it's worth a try.*

She dialled the number and a woman answered in a language that sounded like German. "I'm sorry, I only speak English," Ava said.

"Liechtenstein Private Estate Bank," the woman said.

So much for that plan, Ava thought. "Georges Brun, please."

"Who shall I say is calling?"

"Never mind," Ava said, and hung up.

She had no one else related to this case to talk to, or rather no one who would talk to her. Either way it made no difference. All she had left were the wire transfers, and she had no reason to believe they would contain information she didn't already have.

12

THE WIRES HADN'T ARRIVED BY SEVEN THIRTY, AND Ava was scheduled to join Uncle at eight at the Shanghai restaurant on the Kowloon side. Reluctantly she left her hotel and walked to the Star Ferry. This time she sat in the stern so she could look back at the magnificent skyline, which expanded as she moved farther away from shore.

Uncle was, as usual, already at the restaurant when she arrived. She hadn't even sat down before he asked, "The banker called you?"

"Yes, and he was helpful."

"Good. My friends want to know."

Ava could only imagine what the banker had been told.

"What did you find out?"

"Nothing of any substance, but there may be some leads I can pursue."

"So it is not over?"

"Not yet. Close, but not yet."

He looked at the menu. "What kind of Shanghai food does your mother like?"

"Do they have drunken chicken?"

"Yes, and the stewed sea cucumber."

"Steamed buns?"

"Of course."

"Add a soup and that should be enough."

"They have a Shanghai soup with pork, baby bok choy, and bamboo shoots."

"Perfect."

They talked idly while they ate. Ava's last case had involved bringing two of Uncle's men, Carlo and Andy, from Hong Kong to Las Vegas. Ava said some nice things about their contribution and asked what they were up to.

"Carlo has a bookmaking sideline, and Andy and his wife own a noodle shop near the Kowloon train station," he said. "They were sorry they did not get to see more of Las Vegas. Carlo said you were a very tough boss. He meant that as a compliment, of course."

They left the restaurant at nine. Sonny was waiting outside for Uncle, the Mercedes running. She hadn't seen him there when she arrived. "I am going for a massage," Uncle said. "Call me tomorrow and let me know if you are staying."

Ava rode the ferry back to Central, the view of the skyline now almost overpowering. She had tried to explain it to an American friend one time and all she could compare it to was Times Square — ten times over.

When she arrived at the Mandarin, she asked the concierge if any packages had arrived for her. She was told that an envelope had been taken to her room a half-hour earlier.

Ava opened the door to her room and saw the envelope on the floor. She picked it up and went over to the desk, then opened it and smiled.

As the Kowloon banker had said, there had been seventeen

wire transfers, and the envelope contained copies of them all. As she expected, fifteen wires had been sent to the Liechtenstein bank. The other two were more interesting. One, for US$100,000, had gone to a bank account in Dublin in the name of N. O'Toole, five years ago; the other, for $20,000, had been sent to a Jan Harald Sørensen in Skagen, Denmark, two weeks after the O'Toole wire.

It was just past nine o'clock in Hong Kong, late afternoon in both Dublin and Skagen. Ava found the Dublin bank's phone number online and dialled the number. It took her two minutes to work through the prompts and get to a person.

"Hello, my name is Ava Lee. I work at the Kowloon Light Industrial Bank in Hong Kong. We've been asked to send a wire transfer to an account at your branch. Before transmitting it I wanted to confirm the account number and the holder's name."

"Yes, go on," a woman replied.

"The account is in the name of N. O'Toole, and the number is 032-6567-4411."

There was a pause. "You said you were going to send a wire?" the woman asked.

"That was the plan."

"You should change it. That account was closed three years ago."

"That's strange. Mr. O'Toole gave us the number himself."

A longer pause. "There was no Mr. O'Toole on this account, just a Mrs. O'Toole."

"Are you absolutely sure about that?"

"Let me double-check," the woman said. "Yes, it was Mrs. O'Toole. It's quite clear."

"And the N was the first letter of what name?"

"It doesn't say, and I'm actually surprised that you wouldn't know at your end. I mean, you're the one sending the wire."

"We Chinese aren't all that good with Western names," Ava said quickly. "Do you have any information on file that might help me contact Mrs. O'Toole?"

"No."

Ava started to phrase another question when the line went dead. *Maybe the Danes will be more co-operative*, she thought, and dialled the number of the bank in Skagen.

She got a live person at the Skagen bank on the second ring. She repeated her story about preparing to send a wire transfer and passed along the account number and the name Jan Harald Sørensen.

"Yes, we can confirm it," a woman said.

"Would you also have contact information for Mr. Sørensen?" Ava asked. "We normally like to put an address on the wire."

"No, we can't give out that type of information."

"It would —"

"No, we don't do it under any circumstances," the woman said and hung up.

Bankers in Europe aren't very accommodating, Ava thought. *But then, they aren't connected to Uncle and his network of friends.*

She went online and spent the next fifteen minutes trying to find a Jan Harald Sørensen in Skagen, a town with a population of fewer than ten thousand people. She found a number of Sørensens, but no Jan, Harald, J.H., or even J.

She pushed her chair back from the desk and walked over to the window. She had the name of a Liechtenstein bank that wouldn't talk to her and the names of two people she couldn't locate. She knew that the bank had some kind of connection to Mrs. O'Toole and Mr. Sørensen, whoever they were. She also knew that it had been directly responsible for setting up the second Great Wall company account at the Kowloon bank, and the money from the forged art sales had flowed to them. Given that the company existed for the sole purpose of selling forged art to the Wongs, it made sense to her that this somehow linked O'Toole and Sørensen to the scam. *But how?* Ava thought. *Were they agents who set up a deal or two? Were they artists? Were they the painters who created the fakes?*

Ava caught herself. She went back to the desk and leafed through the wire transfer copies. What it came down to, she finally decided, was that she had to assume that O'Toole and Sørensen were directly linked to the forgeries and were — a big leap in logic, she knew — probably the painters who had been used. *It's the only connection I have to pursue,* she thought, as she started to call London.

"Frederick Locke."

"This is Ava Lee."

"Ms. Lee, I didn't expect to hear from you so soon."

"Something's come up," Ava said. "Do you know an Irish painter from Dublin named O'Toole?"

"Maurice O'Toole?"

"All I have is an initial, N, and I've been told the person is female."

"I don't know any female artists named O'Toole."

"I thought it was a bit much to expect."

"And if it's Maurice you're after, he's been dead for some time."

"Did he do fakes when he was alive?"

"Not that I know."

"Are you being circumspect?"

"No, Ms. Lee, I'm not. I'm telling you I have no idea whether Maurice O'Toole painted forgeries or not."

"Okay," Ava said. "Now I have another name for you: Jan Harald Sørensen. He's Danish, I think, and lives in Skagen."

"Sorry again. I've never heard of him, although Skagen does have a very famous art colony, and the fact that I'm not familiar with him doesn't mean he doesn't exist and doesn't paint."

Ava sighed. "I think I'm just about ready to pack this in. I'm running out of doors to go through."

"I wish I could be more helpful."

"I understand, and thanks for taking the time. By the way, if my hunch is right, the two Dufy paintings among those Brian Torrence wants you to authenticate are the real deal."

"How do you know that?"

"I've found a financial trail that indicates they were purchased like the other three that are genuine."

"I'll take a close look at them as soon as I possibly can."

"Look, if you can think of anything about an O'Toole or a Sørensen, call me on my cell. I think I'll be leaving Hong Kong tomorrow, but I'd still be interested if you uncovered anything."

Ava closed her Wong notebook. She doubted it would be opened again. Liechtenstein wasn't going to give her the information she wanted. She had a dead Kwong and a dead O'Toole, and that left her with exactly one lead. If she wanted to pursue it she would have to fly to Denmark and tromp around Skagen looking for someone named Jan Harald Sørensen, and if she found him, she had to hope he actually was an artist. That was too small a needle in too big a haystack.

She opened her laptop and emailed her travel agent, telling her to book the next day's Cathay Pacific flight to Toronto. Then she let Mimi and Maria know she was heading back to Toronto. Maria answered immediately. I'll meet you at the airport.

Yes, I'd like that, Ava replied.

Before turning off the computer she wrote to her father. She asked how the cruise was proceeding, told him that the Wuhan job wasn't going to materialize, and then, almost as an afterthought, wrote, I met Michael at dim sum yesterday. He looks very much like you, and acted very much like you. It felt strange even writing his name.

She wasn't sure what time she had fallen asleep but she knew it was just past two a.m. when she woke, the digital clock glowing next to the phone that rocked her into consciousness. "Ava Lee," she said.

"This is Frederick Locke. I'm sorry for calling so late, but I knew you were going to be travelling and I thought you'd want to know what I'd found out before you left."

"Found out?"

"The two paintings by Dufy — I think you were correct. I had a quick, intense look at the provenance and it seems to hang together."

"That's good. I'm sure the Wongs will be pleased."

"And while I was looking into that, I had one of my assistants do some research on your O'Toole and your Sørensen."

"And?"

"I had her check into Maurice O'Toole, and it emerges that he was married to a woman named Nancy. She managed his business affairs before he died."

"Did she locate Nancy?"

"Yes, she died three years ago."

Ava groaned. "Great. Everyone I need to talk to is dead."

"The thing is, my assistant also said that Maurice was known to do a bit of funny stuff now and then. The idea of his painting some fakes isn't out of the question."

"How could I confirm that?"

"I don't know."

"Did they have children?"

"No."

"Then it's a long shot that any records still exist."

"I agree."

"One more dead end, pardon the pun."

"Don't be gloomy. We haven't talked about Sørensen yet."

Ava detected a touch of excitement in Locke's voice, and whatever disappointment she felt vanished. "I'm listening," she said.

"My assistant thought the name sounded vaguely familiar and went hunting through some Danish art databases. The reason we couldn't find Jan Harald Sørensen is that he paints and sells under the name Jimmy Sandman."

"Strange name."

"Strange man. The name was originally a nickname his Skagen colleagues pinned on him because of his habit of scouring the beach every morning for driftwood, which he used to paint on. His paintings were focused on the seas and beaches around Skagen and were filled with repetitive characters: a Lutheran minister in his religious garb, a black-haired woman with bright red nipples, and a mournful clown-type character that was his take on himself. He is very, very talented, but limited in imagination and range."

"Is he alive?"

"Well, there's no record of his passing."

"Is he in Skagen?"

"I have no idea."

She began to weigh her options. "Is he talented enough to have done at least some of the forgeries?"

Locke didn't respond right away, which pleased Ava. He was at least taking it seriously.

"I think he is," he said.

"What else can you tell me about him? Age? Any physical description? Married?"

"Definitely married. He has seven children with a woman named Helga. Age, mid-forties. How does he look? Well, in the photo I have, he has a thin, rakish beard that runs around a very ample jawline. He is a rather plump man."

"The data you have, what does it say about his residence?"

"Skagen, but the information is old. He could have had two more children, gained another twenty pounds, and moved to Norway by now."

"Is Jimmy Sandman his legal name?"

"I think it is."

"You think?"

"It does say he changed his name, but I have no idea if he actually did it in the formal sense."

"Are you always this careful?"

"Yes, I am."

"Good, I like that," Ava said.

"What are you going to do?"

"I don't know."

13

SHE TRIED TO GET BACK TO SLEEP AND DID MANAGE to log half an hour here and there, but her mind was too active to sustain her slumber. She had been one phone call away from catching her flight to Toronto, and now she was locked in an internal debate about whether to go there or head to Denmark.

After the call from Locke, Ava had gone online to research Jimmy Sandman. She found most of the material that Locke's assistant had uncovered, but not what she was really looking for — an address, a phone number, anything that could help her actually locate him.

Knowing he was already up, Ava phoned Uncle at six thirty and explained to him what she had found.

"It sounds flimsy," he said.

"I know, but it's all I have. Kwong's dead, the O'Tooles are dead, and there's no chance of getting anything out of Liechtenstein. The only path I can see is through this Sandman."

"And you are not even sure he was involved."

She had thought about that during her restless night.

"No, I am sure, actually. It makes too much sense not to be true. Why would the numbered company wire money to O'Toole and Sørensen otherwise?"

"They did it just once."

"I know, but there had to be a reason for that as well."

"You sound as if you are trying to talk yourself into going to Denmark."

"Uncle, even with the genuine paintings factored out, we're looking at a seventy-million-dollar fraud here. I'm trying to convince myself that I have a chance to recover some of it."

"And this Sandman is the link?"

"The only one I have, but I think he's a good one. And if I can get to him, I'll convince him to lead us directly to the people who orchestrated this."

"Then I think it is worth pursuing. It should not take more than two or three days, and it will show Wong May Ling that you have taken your commitment to her seriously."

"Seriously enough that I'm going to phone her in a few hours and tell her it's time she called you to settle on a fee."

"You are that confident?"

"No, of course not. You know I don't take things for granted. But on the chance that I can get some money back, I want to have an agreement in place. It's just good business, and May Ling knows all about good business."

"When will you leave?"

"Today. I just need to put a flight schedule together. I have no idea how to get from here to there. My agent is still up, so I'm going to contact her when I hang up with you."

"Let me know your schedule. We will take you to the airport."

Ava had been using the same travel agent for years, and even in the age of online bookings she liked the assurance of having someone cover her back if she ran into problems. Squabbling with airlines was not on her list of favourite activities. She emailed her new destination and asked for options.

Half an hour later she had a reply. She couldn't get to Skagen by air; the closest airport was Aalborg, about an hour's drive away. Every schedule to Aalborg involved at least two stops, and all of them landed her via the same local carrier at 11:20 the following night, so it came down to airline and airport preference. She opted for Lufthansa and a Hong Kong–Frankfurt–Copenhagen–Aalborg route because it was a few hours' less flying time.

Ava told her agent to book the flight, check her into an Aalborg airport hotel, and rent a car for her for the following day.

She phoned Uncle. "My flight is at one forty. Could you pick me up at eleven?"

"We will be there."

She made herself a cup of instant coffee and collected the *South China Morning Post* that was waiting for her at the door. Iran. Afghanistan. Pakistan. North Korea. Thailand in some kind of upheaval again. On the cruise she hadn't missed reading about any of it.

She thought about going for a run, but a quick look outside negated that idea. The sky was dark, the rain pelting down sideways as it crossed Victoria Harbour. Instead she emailed Mimi, Maria, and her father to let them know about her change in travel plans. She knew Maria would be disappointed and would start to worry again, so she stressed the urgency of the business that kept her away from Canada.

At ten o'clock she called May Ling on her direct office line. Briefing clients was a tricky business. Uncle believed it was always best to under-inform, to keep expectations to a minimum. If anything, Ava was even more closed.

"Ava, I was hoping to hear from you."

"I'm leaving Hong Kong in a few hours. I have a small lead I'm following up on."

"Where are you going?"

"It doesn't matter."

"Does it have anything to do with the banking information I gave you?"

"That was very helpful, thanks."

"You must be making progress of some kind."

"Actually, we managed to confirm that two more of your paintings are genuine. Someone from Harrington's will probably contact you today with the details."

"That doesn't have anything to do with your leaving?"

"No," Ava said. "I have a small lead I have to follow up on. And I want to repeat the word *small*. It may come to absolutely nothing."

"When will you know?"

"A couple of days."

"And if it comes to something?"

"It would be a piece of the puzzle, nothing more than that. Certainly nothing conclusive."

"And you can't tell me?"

"It's better if I don't. There are too many ifs attached to it."

"And if it comes to nothing?"

"Then my work for you is done."

"I hope not."

Me too, Ava thought, and then said, "I'll call you when I know something definite."

She was packing her bags when she got a call from the lobby. Uncle was early. She quickly organized the rest of her things and rode the elevator to the lobby, where Uncle was waiting for her.

"I spoke to May Ling and told her about the other two paintings being genuine," she said as the car eased out of Central.

"What was her reaction?"

"Hardly enthusiastic."

"The fakes are weighing more heavily on them."

"I also told her I was leaving Hong Kong, but I didn't say where or why."

"Wise."

"I also think you shouldn't call her about our fee — she'll read too much into that. Let's wait until I see what happens in Denmark. There's no point in even talking about money unless I can find this Sandman."

"I agree."

"I arrive late tomorrow night, their time, so I won't know anything until the next day at the earliest. Have you been to Denmark?"

"No. They make good beer — that is all I know," Uncle said. "I do not imagine we have any people there, but I will see who is close by."

"I don't think I'll need any people. These are artists and art agents and galleries I'm dealing with."

"You never know."

14

IT REMINDED HER OF VANCOUVER — THE AALBORG weather, that is. Cold, damp, lingering. It had been wet when she arrived the night before on the Cimber Sterling flight from Copenhagen, and it was the same in the morning as she rode a taxi back to the airport to get her rental car. The airport had been deserted and the rental booths shuttered when her flight arrived, so she had taxied to the Hotel Hvide Hus, where she spent most of the night wide awake, wondering exactly what she expected to find in Skagen.

The car rental opened at eight and Ava was there ten minutes later. The woman behind the counter was dour, almost grim, her conversation devoid of pleasantries. Ava had booked a BMW but there wasn't one available; the woman informed her she was getting a Saab. Ava had asked for a GPS system; the woman said she didn't need one, but Ava argued with her to get it.

The drive did turn out to be simple, almost a straight run on route E45, from Aalborg northeast to the coast and then north past Frederikshavn to Skagen, at the northernmost tip of the Danish peninsula. The countryside — what she could see of it through the mist and rain — was mainly marsh. The villages she passed, their homes and shops pressed tightly against the road, were uniform and neat: rows of brick houses, red tile roofs, and lace curtains hanging in almost every window.

She drove into Skagen at ten thirty, found the downtown area easily enough, and parked her car in a public lot that held only one other vehicle. As she got out she had a feeling of déjà vu. She could have been in downtown Banff, minus the Rocky Mountains. Skagen had the same touristy feel, its main street lined with souvenir shops, coffeehouses, boutiques, dainty restaurants, and, in this case, art galleries. She counted four within sight and headed for the nearest one. It was time to jump into the haystack.

A middle-aged blonde woman with a heaving chest was fussing with a group of small paintings. She took a glance at Ava and then turned back to what she was doing. There was no one else in the gallery. Ava stood, staring, waiting. The woman ignored her. Finally Ava said, "Can you help me?"

"The prices are on the works," the woman said in heavily accented English.

"That's not the kind of help I'm looking for."

"Then what can I do?"

"Do you know a painter called Jimmy Sandman?" Ava said to her back.

"We called him Jimmy the Sandman," she said.

Ava hadn't expected it to be so easy. Then she noted the past tense. "Excuse me, did you say 'called'? Has something happened to him?"

The woman finally turned towards Ava, a look of mild surprise on her face when she actually looked at her. *Is it because I'm Chinese?* Ava thought. *Is it the Adidas jacket and pants?*

"Yes, he left town."

"He moved away?"

"Years ago."

"Do you know where he went?"

"No."

"Does he have any friends, any relatives in Skagen I could speak with?"

"Jimmy was a strange man. Not many people wanted to talk to him, let alone be friends with him."

"There must have been someone. Another painter, maybe."

Ava watched as the woman searched her memory, almost painfully. "He and Jasper drank together sometimes."

"Jasper who?"

"Kasten."

"And where would I find Jasper Kasten?"

"At the Skaw."

"Pardon?"

"*The Skaw.*"

"I did hear you. I just don't what the Skaw is."

"Come with me," the woman said, walking towards the door. She opened it and pointed to the left.

"See that hill at the end of street? If you climb it you can look down on the Skaw. Jasper goes there every morning to paint."

"How will I recognize him?"

"He wears a red anorak."

The rain had thankfully let up, but the closer Ava got to the hill, the brisker the wind. It was a good ten-minute walk, which she found invigorating. Steps had been built into the side of the hill, which was actually an enormous sand dune. Up she went, leaning into the wind, glad she had worn her running gear. A roaring noise was coming from the other side of the dune, and the closer she got to the top the louder it got. She couldn't imagine that it was just waves rolling in; the wind wasn't that strong.

She spotted Jasper Kasten squatting on a camp stool, a canvas on an easel in front of him. His back was to her, his focus on the scene below: a huge expanse of beach. But it wasn't the beach that seemed to hold his attention, and very quickly she saw why. The sea beyond was being whipped into some kind of frenzy, the water spewing into the air like a geyser. The roar she was hearing came from the same source, but now that she was closer she could hear a distinct screech coming from what seemed to be the centre of the geyser.

The cloud cover had broken, streaks of blue now appearing where there had been only a grey shroud. The clouds were moving quickly, leaving gaps for the sun to peek out, and when it did, it created a pattern of rainbows over the water. Ava was a city girl, most comfortable when she had concrete under her feet, but even she found the seascape breathtaking.

He didn't hear her coming and she had to move into his line of vision to get his attention. He looked up, annoyed. He had pale blue eyes, thin lips, a pointed chin, and huge jug ears. "Mr. Kasten?" she said.

"Do I know you?" he asked in English, his manner easing.

"No, I was referred to you by one of the women in town."

"That sounds dangerous."

"I'm looking for someone and they said you might be able to help me."

"Who?"

"Jimmy the Sandman."

"Good God, I haven't heard that name in a while."

"So you know him?"

"Of course," he said, looking out at the sea as if he had already lost interest in the conversation. "Beautiful, isn't it?"

"I've never seen anything like it," Ava said.

"That there on the right, that is the Kattegat strait. It flows up from the southeast and the Strait of Denmark. And there on the left, that is the Skagerrak. It comes from the North Sea. They meet here, crashing into each other in some kind of perpetual war, neither of them ever making headway, just smash, smash, smash in futility. Some days are better than others. Today is almost perfect. The wind is strong; the light flickers."

She looked at his painting. "You come here every day?"

"I do."

"And you paint the same thing?"

"It is never the same. That's why I find it so beautiful."

"I was told Jimmy painted scenes like this too."

"He painted this one, except he couldn't resist sticking in those ridiculous characters of his."

"On driftwood?"

"Yeah, the crazy bastard."

"What do you mean?"

"You would have thought he'd invented the idea of painting on driftwood. He used to scour this beach every morning looking for what the tide had brought in. He used to go nuts if anyone else got there first or was looking when he was. There was more than one fight down there."

"Do you know what happened to him?"

"Why are you interested?"

"I'm looking for him. It's business-related."

"Business? That's a word I'd never associate with him."

"Do you know what happened?"

"He left."

"When?"

"Four or five years ago."

"Why?"

"His wife, I think. She found it too crowded here."

"Crowded?" Ava said in disbelief.

"In the summer we get overrun by those fucking German tourists, but most of the time it's like this. Me, a couple of other painters, and a few guys on the beach throwing sticks for dogs to chase. The wife was a bit of a nut job, used to nag him something awful. Though when you think about all the kids she had to look after, maybe she had a reason."

"Do you know where they went?"

"No."

"Do you think anyone you know would know?"

"I don't know him, but Jimmy had a brother in Hirtshals."

"What's his name?"

"Ronny. He owns a fish plant, Sørensen Fiske. It's right on the main pier in Hirtshals."

"Is that far from here?"

"Straight west about forty kilometres. Just follow the concrete bunkers."

"Bunkers?"

"During the Second World War the Germans dotted this entire coastline with them, to defend themselves against an attack that never came. The walls are so thick we can't rip them down. That's why some of the fuckers come back here every summer — to relive the old glory days."

"Thanks for the help," she said, not particularly wanting to hear a rant about the Second World War; she'd heard them often enough when Chinese spoke about the Japanese. Different continent, different occupiers, same hatred.

15

SHE PUNCHED SØRENSEN FISKE INTO HER GPS AND UP it popped, a half-hour drive if she kept to the speed limit.

Hirtshals was smaller still than Skagen, and she had no trouble wending her way through town to the harbour. There was one large jetty that, according to signs in Danish and English, handled ferry traffic. The others seemed devoted to fishing boats. Ava was surprised to see so many of them in port. Around the outer perimeter of the harbour were a number of what looked like fish plants, and at the far end she saw the sign SØRENSEN FISKE.

She parked the car at the far end of the harbour lot and started to cover the two hundred or so metres to the plant. She had walked about a hundred metres when the smell first became noticeable. She couldn't identify it at first, but the closer she got to the plant, the more intense it became. And then she realized what it was: urine.

She gagged and began to breathe through her mouth. Every four or five breaths she would try her nose again, hoping the odour had abated. It just got worse — the raw, overpowering smell of piss. She felt as though she were

walking in a cloud of it and the pale overhead sun was caus-
ing it to ripple up from the pavement. It reminded her of a
street corner, a block from her hotel in Ho Chi Minh City,
that served as a toilet for street vendors and drunks. She
had to walk past the corner twice a day, and she could smell
the urine from at least twenty metres. Ho Chi Minh was
child's play compared to Hirtshals.

She was breathing entirely through her mouth when she
got to a wide-open plant door, from which the urine smell
was obviously escaping. She looked inside and saw six men
labouring. They were picking up grey fish that looked like
small five-pound torpedoes. They lifted each one by the tail
and then drove the head onto a spike that was attached to
a bench. They then cut across the back of the fish's neck,
gripped the skin with pliers, and ripped it off.

All the men were in rubber boots and overalls. None of
them of them wore shirts. Their chests were massive, their
forearms even bigger. One of them spotted Ava standing in
the doorway and yelled something at her in Danish.

She stepped inside, trying not to breathe. "I don't speak
Danish," she said.

"We already have a Chinaman who buys our fins," he
said in English.

"I don't want to buy fins."

"And we have a contract in the U.K. for all the meat."

"I don't want the meat."

"Then what do you want?"

"I'm looking for Ronny Sørensen."

"He's in the office," he said, pointing to a cubicle on the right.

She walked to the door and knocked. She heard something in Danish and assumed it was *Come in*.

A short, fat, bald man looked up at her when she opened the door. "Erik told you, our fins are all sold," he said.

"Are you Ronny Sørensen?"

"I am."

"My name is Ava Lee. I'm trying to locate your brother, Jimmy."

"You mean Jan?"

"Yes, the one and the same."

"Why?"

"Business."

"Jan doesn't do business."

"Painting business."

"That's not business. *This* is business," he said, motioning to the plant.

Uninvited, Ava sat in a chair across from the desk. "What are those fish anyway?" she asked.

"Sand sharks, dogfish, rock salmon, whatever you want to call them. Every market puts its own name on them."

"And that stench?"

"Uric acid. It is natural to the fish — nothing to do about it. If you want to process dogfish, you have to learn to cope with it. Me, I don't notice it anymore. The men, the same, though it's hard on us when we leave here. The smell gets into your clothes, which is why the men work in as little as they can. Still, my wife swears it gets into your skin. Nothing to do about that either. It puts money in the bank, and in this town we're about the last fish plant still in full production."

Ava wondered if her nylon jacket would absorb the urine smell, and was thankful she hadn't worn her good clothes.

"Where do the fins go?"

"New York, to a Chinaman, and from there God knows. Probably China. The meat goes to the U.K., to the fish-and-chippers. They don't have much cod anymore so they use the dogfish. They call it rock salmon. Sounds better, I guess."

"Yes, it does," Ava said. "Mr. Sørensen, I was asking about your brother."

"Haven't seen him in years."

"But do you know where he is?"

"Why?" he repeated.

"I have a client who bought several of his paintings. They're in the market for more but haven't been able to locate him."

"Jan's paintings were never in any great demand."

"Times change; things get trendy."

"Jan is trendy?"

"He has a growing following."

"Son of a bitch! I'm surprised."

"So, Mr. Sørensen, do you know where I can find him?"

"He's in the Faroe Islands."

She had heard the name but just couldn't place it. A vision of travelling to some South Pacific atoll surfaced in her head. "Where are the Faroe Islands?"

"In the middle of absolutely fucking nowhere," Sørensen said.

"That's helpful."

He laughed. "It's true — the middle of nowhere. They're about 800 kilometres southeast of Iceland, 650 kilometres north of here, and 800 kilometres northeast of Scotland, in the North Atlantic. The Faroes are the kind of place you don't arrive at by accident, unless of course you're some stupid Viking who got shipwrecked there two thousand years ago."

"Why did Jan go there?"

"Helga."

"His wife?"

"The fat cow is from there, never wanted to leave, and she nagged him all the time about going back. He finally gave in to her."

"How can I contact him?"

"You can write him a letter."

"Do you have a phone number for him, a house number or a mobile?"

"He doesn't have a phone."

"Email?"

"Don't be stupid. This is my brother we're talking about, a man who doesn't have much use for the outside world. He's living in a fishing village about half an hour from Tórshavn, the capital. It isn't enough that he wants to live in one of the most isolated countries in the world; when he gets there, he has to isolate himself even more."

"Do you have an address for him?"

"Yes."

"Can I get it?"

"I'm not sure he would appreciate that."

"Mr. Sørensen, all artists like to know their work is appreciated. I'm not trying to sell him a magazine subscription or a mobile phone plan; I want to buy some of his work."

He searched her face for a lie. Ava tried to smile, but it was difficult to make it natural when she was still breathing through her mouth.

"Okay, I guess it can't hurt," he said. He wrote the number on a yellow Post-it pad, tore off the sheet, and passed it to her.

She read, "Jan Sørensen, Tjorn, Faroe Islands."

"The village has fewer than a thousand people. You can't fart without everyone knowing. I write to him, I send him things, and I know the letters always get through because he always replies."

"He still has a bank account in Skagen," she said.

"How would you know that?"

"When we were trying to trace him, my client still had that information from their last transaction."

"The statements come here. I bundle them and send them every six months or so."

Ava saw a tiny opening. "I may actually go to the Faroes to see him. Would you like me to deliver his mail for you?"

"No," he said.

So much for that, Ava thought. "If I were going to the Faroes, Mr. Sørensen, what would be the best way to do it?"

"There is a ferry from Hanstholm."

"And how long a journey is that?"

"Close to two days."

"Ah, how about flying?"

"You can fly."

"From?"

"I'm not a travel agent," he said.

"That's true," Ava said, standing up.

"Tell me," he said, looking up at her. "Those shark fins, what do they do with them?"

"They make soup."

"I know that, but what kind of soup?"

"What do you mean?"

"I hear that it is a special kind."

"Well, it's traditionally served on special occasions: weddings, birthdays, honouring someone."

"So it's expensive, huh?"

She wondered what he was selling the fins for — maybe a couple of dollars a kilo. How would he react if he knew that a bowl of shark fin soup with only a few shreds of meat in it could cost anywhere from ten to fifty dollars? "I don't know. I'm not in the fish business."

Ava left the plant as quickly as she could, breathing through her nose every ten paces or so to test the air, but this time the odour didn't abate even when she had reached her car. She climbed inside and the smell came with her. She had no doubt that it had penetrated her hair. It was starting to rain again, a cool, steady drizzle. She rolled down the driver's-side window and drove away.

It was eleven thirty, still early morning in Toronto, and her travel agent wouldn't be up yet. She found an Internet café on the outskirts of the town. The place was empty. She went online to search for flights to the Faroe Islands. There was a direct flight from a place called Billund at two thirty. She checked a map; it looked like a two-hour drive. She couldn't make it. The only other option was to fly from Aalborg to Copenhagen and catch an evening flight from there.

Ava drove from Hirtshals to Aalborg with the window still down. She was getting wet, but it was preferable to the stench. The flight from Aalborg left at three, and that gave her just over two hours to kill. She checked back in to the Hvide Hus, only too happy to pay the full day's rate for a chance to shower.

The first thing she did in the room was strip off all her clothes. She found two plastic laundry bags in the closet, packed her clothing and running shoes into one, and then double wrapped it in the second bag.

Then she stepped into the shower and scrubbed and rescrubbed every pore of her body. She washed her hair three times. She stepped out of the shower and towelled herself off, then put on her blue-and-white pinstriped shirt and cotton slacks. She finished off the look with her new cufflinks and her gold crucifix and applied a generous spray of Annick Goutal perfume. The laundry bag sat on the bed. She sniffed. No urine smell. She packed it into her carry-on.

The same woman who had rented her the car that morning was at the booth when Ava took it back. She took the keys, noted the mileage, and passed Ava her credit card slip to sign, all without saying a word.

The flight from Aalborg was supposed to take just less than an hour, but it left late and she had to run to catch the Atlantic Airways flight in Copenhagen. That flight was scheduled to last two and a half hours, and because the fare difference between business class and economy was so large, Ava had booked economy. About ten minutes after takeoff she realized she had made a mistake. For the next two hours the liquor trolley made steady trips up and down the aisle. Passengers were buying doubles of everything. Ava had never seen anything like it.

"This is their last chance," the man in the seat next to her said. "The islands are dry. Liquor can't be bought anywhere there, not even in hotels. And Customs is very strict about people bringing in alcohol. So this is their last chance to load up."

"Thank God it isn't a longer flight," Ava said.

"Oh, it could be."

"I'm sorry?"

"Vagar Airport gets a lot of mist and quite often the plane can't land. They usually divert us to Reykjavik."

"Iceland?"

"It isn't so bad, though the people there are more depressed than ever since the country went bankrupt."

"How are the Faroe Islands?"

"People there are always depressed, or maybe I should say morose, regardless of what's going on. It's definitely a place where the glass is permanently half empty."

"You are Faroese?"

"No," he said, extending a hand. "My name is Lars. I work for the Danish government. We still heavily subsidize the islands, and I fly there every month or so to make sure the money is being spent as it should be."

"I'm Ava."

"What on earth is taking you there?"

"A painter, an artist."

"In the past you would see the occasional Japanese person there; they came to buy fish. There isn't much fish left, so no more Japanese. You will be an exotic sight. You can expect to be stared at."

"I'm Chinese, not Japanese."

"Still, a very unusual sight in the Faroes. The population is about ninety-four percent Faroese — old Viking — and the rest a mixture of Danes, Norwegians, and Icelanders. There are only about forty thousand people. They're outnumbered by sheep more than two to one."

"I don't have a hotel yet. Will that be a problem?"

"It shouldn't be. Tórshavn has lots of them, and at this time of year there aren't many tourists."

"The artist lives in a village near there, Tjorn."

"I know the place. Quite picturesque. The Russian trawlers use it as a base. There's a hotel there, actually, sort of a fisherman's hotel. It's not bad."

"How about the weather? I didn't bring a jacket — none that I can wear anyway."

"It will be cool and most probably wet. It rains about 260 days a year. You can buy a locally handmade sweater at the airport; that should do you."

"No snow?"

"Surprisingly, very rarely. The North Atlantic Current flows right around the Faroes and gives it moderate temperatures. Nothing warm, mind you, but you know, ten degrees in the summer, two degrees in the winter, that type of thing."

It was pitch black outside as they banked and started their descent into Vagar Airport. When Ava finally saw lights, they shone through a window that was streaked with rain.

For an airport so small there was a large contingent of customs officers standing behind a long wooden table. She soon saw why. They went through nearly every carry-on bag and patted down many of the passengers. Bottles of alcohol of all sizes began to cover the table. By the time she got to an officer there was enough to start a small liquor store.

Behind her was a row of wheelchairs occupied solely by men who looked too drunk to walk. As the chair behind her rolled, she could hear the clinking of bottles.

Lars walked with her into the terminal. He pointed out the sweater shop and a tourist information booth. "It's about a one-hour ride by car into Tórshavn since they built the tunnel under the sea from Vagar to Streymoy. Before that it was a couple of hours by ferry. We can share a cab if you want," he said.

"Let me get my hotel sorted first. Would you mind waiting?"

The woman at the booth seemed startled when Ava approached her, and even more so when Ava asked about the hotel in Tjorn. "Are you sure you want to stay there?" she asked.

"Is it clean?"

"Of course."

"Are there rooms available?"

"I'll call," the woman said.

The conversation was entirely in what Ava assumed was Faroese. When it was done, the woman gave her a little smile and said, "Yes, there is a room, and it's one with a bathroom."

"I'll take it."

"They're holding it."

"They don't even have my name."

"They don't need it. I told them who you are."

"But you don't —" Ava began, before realizing what the woman meant. "Thank you."

She went back to Lars. "I'm staying in Tjorn."

"Then you should catch your own taxi. It will cost you about 180 króna."

"What is that in U.S. dollars?"

"About forty, but most of the drivers won't take U.S. dollars. There's a bank machine over there if you need it."

"Thanks for all the help."

"If you're in Tórshavn for dinner or something, give me a call. I'm staying at the Town House Hotel and I'm always glad to have company."

She waved goodbye and wandered over to the gift shop. When Lars mentioned sweaters, she had imagined bulky knits in greys, blacks, and browns. But in the far corner she saw an explosion of colour and the name STEINUM above a rack that held some of the most exquisite knitwear Ava had ever seen. The sweaters were a riot of blues, reds, and yellows, with strange geometric shapes running around the edges. They were like pieces of art, no two the same. She checked the label: HANDKNIT, FAROE ISLANDS.

She had a hard time deciding which one to buy, so she bought two.

"These are beautiful," she said to the cashier.

"Jóhanna av Steinum — she is Faroese."

Ava pulled on the most colourful one, the fit tight, slimming. *I'm like a Fauvist painting come alive*, she thought.

16

THE HOTEL WAS A LONG, LOW BUILDING OF ONLY TWO storeys that sat at the base of a mountain, looking out directly onto the harbour. Tjorn was small. The main street, or what Ava assumed was the main street, ran for only about two hundred metres, separating the harbour from the town. The majority of the residents seemed to live above the harbour, their house lights beaming from the mountain side. She saw a number of fishing boats tied up at the wharf, and at least one of them was Russian, judging by its Cyrillic name.

She was met at the hotel door by a woman in denim shirt and jeans who looked like a slightly older version of Mimi. "I have been waiting for you. My name is Nina," the woman said in English.

"I'm Ava."

She led Ava to the lobby desk. She passed her a registry form and a key attached to a wooden stick. "I held the room with the bathroom for you."

"*The* room?"

"Yes, only one room has its own bathroom; the others

share. The Russians landed half an hour ago and the captain wanted your room, but I held it for you."

"Thank you," Ava said. She was beginning to think that Tórshavn might have been the better option. "Will my cellphone work here?"

"If you have Bluetooth it should."

"How about the Internet?"

"Not from your room, but you can always use my desktop if you need it."

"How about food?"

"The restaurant is still open. We serve for another hour."

Ava filled in the form and gave the woman her passport and credit card. "What kind of food do you have?" she asked.

"Sheep," the woman said.

"Lamb?"

"No, sheep."

"That's all you have?"

"We have run out of everything else."

Ava had eaten on the plane, not much, but enough to keep her going until morning. "I'm not really hungry, thank you anyway."

"If you do not mind me asking, what brings you here? We don't get many visitors who are not fishermen. We certainly do not get attractive young women, and Asian at that," the woman said with a quick smile.

Is she flirting with me? Ava thought. "I'm here to see an artist."

"Jan Sørensen?"

"Why, yes."

"That was an easy guess. He is the only artist we have," the woman said. "Does he know you are coming?"

"No."

The woman looked pained.

"Is that a problem?"

"He is a funny kind of man. Keeps to himself, doesn't mingle, doesn't even hardly talk. Some of us think it is because he is a Dane and thinks he is too good for us. Others think he is just a bit mad."

"What do you think?"

"I lean towards mad."

"He's married, right?"

"Helga, a down-to-earth Faroese girl. They have seven kids. She runs the house, runs the kids, and runs him, I think."

"Where do they live?"

She jerked her head to the right. "Up the hill, on the street that runs along the right side of the hotel."

"Does it have a number?"

"It has a purple door."

Ava checked her watch; it was almost ten o'clock.

"They will still be up, if that is what you are thinking. People here eat late and sleep late."

"I'll think about it."

Her room was on the main floor, just three doors away from the lobby. She unpacked her carry-on, shoving the laundry bag into the closet. She thought about having her clothes washed but didn't think she'd be in Tjorn long enough to get them back in time.

She walked back into the lobby and peered into the restaurant. There were three clusters of men eating what she assumed was sheep and drinking from bottles of what looked like vodka. She imagined they had brought the liquor from the boat. They looked at her with more interest than she liked, and she quickly backed away from the door and headed outside.

It was still drizzling, enough to dampen her hair but not enough to make her really wet. *What the hell,* she thought, and started up the street.

Sørensen's house was the fourth on the left. It was a two-storey brick structure, square, solid, with a window on either side of the purple door and three windows in a row above it. The downstairs windows were lit, the occupants shielded by the same type of lace curtains she had seen in Denmark.

The door had a large brass knocker. Ava swung it three times and then waited. The door opened a crack. A pair of bright blue eyes stared at her. A woman's eyes.

"Hello, my name is Ava Lee. I apologize for dropping in on you like this, but I'm here to speak to Mr. Sørensen about his work. I was given this address by his brother, Ronny, who said it would be all right for me to come."

The door opened enough for Ava to see who was behind it. This had to be Helga. About five feet tall and almost as broad. She was wearing a floral-patterned muumuu over bare legs and feet that were in sheepskin slippers. Her face was framed by a mass of frizzy light brown hair and her skin was pale and fleshy, with deep wrinkles etched at the corners of eyes that were alert, watchful. "We weren't expecting anyone."

"I know, I'm sorry. I would have written but I didn't have that much time, and I didn't know how else to contact you."

"What do you want?"

"As I said, I want to chat with Mr. Sørensen about his work, perhaps buy some pieces. I have a client who has several of his paintings and he's expressed an interest in buying more."

"What work?"

"The beach scenes."

"He doesn't do those anymore."

"Then maybe I could see what he has been working on."

Helga turned her head to look back into the house but didn't speak.

"We'd pay cash," Ava said.

"Come in," Helga said.

From the entrance Ava could see a dining room on the left, its long, empty table surrounded by twelve chairs, the walls covered in paintings. On the right was the living room, which had a wood-slat couch, two chairs, and a coffee table that was as bare as the one in the dining room. Everything was in perfect order, made all the more perfect by the aroma of fresh baking.

"Jan is upstairs; I'll get him. You can sit there and wait," she said, motioning to the living room.

More paintings hung there, most of them of the Tjorn harbour and all of which featured a bald man and a woman with bright red nipples. When Jan Sørensen walked into the room, she knew who the bald man was, and she imagined that Helga must have remarkable nipples.

He was only about five foot six and he was fat and soft, not a man used to manual labour or physical exertion of any kind. His eyes were as blue as Helga's, his skin as fair, and the same lines were etched beside his eyes. They could have been twins if she were taller.

"There was a dealer here from Copenhagen about six months ago. He tried to steal my paintings for next to nothing. Are you with him?" he said aggressively.

Ava stood and offered her hand. "My name is Ava Lee,

and I have nothing to do with a dealer in Copenhagen."

"Then who do you work for?"

So much for easing into this, she thought. "I work for a Chinese collector."

Sørensen looked baffled. "Chinese? I've never sold to any Chinese."

"They were purchased indirectly."

He looked at his wife. "I told you that agent was screwing us over."

"Can I sit?" Ava asked.

"Please," Helga said. "Can I get you anything? I just baked some muffins, and we have coffee and tea."

"Coffee would be fine."

"We only have instant."

"Perfect," Ava said.

She sat on one of the chairs and Sørensen sat on the couch facing her. He looked as if he wanted to ask her something, and she prepared herself. But he held back until his wife came back, with one cup of coffee. *That's interesting*, Ava thought.

"What paintings did your client buy?" he asked as the cup was placed on the table in front of Ava.

"Some Skagen beach scenes," she said.

"How much did he pay?"

"It varied."

"How much?"

Ava couldn't see how to avoid giving him a number. "On average, about five thousand," she said.

"Kroner?"

"U.S. dollars."

"That fucker!" he yelled, leaping to his feet.

Helga tugged at his arm, and for a second Ava was reminded of May Ling Wong trying to calm her husband. There was a strange kind of symmetry.

"He has never paid me more than five thousand kroner — that's about a thousand dollars!" he said to his wife.

"I know, Jan, I know. Now sit down; you don't want to scare this young woman."

He collapsed onto the couch.

Ava looked at the paintings on the wall. How was she going to get from them to Fauvist art? Her decision to walk up the hill had been taken too lightly, she now thought. She normally liked to prepare for meetings, imagining different scenarios and how they would play out. This was all too ad hoc. And now she was stuck.

"Can I speak frankly?" she said, talking to Helga more than her husband.

"Of course," the woman said.

"I'm going to buy some of Mr. Sørensen's paintings — the ones hanging here on the wall, if you'll sell them to me — but they aren't the real reason I came to see you."

They both looked at her, faces blank.

"What I really want to know is if Mr. Sørensen has ever dabbled in Fauvist art?"

She had seen photos of cattle getting hit between the eyes with a stun gun. Their reaction wasn't any different.

Jan slumped back on the couch, his anger replaced by something else. Resignation? Fear? His wife gathered herself more quickly, a determined look settling across her face. "We don't know what you're talking about," Helga said.

"I didn't come here to cause any harm to you, your husband, or your family," Ava said quickly. "I'm not the police and I don't work for any legal authority. I'm just trying to help a client solve a riddle."

"We don't know what you're talking about," she repeated.

"About five years ago, someone sent a money transfer to your husband for twenty thousand dollars. I believe that money was payment for producing paintings in the style of various Fauvist artists, which were sold as genuine works for considerable amounts of money. Now, I don't know if the money you received was a down payment or if there were additional payments, but I do know for certain that the payment was made. I have the bank records."

Helga glanced at her husband. Ava knew the look: her mother had used it often enough with her. It said, *I told you so.*

"How many paintings did you do?" Ava asked.

Sørensen turned and stared at his wife. She was looking into the dining room. Ava could almost see her calculating how much Ava might actually know. Jan Sørensen wasn't going to say anything, Ava knew. He was waiting for his wife to assume control.

"Mrs. Sørensen, the people I represent are very wealthy. They believe they've been cheated and they've hired me to find out what happened and to remedy it. They have no interest in pursuing you or your husband. In fact, they're prepared to pay you if you'll assist them in getting to the bottom of this. And not only will they pay you, I guarantee that your husband's name will never be connected to this affair."

"How much money are you talking about?" Jan said.

His wife shushed him as Ava leapt in. "Twenty thousand."

"Kroner?"

"Dollars."

Jan Sørensen started to speak but his wife shushed him again, and this time accompanied it with an elbow into his side. She stared at Ava, searching for a lie.

"We will pay you, and your husband has nothing to fear," Ava repeated.

Helga Sorensen plucked at the folds of her dress.

She's calculating, Ava thought. "Money in the bank and absolutely nothing to fear," she said.

The woman looked at her husband. Ava knew he had been ready to say yes the moment she said twenty thousand. "My husband and I will need to discuss this," Helga said deliberately. "That is not an admission of anything, you understand. We just need to discuss this."

"Do you want me to step outside?"

"No, it will take longer than that. Where are you staying? In Tórshavn?"

"No, here, at the fisherman's hotel."

"Come by in the morning. The children leave for school at eight twenty. Anytime after that."

"I'll be here," Ava said.

Helga Sørensen walked Ava to the door, opened it, and eased her onto the street without saying another word.

The rain was coming down hard now, and Ava was soaked when she got back to the hotel. Nina was still at the desk. "How did it go?" she asked.

"Better than I expected," Ava said. "It was worth getting wet. Now I just want to jump into a hot shower."

"I would do it quickly if I were you. The Russians will finish drinking soon and make a dash for the other bathroom and use up the hot water."

"I'll beat them to it, then," Ava said, heading for her room.

She stripped, showered quickly, towelled herself dry, and climbed into bed in underwear and a T-shirt. It had been a long day and now she was exhausted. She thought about calling Uncle and decided it was premature. She had met no-nonsense women like Helga before. She was confident she would be able to cut a deal with the Sørensens, but she wanted to have a dollar amount established and she wanted to have a name before phoning Hong Kong.

She was dozing, barely asleep, when she heard noises in the corridor. She thought about putting tissue in her ears when she heard Nina's voice. At the same time her door handle turned back and forth. Someone was trying to get into her room.

She walked to the door, and as she did, the handle jerked more violently. She heard men's voices in what sounded like Russian. She stepped back. Then Nina screamed, a mixture of fear and anger. Ava opened the door, took one step into the corridor, and walked almost directly into Nina.

Three men were to her immediate right, staring at Nina, who in turn was glaring at them and gripping an axe.

"We want to use your bathroom," one of the men said to Ava in English.

"Get away," Nina said.

The men were in a tight cluster. They began to separate, forming a semicircle around Nina and Ava. Ava thought they looked to be in their late twenties or early thirties. "Nina, back up. Stand next to me," she said.

As Nina did, the men inched closer. "Please go away," Ava said.

None of them were that big. One was close to six feet but wiry; he wore a greasy grey T-shirt. The other two were shorter and looked almost scrawny under their thick black woollen sweaters. Even from several feet away she could smell the odour of fish on them. They were grinning at each other and speaking Russian. She saw them looking at her underwear. The taller one moved so close that Ava could smell the liquor on his breath.

"What are they saying?" Ava asked Nina.

"I don't want to repeat it," she said, gripping the axe tighter.

"Tell me."

"They're saying they have never had ... never had Chinese cunt."

"Ah."

"I'm sorry I said that."

"Don't be. I expected it was something like that."

"I won't let anything happen," Nina said, waving the axe.

Ava took another step forward so that she was in front of Nina. "Put that down. I want to look after this without worrying about getting accidently clipped."

The three men were talking among themselves again. The one to her right laughed and reached out to grab her breast. Ava moved so quickly that his two friends froze as they tried to comprehend why he was on the ground, both hands holding his nose, which was spread across his face and spurting blood.

Before they could react, she took out the tall one, driving a phoenix-eye fist into the top of his belly, where nerve endings are grouped. He convulsed, gagging, as he fell to his knees.

The last one standing yelled something she couldn't understand and then swung a fist wildly in her direction. She sidestepped him and hammered her middle knuckle into his ear. He collapsed, falling sideways, his head bouncing off the wall and then hitting the floor.

"Good God," Nina said.

Ava stepped back into the doorway. "Those two will be okay in a while, but I probably broke that one's nose. He'll need a doctor." She stood over the wiry one, the one who had spoken to her in English. "How did you enjoy your Chinese cunt?" she asked.

"Go back into the room," Nina said. "I'll get the captain and we'll clean up this mess."

Ava stepped into the room and shut the door, turning the lock. She had trouble getting back to sleep. There was lot of commotion in the corridor, but after about half an hour it quieted down. She was finally nodding off when she heard a gentle rap at the door.

"Who's there?" she asked.

"Nina."

Ava got up and opened the door. Nina stood there with a bottle of cognac in one hand and two glasses in the other. "My nerves are rattled. I need a drink."

"I thought that was illegal here," Ava said.

"The Russians are good for some things."

"How are they taking this?"

"The captain was furious with those men," Nina said, walking past Ava into the room. "He will discipline them in his own way. He is a good man. He has been coming here for at least ten years."

Nina put the glasses on the dresser and filled them. Ava

closed the door and turned the lock, then walked over and sat on the edge of the bed. Nina joined her. "*Skol,*" she said, taking a slug.

Ava took a small sip. Cognac wasn't her kind of drink.

"Look at me," Nina said, holding out a hand. "I'm still trembling."

"It was a shock."

"Not to you, evidently. Just how did you do that, take out those men?"

"I've been training in martial arts since I was a teenager. It was no big deal."

"I've never seen martial arts like that."

"It's called bak mei. It's a very old discipline."

"And effective."

"I probably overreacted," Ava said. "I mean, the three of them were pretty drunk, and not exactly tough guys. But he shouldn't have reached for my breast."

"No, I think you were perfect," Nina said, her cheeks slightly flushed. "I think you *are* perfect."

She's coming on to me, Ava thought. "Nina, I'm tired and I really need to go to sleep."

"Oh, sure, I am sorry for disturbing you," she said, now flustered as well as flushed. She rolled her glass between her palms, downed the last of the cognac, and looked awkwardly at Ava.

Ava found the awkwardness endearing. "Do you want to join me?" she asked.

Nina, looking down at her glass, slowly nodded.

"Then take off your clothes, turn off the light, and get into bed."

17

AVA WASN'T SURE WHAT TIME IT WAS WHEN SHE WOKE.
Nina was perched on the side of the bed, already clothed.
She leaned down to kiss Ava on the forehead. "I have to go.
There's a meeting in Tórshavn that I have to be at, which
ends with a dinner tonight."

"I may not be here when you get back. If things go well
this morning, I'll be leaving later today," Ava said.

"I left my phone number, my email, and my home address
on a piece of paper. It's on the dresser. If you want to keep
in touch —"

"I just might."

Ava checked her watch as Nina closed the door. It was
seven o'clock. She hauled herself out of bed and went over
to the window. If the sun was up it was doing a good job of
keeping out of sight; the sky was so grey it verged on black.
She felt like a run — there was nothing like a run after good
sex. Then she remembered that her running gear was out
of action, and at almost that exact moment the sky opened
and the rain began to pelt. *It just wasn't meant to be*, she
thought.

There was a kettle and two sachets of instant coffee in the room. She boiled the water while she showered and then sat on the bed with a towel wrapped around her and drank two cups in quick succession. She thought about the Sørensens. If there was going to be a deal with them, it would have to be papered, however roughly. If they were going to tell her who had orchestrated the fraud, she wanted it in writing, signed and sealed. She called the front desk and a man answered.

"Nina said I could use the hotel computer," Ava said. "Can I come down in about fifteen minutes?"

"I don't see why not. It's in the back office here."

She dressed, the second Steinum sweater going over the black Brooks Brothers shirt. Mimi teased her constantly about her almost monochromatic taste in clothes. If it wasn't black, grey, white, or a muted blue or pink then it wasn't for Ava. But as she looked at herself in the mirror, all lit up like a Christmas tree, she thought the bright colours suited her and the tight fit showed off her curves.

The man at the desk looked to be about the same age as Nina, and Ava had a passing thought that he might be her husband. He pointed to a door behind the desk and she walked into an office that was only large enough to hold a metal filing cabinet and desk, a photocopier, and a swivel chair. Ava figured four people might be able to squeeze into it if three of them were standing. The walls were bare and there were no pictures on the desk or the cabinet. She sat at the computer and began to type. Twenty minutes later, she printed three copies of a document that left spaces for the dates and names to be filled in.

She walked into the lobby and looked out onto the harbour. It was set in a cove, three sides surrounded by mountains of bare rock split here and there by streams of water tumbling into the sea. The mountaintops were shrouded in mist, and in the distance she could see a faint rainbow.

"The Faroe Islands: nothing but mountains, rain, and sheep," a voice said behind her.

She turned and saw a burly man with a thick black beard; he was wearing a heavy black sweater. "I am the captain of the fishing boat out there," he said. "My name is Mikhail."

"I'm Ava Lee."

"I have been coming here for years and I never get used to how barren and isolated it is," he said. "When we could catch all the cod and haddock we wanted, it wasn't so bad. But now all we get is some perch and bluefish, and I am beginning to wonder if I'm not long for this place."

"Does it always rain like this?"

"No. Sometimes it rains harder, sometimes it just drizzles."

"I'm a sunshine girl."

"Then this isn't the place for you."

"I'm leaving today," she said. "You can have your room back."

"I am sorry about last night," he said.

"Me too."

"Those three men will not crew with me again. I have been at sea for twenty-five years, and I have always been aware that people think *fisherman*, think *Russian*, and then think *animal*. That is not me, and it won't be any man who signs on with me. So they will be gone."

"That's not necessary on my account."

"It is on mine."

"And I probably overreacted. I could have handled it better."

"The nose will mend, the other two will live. What will be worse for them is that the crew will taunt them for the rest of the trip about being beaten up by a hundred-pound girl. And then word will get around to the rest of our fleet and they will be joked about for years."

"I overreacted," Ava repeated.

"They are sitting in the restaurant. They would like to apologize to you."

Ava looked out again at the harbour. The rain was finally letting up and she figured she could make it to the Sørensens' without getting soaked. "No, that's not necessary," she said. "And now I really have to go; I have a meeting. But thank you."

Before the Russian could say a word she was gone out the door, making a hard right turn, and heading up the hill.

Helga Sørensen greeted her at the door. She was wearing a nicer dress, pantyhose, and a layer of makeup, and her hair was brushed back and coiled in a bun. Ava knew which one she would be negotiating with. "Where is Mr. Sørensen?" she asked.

"Upstairs. We do not need him."

"No, I do. There are questions I need answered, papers I need signed."

"Let us settle the money first," Helga said.

"I need to know that he'll answer my questions."

"As best he can."

"And that he will sign the papers."

"You said he would be kept out of this."

"I can't go to the person or people who organized this fraud with only his word. I've prepared a statement that I would like Mr. Sørensen to sign. It isn't perfect and it isn't meant to be legal. It's just an admission that he painted some of the artwork in question. I need to know what he painted, when, for whom, and how much he was paid. It won't go any further than me."

"Can I see it?"

Ava pulled a copy from her Double Happiness computer bag and passed it to Helga.

"The point is that they need to know that I actually know what happened, that I'm not guessing or making any charges that are unsubstantiated."

"There is no money mentioned in here."

"I didn't think you would want them to know you've been paid to cooperate. Don't you think it looks better all around if they believe you did this out of good conscience?"

"Better for you too."

"Yes, that's part of it."

"So what about the money?"

"I'll have twenty thousand wired to any bank account you want, once he signs."

"Twenty is not enough."

"I thought we had agreed —" Ava said.

"No, I said that my husband and I needed to talk. That is how things were left. And now we have talked and twenty thousand isn't enough."

She's good, Ava thought. "What number do you have in mind?"

"Eighty."

She wants forty, Ava thought. "That's more than you received for doing the paintings."

Helga sat stone-faced.

"I'll send you twenty-five."

"Eighty."

"Thirty."

"My husband insists on eighty."

"You need to meet me halfway. I'm quite sure my people will never approve eighty."

"Halfway?"

"Forty. Mrs. Sørensen, I've already doubled my original offer."

"All right, we'll settle for forty."

"Okay, I'll send you forty, but I want Jan to go over these papers right away, fill in the blanks, and sign three copies. If he can do that in the next hour, I can have the money in transit to you today. It might even hit your bank account by lunch. If he dawdles, I won't be able to get it out of Hong Kong until tomorrow."

Helga Sørensen stood up and walked to the foot of the stairs. "Jan!" she shouted.

Ava heard footsteps above her.

"Come down here," Helga said.

When he appeared, his wife grabbed him by the elbow and led him into the dining room. "We have to fill out these papers for the woman."

Helga came back into the living room. "I need to help him," she said. "I have this information filed and he doesn't remember so well."

"I'm not going anywhere," Ava said. "But if you give me your bank information, I'll get things started on my end."

"I'll be back."

She disappeared up the stairs. When she came back a few minutes later, she handed Ava a blank cheque from a Tórshavn bank. "I thought you had an account in Skagen," Ava said.

"Haven't used it in years," Helga said.

But you didn't close it, Ava thought. *How lucky is that?*

As Helga and Jan Sørensen began to fill in the gaps in the statement, Ava called Hong Kong.

"*Wei.*"

"Uncle, it's Ava."

"Where are you, Denmark?"

"No, the Faroe Islands."

"Where is that?"

"Somewhere in the North Atlantic, between Iceland and Norway."

"You had success in Denmark?"

"Some. I think I've located one of the artists."

"Have you told May Ling?"

"No, and I'm not going to."

"Probably best."

"Uncle, I need you to call the accountant to organize a wire transfer. It's for forty thousand U.S."

"When do you want it sent?"

Ava looked at Helga and Jan huddled together at the dining room table, he writing intently as she read from various files. They were going to give her what she wanted. "Send it now and get him to scan the wire confirmation and email it to me."

"I will have it done . . . Are you getting close?"

"Maybe once removed."

"Keep me informed."

"I will," she said.

She hung up and pulled her notebook from the bag. She opened it to the page where she had listed the paintings. If she was correct in her assumption, Sørensen had started painting the fakes five years ago. The Wongs had stopped buying two years ago. During the three-year gap, they had bought seven paintings that Torrence thought were fakes. Those paintings were what she expected to see on Sørensen's statement.

Helga came into the living room with Jan in tow. He looked sheepish, like a kid who had been caught doing something naughty. "Here," she said, thrusting the papers at Ava.

Six paintings were named, the last six, in the exact order in which the Wongs had purchased them. Sørensen had been paid ten thousand dollars for each one. She turned to the second page and saw the name Glen Hughes, with a London address.

"How did this Hughes find you?" Ava asked.

"Through Maurice O'Toole," Helga said. Her husband nodded in agreement.

"We got a letter from Maurice when we were still in Skagen," Helga continued. "He said he had been doing some work for a dealer and that he was going to have to give it up. They were looking for a replacement and he wanted to give them Jan's name. He wanted to make sure we were okay with it."

"How did Jan know O'Toole?"

"They went to art school together and kept in touch afterwards. They had a lot in common, Maurice and him, both of them drawn to water, to seascapes."

"And they could both copy."

"Of course, it was part of their training. Jan told me he and Maurice spent many hours in galleries copying the masters. They were at the top of their class. When they graduated, they went their separate ways but always kept in touch with letters and cards. Jan had some success in Skagen but poor Maurice could not find a market for his work and became very frustrated, bitter. That is when he started to play around with forgeries. It was just a way to make a living, to get by until his own work made its mark. He wrote to Jan about it — that was before he started on the Fauvists. He developed quite a reputation, he did, in some parts of the art world. It wasn't surprising that those people sought him out when they decided to concentrate on Fauvist art."

"So why did he give it up?"

Jan spoke, his eyes welling. "He was dying — brain cancer."

"Did you know that around the same time you got your first ten thousand dollars, O'Toole's wife was sent a hundred thousand?"

"No. How would I know that?" she said.

"Why do you think it was sent?"

"I don't know and I don't care. We were happy to get ten. It bought us this house. It got us out of Skagen."

"How did Jan and this Hughes person connect?"

"Maurice wrote to Jan and explained his problem. He knew we were hard up for money and he thought Jan could pick up the assignment. That's when Hughes wrote to us."

"And you agreed?"

"Obviously."

"Then what happened?"

"Hughes came to Skagen to meet Jan. He brought one of Maurice's Fauvist paintings with him and asked Jan to duplicate it. It took him only two days. Hughes asked us to take over the project when he saw the result."

"Did he explain what the project was? I mean, you knew you were doing something that was probably illegal. Weren't you curious about what he was doing with the paintings?"

"We didn't care."

"No curiosity at all?"

"You have to understand how hard it was for us in Skagen. We lived hand-to-mouth, we never had enough money, and I was tired of Jan begging his brother for loans. We didn't care what Hughes was doing with the paintings as long as he kept paying us ten thousand for each one."

Ava could hardly imagine what it would be like to care for seven children. "How did Jan decide what to paint?" she asked.

"Hughes would write and suggest an artist, maybe a theme, and then leave it to him."

"You sent him the paintings?"

"Yes, to London."

"Did Jan sign them?"

"Of course."

"Did you meet Hughes, Mrs. Sørensen?"

"Yes, that one time in Skagen."

"What kind of man is he?"

"I didn't like him."

"Why not?"

Jan Sørensen was shifting uncomfortably, his eyes on the floor.

"He was one of those overly polite people, the kind who knows he's better than you and lets you know it by talking down to you. And he was too friendly, saying how wonderful our family was when I knew he didn't mean it, and talking about what a great partnership he and Maurice had, and how he was sure he and Jan would be great mates. That's the word he used, *mates*."

"What does he look like?"

"He is a tall man, a full head above Jan. He's thin, bony, his face is long and pointy, and his eyes I found very strange."

"His eyes?"

"Yes, they were so close to his nose, pressing in, almost running into each other. When he looked at me, I had the sensation that he had one big eye instead of two like the rest of us. But one eye or two, he still looked sneaky."

"He kept his word, though?"

"What do you mean?"

"He always paid you in full, on time?"

"He did."

"When was the last time you heard from him?"

"It was almost two years ago. He wrote to say he had terminated his agreement with the person buying the Fauvist art and that he was going to have to stop buying from us. We wrote back saying there had to be a market somewhere for the forgeries, and that if he wanted, Jan could paint in other styles. He responded by saying that we misunderstood the nature of the commission — that he wasn't in the business of selling forgeries, that the customer he had was knowingly buying fakes. He said they loved the Fauvists, couldn't afford originals, and were very happy to hang Maurice's and Jan's interpretations. He underlined *interpretations*."

"Did you believe him?"

"Was it true?" she asked. "What Hughes said about the customer?"

"I wouldn't be here if it was true," Ava said.

Helga looked at her husband. "I told you it was a lie," she said, then turned to Ava. "My husband is too trusting at times. He believed that story."

"Have you heard from Hughes since?"

"No, and we wrote to him twice, and to the gallery. No answer."

"Did you keep his letters?"

"All of them."

"Can I get the one he sent two years ago to end your relationship?"

"I'm not sure —" Helga began.

"I'll make a photocopy. You can keep the original."

"I think that will be okay."

"Good. Why don't you get it for me."

Helga returned with a fistful of letters. "I thought you might as well have the other ones too, the ones asking him to paint this guy and that guy."

"Do you want to walk down to the hotel with me?" Ava said.

"Why not?"

Jan Sørensen sat quietly as his wife got her coat. *He's like a child*, Ava thought, *one of those men who can't survive without a strong woman*. And Helga fit that bill.

Helga reappeared with a coat and a Burberry umbrella that was ratty even for a fake. "I shouldn't be long," she said to Jan.

He stood and walked with them to the door. "Excuse me, but do you still want some of my paintings?" he said to Ava.

"Jan, the business is done," his wife said.

"But last night she said —"

"Actually, I wouldn't mind having a painting," Ava said. "The thing is, I don't want to take it with me."

"We'll send it," he said.

Ava gave her business card to Helga. "Send it to this address. Choose any painting you want and send me an invoice."

Helga glanced at her husband and then turned to Ava. "I see no need for an invoice."

Ava smiled. "Thank you."

They walked down the hill side by side, Helga's arm linked with Ava's for support. She outweighed Ava at least two to one and wasn't completely steady in a pair of shoes with small heels. Helga kept glancing left and right, as if anxious about who was observing them, or maybe hoping that someone would see her walking side by side with the exotic young Chinese woman.

The same man was behind the desk at the hotel, and he nodded as they walked into the lobby. "Can I use the office again?" Ava asked.

"Sure."

Ava went into the office with Helga. She sat at the computer and signed on while Helga hung over her shoulder.

"Do you know how to use a photocopier?" Ava asked.

"No," Helga said.

Ava took one of the letters and placed it face down on the glass. She pointed to the COPY button and hit it. "That's all you have to do," she said.

While Helga copied the letters, Ava checked in to her email. The wire had been sent. She opened the attachment and pressed PRINT. "Your money has been sent already," she said.

"Thank you," Helga said, focused on the photocopier.

It was just past nine o'clock — three a.m. in Toronto —

and Ava knew there was no way she could reach her travel agent. She logged on to the Atlantic Airways site and searched for a flight that would get her to London. There was a 2:45 p.m. flight from Vagar to Copenhagen that would connect with a Cimber Sterling flight to Gatwick, getting her into London just before nine in the evening. "I'm thinking I would like to leave today," she said, pulling the copy of the wire confirmation from the printer and handing it to Helga, "but if you want to me stay until the money is in your bank account, I will."

Helga read the document and said, "You can go."

Ava booked the flights and then looked for a hotel. The Hughes Gallery was on Church Street in Kensington. Two months earlier, while on the job for Tommy Ordonez, the Filipino billionaire, she had been in that exact area, at the Fletcher Hotel, and had enjoyed its proximity to Kensington Gardens and Hyde Park. It was right on the High Street, directly across from the gardens, and a short walk from Church Street. The room rate was 235 pounds a night — Hong Kong Peninsula Hotel rates. She clicked onto their website and reserved a room.

Glen Hughes had written to the Sørensens on gallery stationery. The letterhead listed a phone number and a general email address. Ava punched the number into her cellphone. A woman's voice answered, "Hughes Gallery."

Well, it's still open for business, Ava thought. "Could I speak to Mr. Hughes, please?" she asked.

"He doesn't arrive until ten."

"Do you expect him today?"

"Of course."

"And what is your closing hour?"

"We're open from nine to six every day but Sunday."

Ava hung up and returned to the computer. She drafted an email saying that she was the representative for a Hong Kong–based art collector and was in London on a scouting expedition. She asked to drop by the gallery at eleven o'clock the next morning to meet with Mr. Hughes. She sent the email without much optimism. If there was no response, she'd phone again when she got to London, or if necessary make a cold-call visit.

Helga had finished making the copies and bundled the letters together. She handed Ava her set. "I want to say that I'm very thankful for the money. I just need you to understand that I am still concerned that Jan's name doesn't get dragged through the mud because of this. He is a good man and a good painter, and we are forever hopeful that he will find an audience for his own work."

"I will do everything I can to protect his reputation," Ava said.

She walked Helga to the hotel door and stood outside in the drizzle, watching the stout woman make her ascent up the hill. After ten steps or so, Helga turned, smiled, and waved. Ava felt a touch of guilt as she waved back. The truth was, she wasn't at all sure she would be able to keep Jan Sørensen's name secure.

When she returned to the hotel, the front desk had been abandoned. She saw that the man who had been there was now in the office, using the computer. She stared at his back, willing him to see her and voluntarily give it up. He ignored her. "Will you be long?" she finally asked.

"A few hours," he said.

"Could you book me a taxi for the airport?"

"What time?"

"My flight is at two forty-five."

"I'll have a taxi here for one," he said.

In her room, she went through the letters from Hughes to Sørensen. The last one was a completely self-serving, cover-your-tracks kind of letter. The others were more straightforward, each one asking Sørensen if he could do a work "in the style of" a specific artist. The first four comprised a list of most of the Fauvists — Dufy, Vlaminck, Derain, Braque — while the last two wanted repeats of Vlaminck. There was never a hint that Hughes was engaged in anything shady, although in the letter requesting another Vlaminck he did mention that the customer had been absolutely thrilled with the latest work.

Ava pulled out her notebook and recapped the morning's meeting. She then slid the letters inside the notebook and placed it in her bag. She lay on the bed. The sheets still smelled of Nina's perfume. The scent was a bit raw, like Nina herself. She thought about calling Uncle and then dismissed the idea. She had nothing new to add, just a name. And until she met with Glen Hughes, that's all it was — a name.

18

AVA FOUGHT HER WAY OUT OF GATWICK AIRPORT TO catch the express train to Victoria Station, and then she fought her way through the station to catch the tube to Kensington High Street. It was close to ten o'clock when she finally walked into fresh air, air that was as cold and damp as in Skagen or Tjorn. Curaçao seemed a long way away. She was happy she had worn one of her Jóhanna av Steinum sweaters, sweaters that she liked so much she had bought one each for Mimi and Maria at the Vagar shop before leaving.

From the station she had a short walk, past a Marks & Spencer and a Whole Foods, along the High Street to the hotel.

Ava was relieved to check in and get to her room. It was a spectacular modern blend of black, red, and white — sparse, functional, yet still somehow luxurious. A bottle of chilled mineral water and a bowl of fresh fruit were on the coffee table, accompanied by a welcoming note from the hotel administration.

She was hungry, and called the front desk. The concierge informed her that the main restaurant was still open. She quickly unpacked and then got two laundry bags from the closet. She put the black Brooks Brothers shirt and cotton slacks in the first bag, and in the other the laundry bag from Aalborg with her running gear. She carried the bags downstairs and deposited them at the front desk. "Is there any way I could get these back early tomorrow?" she asked.

"Is nine a.m. soon enough?" the desk clerk said.

"Yes, thank you," Ava said, pleased with the five-star service.

She walked into the Fletcher's dining room and was immediately led to a seat. She ordered sautéed langoustines with crab tortellini in a shellfish bisque as a starter, and pan-fried black bream with truffle mashed potatoes as her main. Everything came in rapid succession; she barely had time to drink half her bottle of white burgundy. She took the balance back to her room in an ice bucket.

She turned on her laptop; there were more than twenty new emails in her inbox. She quickly deleted the spam, skipped reading any she didn't think were urgent, and then opened the three she had received from Mimi, her father, and Maria.

Mimi's was, as usual, filled with the trivia of her life, but when Ava neared the end, her interest spiked.

Derek and I have decided that both our condos must go. He wanted to keep his because his father bought it for him as an investment, but I don't want him to have a place to bolt to if things don't work out. He's agreed. Happy me! So we start out on a level footing. I have two real estate agents scouring the

midtown area for a house. I really like the area between Bayview Avenue and Mount Pleasant Road,
south of Eglinton. Lots of young professionals with
kids and dogs and nannies.

Ava couldn't imagine either Mimi or Derek in that envi-
ronment. But then, she hadn't ever contemplated that they
could be a couple. Ava also noted that Mimi wasn't asking
for her opinion.

In the last paragraph of the email, Mimi mentioned
Maria. Ava paled as she read, Maria and I had lunch yesterday. She told me that her mother is flying in from Bogota
for a Toronto holiday. She says she wants to introduce you
to her mother but she's not really sure how you would react
to that idea. She also said she wasn't sure how her mother
would react, but that it was time to find out.

Introduce me as what? Ava thought. The last thing she
wanted was to get caught between Maria and her mother.
Ava had never discussed her own sexuality with Jennie
Lee, and she kept her personal life and her friends private.
Jennie knew, of course, about Ava's sexual orientation and
from time to time made vague references, but it was a subject they'd never directly broached and never would, just
as Ava never pried into Jennie's relationship with Marcus.
Neither woman needed explanations, and the respect and
love they had for each other were absolute.

I don't think meeting her mother is a great idea, Ava
wrote to Mimi. Then she turned to Maria's email. It mentioned the lunch and the possibility of Derek and Mimi
selling their condos, and then simply said, And by the way,
my mother is thinking about coming to Toronto for a short

holiday. Ava didn't know how to reply, and decided not to for the time being.

Her father's email was, if anything, even more vague. Cruise goes better. Mummy and Bruce have made some kind of peace. I'm staying in Toronto for an additional week when we get back. I'm pleased that you and Michael connected, though I do find it a bit strange. At some point we need to talk about him.

She read the message three times, questions popping into her head about Bruce, the extra week, and Michael. She started to ask those questions and then stopped. She was on a job and didn't need more distractions. She simply wrote, Glad to get your news. See you in Toronto.

Ava signed out of her email account and accessed Google. She typed in "Hughes Art Gallery." There were more than sixty references, though none of them were less than two years old. If she hadn't actually phoned the gallery she might have assumed it had gone out of business, which would have been sad, given that it had apparently been around for almost a hundred years.

Glen Hughes' grandfather had established the gallery, which his father had taken over and expanded in size and reputation. The business had been passed on to Glen and his brother, Edwin. Many of the Google references were from art journals, which spoke highly of the brothers. Their firm was as knowledgable about the art scene of the past 150 years as the big art auction houses such as Christie's, Sotheby's, Bonhams, and Harrington's. The brothers — Glen most often — were described as specialists in the Impressionists, the Post-Impressionists, and the Fauvists. *Kwong must have known them by reputation*, Ava thought. *That's why he was so willing to take their word at face value.*

She read entry after entry citing Glen Hughes as authenticating this painting and casting doubt on that painting. She began to worry. This was an acknowledged expert she was dealing with, not a fool. The letters he had sent to the Sørensens were open to interpretation. Jan Sørensen's position could be described as not much more than one man's opinion. *No*, she told herself, *it will work*. She turned off her computer and headed for bed.

She fell asleep without much more thought about Glen Hughes. But the emails from Maria and her father crowded into her mind, and it was her father who came to her as she slept.

In recent months Ava had been having a recurring dream about Marcus. She and her father were trying to catch a plane or a ship in some unknown city on their way to some other unknown city. More often than not she lost him in the attempt. This night, for the first time, her half-brother Michael entered the nocturnal drama. Michael and her father were inseparable; it was always she who was getting lost, who was searching. She woke just as the three of them had reached an airport terminal, only to be shuffled into different check-in lines that meandered through different buildings, towards different planes.

It was seven o'clock; she had slept long, if not well. Her father and Michael dissolved from her mind and Glen Hughes re-entered it. She rolled out of bed, boiled water in the hotel kettle, and made her first Starbucks VIA instant coffee of the morning.

She quickly downed two cups, scanning the morning

newspapers, and then thought about taking a calming run before she remembered that her tracksuit was at the cleaner's. She pulled a Steinum sweater over her T-shirt and Brooks Brothers black linen pants and headed downstairs and out onto the High Street. It was another dreary day, without a patch of blue in the sky. She crossed the High Street and began to walk briskly up Church.

The Hughes Gallery was half a kilometre from the hotel. It was larger than Ava had envisioned, taking up the equivalent of two storefronts. A large double door made of a dark wood separated two windows. On the left door the word HUGHES was affixed in brass letters; on the right door was GALLERY. Both windows had the name painted discreetly in the lower left corner. There was a solitary painting in each window, artists Ava had never heard of, their style distinctly abstract. She looked inside. The gallery ran so far back that she couldn't see the end of it, only a jumble of statues and paintings.

She turned and walked back to the hotel. The gallery was impressive and looked prosperous. That only reinforced the doubts she had about her ability to leverage Glen Hughes.

The weather was starting to turn nasty; the wind picked up and the sky began to spit rain. Despite the sweater she felt a chill. By the time she reached the High Street the rain had intensified and she knew a run was now out of the question.

As she walked into the lobby she saw her dry cleaning hanging near the concierge's desk. It was ten to nine. *Pretty damn good timing,* she thought, as she carried it to her room.

She hung up her clothes in the closet and went to the window. The rain was now lashing sideways.

Ava made herself another coffee and then sat at the computer. She logged in to her emails with little expectation, but near the top of her inbox was one from the Hughes Gallery, saying Mr. Hughes couldn't see her at eleven but was available at ten. She replied, saying she'd be there.

She showered quickly, not bothering to wash her hair. Standing naked in the bathroom, she applied a touch of lipstick and a hint of mascara and dabbed her Annick Goutal perfume on her wrists and at the base of her throat. She brushed her hair and then pulled it back and fixed it with her ivory pin. She went to the bedroom and put on a bra and panties, her black Brooks Brothers shirt with modified Italian collar, and black linen slacks. The Shanghai Tang cufflinks looked perfect against the black. She fastened the gold crucifix around her neck and then added the Cartier watch. Then she slipped on the new alligator heels and stood back to look at herself in the full-length mirror. *Professional and ready for battle*, she thought.

She heard thunder and walked back to the window. The rain was still pelting down. She packed the Sørensen letters in her Shanghai Tang bag and headed downstairs to the business centre to make an extra copy of the documents for Hughes in case the need arose.

On her way out, the concierge offered her a choice of umbrellas. She took the largest one, which had WILSON GOLF printed on it. Even with the umbrella she felt the effects of the rain as it splattered off the sidewalk and wet her shoes and slacks. The walk felt twice as long as it had earlier, but when she got to the gallery door it still was only ten to ten. She tried the door but it was locked. She huddled in the doorway, the umbrella pointing towards the street.

"Come in, come in," a woman's voice said suddenly as the door opened behind her.

Ava slid in and was greeted by a tall, slim young woman with a mop of blonde hair styled into an über-chic Afro. She wore a short, tight red designer dress that showed off her long legs.

"You must be Ms. Lee. My name is Lisa. Mr. Hughes is in the back. Let me take you there."

Lisa guided Ava through the space, which was filled with numerous paintings, statues, and ceramics. When they reached the other end of the gallery, Lisa opened a door and led Ava into the office area. All the doors were closed but one, which opened into an office where a tall man in a brown suit sat at a desk. He had thick dark blond hair and a long, thin face and pointed chin. When he looked up at Ava, she saw that his clear blue eyes were not close-set the way Helga Sørensen had described. Ava felt her stomach sink.

"Mr. Hughes, Ms. Lee is here," Lisa said.

Ava stood in the doorway to the office.

Hughes stood and extended his hand. "I'm Edwin Hughes," he said.

"Ava Lee."

"Have a seat," he said, pointing to a chair across from his desk. "Would you like anything? Coffee or tea?"

"No thanks," Ava said, noticing the painting on the wall behind him. It was the Tower Bridge. "A Derain?"

"Yes, that's very observant of you."

She continued to stare at the painting as she struggled to find a way to initiate the conversation.

"So, Ms. Lee, you represent a Hong Kong firm?"

"I do."

"We haven't done much business in Hong Kong. Japan has been kinder to us as a market."

He has a lovely voice, she thought. *And he paces his words quite carefully.* "I don't mean to be impolite, but I was actually expecting to see Mr. Glen Hughes," Ava said.

"My brother is no longer associated with this part of the business," he said calmly.

"I see."

"I assure you, whatever gallery business you were planning to discuss with him, you can discuss with me."

"I'm not so sure that's true."

He looked quizzical. "Ms. Lee, you are sounding mysterious."

"I'm sorry, this is awkward."

"Awkward? That's rather a strange word. It's paintings you're here to discuss, I presume."

"Yes, it is."

"Then there's no reason to feel awkward. That is my business, after all."

He said it matter-of-factly, and Ava responded in kind. "I was going to talk to your brother about the Fauvist art he's been commissioning over the past ten years or so, the art he sold through the Great Wall Antiques and Fine Art Gallery in Hong Kong."

"The most recent piece of Fauvist art was painted in about 1910, Ms. Lee."

"I am aware of that. This gallery commissioned the works. They were fakes, of course, designed to mislead my client."

"This gallery did no such thing," Hughes said, his voice

calm but his eyes hardening as he looked across the desk at her.

"I have a signed statement from one of the artists who was paid to paint them, and I have copies of correspondence between your brother and the painter discussing the project. The correspondence from your end is on gallery stationery."

She sat back, waiting for a reaction. Instead he said, in the same even tone, "What foul weather has brought you and word of my brother to my door?"

"Your standard London rain."

He smiled. "Would it bother you if I asked to see the correspondence?"

"No, I brought it with me," she said, opening her bag. She passed him a set of copies.

"Can you give me a moment alone with these?"

She hesitated.

"I'm not going to do a runner out the back door," he said.

Ava stepped into the hallway, trying to focus on the art that was hung haphazardly on every wall. But she couldn't get her mind off the fact that it was Edwin Hughes she was speaking to and not Glen.

"You can come back in now," Edwin said after a few minutes.

When she sat down, he put his feet up on the desk and pushed back, his hands clasped behind his neck. She noticed the shoes — gorgeous brown leather wingtips. "First of all, Ms. Lee, if this correspondence is in any way genuine, and if the charges you're making have any substance to them at all, then you need to be talking to my brother and not me."

"The correspondence is on gallery stationery."

"So you've said. And what does that mean? Someone stole or copied our stationery?"

"Your brother's signature is on those letters."

"So you claim," he said. "And if it is, so what? He was commissioning work on his behalf, not the gallery's."

"He was representing the gallery, the business," she said.

"Don't dare to presume that you understand the nature of our business," Hughes said, his tone rising just slightly. "My brother and I each had our own arrangements. Not everything we did was in tandem."

"He was representing the gallery," she insisted.

"I won't acknowledge that because it is completely untrue."

"The letters —"

"The letters are utter rubbish," he said. "They don't make any mention of fakes or forgeries. The last one, in fact, makes it very clear that he was commissioning copies for a client who knew what he was buying." He paused. "Now here I am defending my brother, when that really isn't my intent."

"Then what is your intent?"

"To tell you that neither I nor this gallery had anything to do with whatever this is."

"My client may think otherwise."

"And what? Sue? Based on those letters? Go ahead."

"A lot of money was spent on those forgeries."

"And where is that money? I assure you, it isn't in our bank account."

"No, it's in a numbered account in Liechtenstein."

He paused, and Ava saw the first flicker of something other than confidence in his eyes.

"I know of no such account."

"Who would?"

"Talk to my brother."

"I'd love to. Where can I find him?"

"In New York."

"You have a gallery in New York?"

"No, he has an office in New York. A few years ago we restructured the business and he opted to go to North America."

Ava thought of the Google entries that were all more than two years old. "Two years ago?"

"Yes, about then."

"There was no mention of his leaving the business in the research I did."

"We saw no reason to make a fuss about it. We did it quietly."

"And I didn't see any reference to him in any new business."

"He's set himself up as a private art consultant, and he's arrogant enough to believe that he doesn't need to advertise his wares. He thinks those who need him will find him."

"And how would I find him?"

"Ms. Lee, you surely don't need my help to do that."

"I imagine not."

"But I have to tell you that when you do find him, you'll get a very similar reaction to mine, though perhaps less polite. My brother has never been afraid to use lawyers, and if you even suggest any impropriety on his part he'll have them down your neck."

"What about unwanted publicity?"

"He couldn't care less."

"And you?"

He put his foot on the letters on the desk and slid them back to her with the heel of his shoe. "Good luck with my brother," he said.

19

AVA WAS LED TO THE CHURCH STREET ENTRANCE,
where Lisa returned her umbrella. She felt as if she were
being deposited on the street like trash.

The rain had let up, easing into a whippy drizzle. She
walked back to the hotel, returned the umbrella to the concierge, and went directly to her room. The maid had been
there already. The bathroom was sparkling, the bed was
made, and a package of bonbons was resting on her pillow.
There was still almost half a bottle of wine from the night
before. Ava poured herself a glass and sat by the window.

She couldn't remember the last time she had felt so
incompetent. At the very least, she should have been prepared for the possibility of meeting Edwin Hughes instead
of, or even with, Glen Hughes. Ava took pride in being organized for meetings, prepared for any eventuality. *How could
I have made such a mess of this one?* she thought. *I didn't do
enough research.* She should have confirmed which Hughes
she was going to meet. She should have known the brothers
had split. She should have known enough about their characters to know how to squeeze them. Instead she went in

ill-prepared, with no discernible strategy other than waving around letters she already knew were open to too many interpretations.

Ava then thought about Edwin Hughes. He had been so calm, so sure of himself, that she found herself believing almost everything he had said, including the fact that her threat to sue him or his brother or the gallery didn't concern him. She hadn't intimidated him; she hadn't even mildly rattled him. The only time he seemed interested in what she was saying was when she mentioned the bank account, and then he had basically thrown her out of his office. She thought of him shoving her letters across the desk to her with his foot.

The real question was whether or not Edwin had anything to do with the Fauvist scam. On balance, she thought that he hadn't. There had been only one signature on the letters sent to Sørensen, and that belonged to Glen Hughes.

The bottom line was that she didn't have any leverage, even in theory, if the Hughes brothers were prepared to withstand lawsuits and bad publicity. And that was assuming that May Ling and Changxing would agree to sue. She felt, despite May's claim, that Wong never would. His face was worth more than $70 million.

So what do I have? she thought. "Sweet bugger all," she said softly to herself.

She was close to packing it in. But she also knew she couldn't give up until she had exhausted every lead. She decided to find out more about the brothers, something she should have done before. She phoned Frederick Locke.

"This case I've been working on, it's led me into some complicated areas. I was hoping you could help," she said.

"Where are you?"

"London."

"You do get about."

"I came here to see a man named Glen Hughes and instead found myself talking to his brother, Edwin."

The line went silent. "Holy fuck," he said finally.

"Is that good?"

"Are you telling me you think the Hughes brothers might be involved in this scam?"

"One of them anyway, maybe both."

"You don't know who they are, do you."

"Only what I read online about Glen."

"They're huge. In our business they don't come much bigger, outside of museums and national art galleries and leading international auction houses. Are you sure about all this?"

"No, I'm not, Frederick. That's why I'm calling you. I thought you could tell me a bit more about them. For example, when I met with Edwin this morning, he said he and his brother had parted company."

"Yes, that's true. It was all hush-hush when it happened but it eventually leaked out. By the time it did, no one thought twice about it."

"What was the cause?"

"No one actually said."

"Were there rumours?"

"Some. There was talk of a financial falling-out. One of the brothers — I think it was Glen — was supposedly playing outside the sandbox, so to speak."

"What is he doing now?"

"Running a business in New York as a private consultant to collectors," Locke said, confirming Edwin Hughes' claim.

She was writing while he spoke. Almost uncon-
sciously she found herself underlining the words *two years*.
"Frederick, it was that Jan Sørensen, the Sandman, who
pointed me in the direction of Hughes."

"So you found him?"

"Obviously."

"And?"

"He painted a good number of the fake Fauvists."

"Are you sure?"

"I have a signed statement from him."

"Good God."

"And he told me that Maurice O'Toole did the others."

"That doesn't surprise me," Locke said. "I did some more
research after our last chat and the boy did have that reputation. I spoke to someone who told me that Mr. O'Toole
was a whiz with Matisse and did very passable Monets and
Manets."

Manet wasn't on her list. She added the name.

"So, Ava, where does this leave you?" Locke asked.

"I'm not quite sure. I don't have what you would call hard
proof of anything. Even Sørensen's statement isn't supported in any concrete way other than that the paintings
exist, and Edwin Hughes seems immune to threats of lawsuits or bad publicity. He tells me his brother will be an
even tougher case."

"Remember what I told you about our business being
filled with hard men? Well, they don't come much harder
than the Hughes brothers."

"I sense that."

"So what to do?"

"I don't know, I really don't know," she said. "I need to do some more thinking. But look, thank you for the information. You've been very helpful. If I have any more questions I hope you won't mind me calling."

"Not at all. My days are quite repetitive and can be a bit of a bore. Call me whenever you wish."

Ava closed her phone and looked out the window, down at the High Street and across to Kensington Gardens. The sky was clearing and people were walking without umbrellas. She decided to try to get in a run before the weather changed one more time. She quickly changed into her tracksuit and left the hotel.

Ava crossed the street, entered the Gardens at Exhibition Road, and then loped across the Serpentine to West Carriage Drive. She ran north from there until she reached the jogging path. Hyde Park and Kensington Gardens ran seamlessly into each other, separated only by the Serpentine. The total area was more than six hundred acres, just smaller than Central Park in New York, and the jogging path was five kilometres long. She normally would have done one full lap after the initial two kilometres or so she had run to the starting point. Today she needed to burn off frustration, and one lap wouldn't cut it.

As she ran, she replayed the past few days. She told herself it was time to call Uncle, May Ling Wong, and her travel agent and head on home. Ava was halfway through the second lap when a scrap of conversation she'd had with Helga Sørensen came to mind, along with something Frederick Locke had just said to her. She headed back to the hotel.

When she got back to her room, she wrapped a towel around her shoulders, pulled out the Chelsea–Kensington phone-book, and looked up George McIntyre, the lawyer she had dealt with on her last trip to London.

The receptionist put her on hold. Ava hoped he remembered her and would take the call.

"Well, well. Is this the Ms. Lee who gets phone calls from the Prime Minister's Office?" McIntyre said.

"Yes, Mr. McIntyre. Thank you for remembering me, and thank you for taking my call."

"Would you believe me if I told you I was afraid not to?"

"No."

"Well, rightly so. I'm just surprised to hear from you and curious as to why."

"I'm calling on business."

"Roger Simmons again, or has Jeremy Ashton been acting up?"

"No, different. I'd like you to do something for me, for a fee, of course."

"And what is that?"

"There is — was, rather — an Irish painter by the name of Maurice O'Toole. He died about five years ago. He was married to a woman named Nancy, who died about three years ago. They had no children but there had to be an estate. Could you possibly find out for me if there was one, and if so, who inherited it?"

"That's all the information you have?"

"That's it."

"What part of Ireland? That does matter."

"Dublin."

"It may take a little time."

"Can you get back to me today?"

"Ms. Lee, you are always in such a rush. The last time you

were here we papered an agreement in a matter of hours when it normally takes days."

"I'll double your fee if you can get me the information today."

"You don't know what my fee is."

"I don't care. I know it will be fair."

"All right, let me work on it."

"Thank you so much. You can call me on my cellphone or at my room at the Fletcher Hotel."

Ava jumped into the shower and took her time washing her hair. She spent another ten minutes drying it. When she came out of the bathroom, her room phone was blinking. It was George McIntyre, asking her to call him back.

"The person you want to talk to is Helen Byrne," McIntyre said. "She inherited everything Nancy O'Toole had. She lives in Donabate, a large village or small town — whichever you prefer — on the Irish coast about twenty kilometres northeast of Dublin."

"That is remarkably fast work."

"Not really. They're very well organized over there; all it took was one phone call. A colleague in a Dublin firm, an old schoolmate of mine, found Nancy O'Toole in the death register and the law firm that handled her estate, all while I was still on the line."

"Do you have an actual address for her, a phone number?"

"Write this down," McIntyre said, giving her the information.

"Is she a relative?"

"I wasn't told."

"Thank you so much, Mr. McIntyre. How much do I owe you?"

"Not a thing."

"Please, I insist on paying you."

"No, I would rather have you owing me a favour."

"And I would rather pay."

"Your owing me a favour is worth more to me."

"Done," she said.

Ava hung up the phone and threw on a clean black Giordano T-shirt. She picked up her cellphone, checked the incoming call list, and saw a Chinese area code. May Ling Wong.

She sat on the edge of the bed and dialled Helen Byrne's number. If this didn't work out, then Ava's next calls would most certainly be to Uncle and May Ling.

"Ms. Byrne, my name is Ava Lee. I'm calling you about Nancy O'Toole and Maurice O'Toole."

"Do I know you?"

"No, you most certainly don't, and I apologize for calling out of the blue like this."

"What kind of name is Lee?"

"Chinese."

"You don't sound Chinese."

"I'm Canadian."

"I have a brother who lives in Canada, in Hamilton."

"Hamilton is quite close to the city I live in."

"What is it you want with Nancy?" Helen said with some force.

"I understand you inherited her estate."

"I'm her sister. We were close all our lives."

"It must have been difficult, her dying so young and so soon after Maurice."

"Cancer is a terrible thing."

"Yes, of course."

"Now you still haven't told me what you want with Nancy."

"It's actually Maurice I'm more interested in."

"That useless piece of shit?"

"Yes, him."

"I never understood what my sister saw in him, never. He didn't work a day in his life, just painting, smoking, and drinking. He didn't womanize, thank God, but I always said that was because no other woman wanted anything to do with him."

"Still, your sister obviously loved him."

"She did that."

"And he did make some money."

"Oh, the last few years weren't so bad for that. He left her comfortable, though a lot of good it did her. She died of lung cancer, poor girl, and she never smoked a day in her life. It was second-hand smoke, the doctor said, that killed her. I always thought it was Maurice's way of reaching out to her from the grave."

"I'm not fond of smokers myself," Ava said, trying to find some common ground.

"Well, they've passed all these new laws here. You can hardly smoke anywhere outside your own house."

"Canada is the same."

Helen paused. "What is it you want with Maurice, then?" she finally asked.

"I'm trying to trace some paintings he did for a client of mine. I was wondering if he left any records behind and if Nancy kept any of them, maybe passed them down to you."

"I've got a shed full of it."

"Pardon?"

"My garden shed is stuffed with his boxes and things."

"You're serious?"

"Nancy couldn't bear to part with his things after he died. She hung on to it all. She lived here with me and kept it in the shed. I just haven't bothered getting rid of it."

"Do you know what's in those boxes?"

"Paper."

"What kind of paper?"

"I have no bloody idea. It could be anything. Maurice was a real pack rat — he never threw anything away."

"Ms. Byrne, is it possible that I could stop by to take a look at those papers?"

"You'd come all the way from Canada for that?"

"Actually I'm in England right now."

"Still, that's an awful lot of trouble for Maurice's leftovers."

"Ms. Byrne, this is quite important to my client. He has some art that he thinks was painted by Mr. O'Toole, and he wants it confirmed. I am prepared to pay you for any assistance you can provide."

"How much are we talking about?" she said swiftly.

"How about a thousand dollars?"

"We use euros here."

"A thousand euros then."

"All right, Ms. Lee, bring the cash with you and you can poke away in Maurice's boxes to your heart's content."

"I'm going to try to catch a flight out of here this afternoon."

"Do you have my address?"

"I do."

"We're about fifteen kilometres from the Dublin airport. Any taxi driver will know where Donabate is."

"Do you mind if I drop by when I get in?"

"As long as you bring the money, you can come at midnight if you want."

20

AT A QUARTER TO FOUR AVA STEPPED OUTSIDE AT Dublin Airport into wet, cold, mean weather. She was beginning to think that all of Europe was sitting under one giant rain cloud. She pulled a sweater from her bag and put it on.

She had called Helen Byrne as soon as she could turn on her cellphone and was now officially expected. She lined up at the taxi stand; to her right was a mass of people huddled inside a fenced area, partially hidden by small trees. "Stupid smokers," the woman in front of her said. "They call that area Sherwood Forest because of the trees. Those idiots would stand there even if it was hailing on them." She was holding a large umbrella and moved it towards Ava so they were both covered.

"Thank you so much," Ava said.

"Are you Vietnamese?"

"No, Chinese-Canadian."

"There are lots of Vietnamese in Dublin these days. Them and Poles. Don't know what restaurants and hotels would do without them. Shut down, probably."

The line moved quickly, and Ava was in a taxi before most of the smokers had finished getting their fix. She asked the driver to take her to Donabate. "A pretty little town," he said. "The surrounding area, Fingal, is just as nice." Ava couldn't see any of it through the rain and mist. "The town is on a peninsula overlooking the Irish Sea," he went on. "It has some fine beaches." Ava wondered how many days a year those beaches could be enjoyed.

The cab stopped in front of a small whitewashed cottage four doors down from a miniature Tesco and six doors from a Boots store. Ava paid the driver, walked up to the front door, and gave the brass knocker a solid rap. She pressed close to the house, trying to keep dry.

The door swung open wide and Ava almost fell inside. "You're not what I expected," a woman said.

Neither are you, Ave thought as she stared up at a tall, gangly woman wearing jeans and a red fleece top zipped to the neck. For some reason she had imagined a small, thin, grey-haired old lady. Helen's hair was dyed blonde, dark at the roots, and combed over to one side. She looked to be in her late forties or early fifties, though it was hard to tell through the thick layer of makeup.

"You're young," Helen said.

"Not as young as I look."

"And I thought you'd look more professional somehow." Ava glanced down at her training pants and running shoes. "Did you bring the money?"

She passed Helen the wad of euros she'd withdrawn from the ATM at the airport.

"Come in," Helen said.

Ava put down her bags in the narrow hallway.

"Do you want to go directly to the shed?"

"Please."

The cottage was tiny, with no more than six rooms. They walked past two closed doors on either side to the back, where the kitchen door opened onto the yard. There was an empty pizza box on the counter. "That's the shed; the door is open," Helen said. "There isn't a light in there and it will get dark in a couple of hours, so you'd better work fast."

The shed couldn't have been more than three metres square, big enough for a lawnmower and some basic gardening equipment. Ava pushed the door open and was immediately hit by a musty smell, the kind that damp paper generates. *Geez*, she thought, *all that way for this.*

Four rows of cardboard boxes were stacked against the far wall, three boxes high. She opened one and saw a row of neatly hung files, each of their tabs clearly marked. Her spirits rose. Then she noticed that the boxes were dated, starting with 1984–85 and the last dated 2004. She loved tidiness.

She scanned the tabs in the most recent box. Many of the files contained mundane documents, business expenses, bank statements. There was a file marked *Jan Sørensen*. She opened it and saw copies of all the correspondence that had gone back and forth between the two men. There was another marked *Hughes Gallery*. And one identified *Derain*. She opened it with a touch of excitement. Inside was a complete record of the life of a painting: the letter from Glen Hughes requesting the work; Maurice O'Toole's reply; an invoice for the finished work, sent to an address she didn't recognize; and a Polaroid photo of the painting itself, with the completion date and a title written across the bottom. *You beautiful man*, she thought.

She pulled down another box and opened it to find an almost exact duplicate of the first, except instead of Derain, there were tabs for Braque and Dufy. The Dufy file was as complete as the Derain. Ava removed the lids from two more boxes and found more of the same. Drops of water began to fall on her head and on the files. *Great*, she thought, looking up at a small leak in the ceiling. Ava thought about asking Helen if she could take the boxes into the kitchen and work there, and then thought better of it. She didn't want the woman standing over her shoulder as she looked through them, and she knew she was going to have to make copies — lots of copies.

She made her way back to the house. Helen was standing in the kitchen with a bottle of beer in her hand. "Back so soon?"

"We need to talk," Ava said. "I can't work in the shed. What I'd like to do is take the boxes to my hotel and work there. It's going to take me a day, maybe longer, to work through them, and I have to take notes and make copies."

"What hotel?"

"I don't have one yet, but give me a minute and I will."

Helen nodded.

Ava called her travel agent in Toronto. "I need a hotel in Dublin, Ireland. I want a suite, something with a proper work area. Book it for two nights." She turned to Helen. "So you're okay with this?"

She shrugged and Ava saw she was doing her own calculations. "Look, we can do a different kind of deal, you know."

"What are you thinking?" Helen asked.

"I'll buy the files from you."

"Now why would you do that?"

"I'll be wanting to have some of the original documents rather than copies. Instead of doing this piecemeal, why don't we strike a deal for the lot?"

Helen sipped her beer, her eyes suspicious. "Have you found something in those boxes, I mean, something valuable?"

"Ms. Byrne, you can go through each and every box before I take it away."

Helen winced. "Not bloody likely. So, okay, assuming you want to buy them all, what kind of price are we talking about? I mean, you were willing to pay a thousand euros just to look at them."

"Another thousand."

"Ten thousand sounds better."

"Ms. Byrne, without me that paper is junk," Ava said.

"Five thousand."

"I'll give you two."

Helen nodded. "When can I see the money?"

"Tomorrow."

"Then the files stay here until then."

"Please, Ms. Byrne, don't make me waste my evening. Let me take at least a couple of boxes tonight. The balance can stay here until you get your money."

Ava's cellphone rang. She listened, said "Thanks," and then turned to Helen. "The Morrison Hotel on Ormond Quay. Do you know where that is?"

"Centre of Dublin."

"That's where I'll be. Come by tomorrow anytime after

eleven with the rest of the boxes and I'll have your money for you."

21

AVA'S SUITE AT THE MORRISON GAVE HER A JOLT OF déjà vu. It had the same bold, bright minimalist look as the Fletcher Hotel — black-and-white furnishings with bright red cushions and duvet cover. But instead of looking down on Kensington Gardens, the view was of the River Liffey flowing slowly by.

She had the bellman put the boxes on the floor in the sitting area and dropped her carry-on in the bedroom. When he left, she took off her still-damp clothing and hung it in the bathroom to dry. Then she opened the Double Happiness computer bag and took out her notebook. She wanted to review her notes, try to create some kind of time-line, before attacking the files.

Her phone rang and May Ling Wong's number appeared on the screen. Ava looked at her watch. It was past midnight in Wuhan.

I can't avoid her forever, she thought. "Ava Lee."

"May Ling."

"It's late for you."

"I couldn't sleep. I called Uncle and he said he hadn't

heard from you. It's been some days now and I'm curious as to how you're doing."

"I don't have much to report."

"But you're still looking — that must mean something."

"It means I'm still looking."

"I'm going to assume that's positive."

"It isn't anything right now," Ava said.

"Where are you? Physically, I mean?"

"Ireland."

"Why?"

"Auntie, please let me do my job. I promise you, the moment I have something to report, I'll call."

The line went quiet. "Ava, I asked you not to call me Auntie," she finally said.

"I'm sorry, May. I forgot."

"Uncle said you were difficult to reach and reluctant to talk about the job at hand. I thought he was exaggerating."

"He wasn't."

"I thought after our chat in Wuhan that we had built a trust."

"May, this has nothing to do with trust, or friendship, or anything other than the fact that I refuse to speculate on how well things are going and when it will end. It's better for you and better for me that way. You don't have unrealistic expectations, and I'm not burdened."

"Ava, if — and I repeat and emphasize the *if* — if you do find something I want you to promise you'll let me be the first to know. I don't want to hear it from Uncle."

"I can do that," Ava said.

"Then I'll hear from you."

"You will."

Ava hung up and dialled Uncle's number. If May Ling had been talking to Uncle, Ava assumed he was still up.

"*Wei.*"

"It's Ava. May Ling just called me."

"She phoned here four times today. I finally spoke to her tonight. She said she wanted to talk to me about our agreement. I think she was just testing, seeing if we were encouraged enough to ask for one."

"What did you say?"

"I told her it was too soon to discuss it."

"Thank you."

"Is it too soon?"

"Yes. I don't have enough to go on."

"I thought London was going to be helpful."

"Not yet. I handled it badly and now I need to find another reason to go back."

"What is your plan?"

"I'm working on one. By tomorrow I might know."

"Call me then, one way or another. This is taking up a lot of time, and I sense you are getting frustrated. Sometimes we just have to walk away."

As Ava hung up she felt a pain in her stomach. She had gone all day without eating, and now she was ravenous. She reached for the room service menu and ordered potato and haddock soup and a steak sandwich made from aged Hereford.

She opened her notebook on the coffee table in the sitting area and reached for the first box, the one with the most recent records. She worked steadily for an hour, stopping only to answer the door when room service called. She opened every file folder and looked at every scrap of paper, taking nothing for granted. Helen Byrne wasn't wrong: Maurice O'Toole had been a hoarder. He kept not only bills and receipts related to his paintings but receipts for every household expense, bank statements, and copies of the cheques he had received. *He would have made a good bookkeeper*, Ava thought. What surprised her was how few sales he had made. In addition to the Derain he faked during that period, he had sold only ten of his own paintings, and they netted him less than the one Derain.

The second, third, and fourth boxes were more of the same. It had taken her close to four hours to go through the paperwork, and all she had when she was done was the same information Helga Sørensen had given her, though more detailed, and she had the photos of the paintings. But it was still only Glen Hughes' signature on the letters requesting works "in the style of," and there was no hint of any impropriety.

She pored over the invoices, deposit slips, and bank statements, hoping she could find something that might link Edwin to the forgeries or expose a bank account other than those she knew about in Liechtenstein and Kowloon. There was nothing. Maurice O'Toole was paid exclusively from the Liechtenstein account, most often by a cheque signed by Glen Hughes. There was no mention in the files of the $100,000 Nancy O'Toole had received from the Kowloon account. Ava made a note to ask Helen if Nancy had been as professional about record-keeping as her husband.

It was eleven o'clock and she thought about going to bed, but her head was too full of O'Toole's files. Ava looked outside at the River Liffey, lit by streetlamps filtering through a fine mist. The heavy rain had abated but it still looked chilly outside. It had been like this since she had arrived in Europe, and her mood was beginning to take on the character of the weather. Every time she thought she had found a ray of sun, a dark cloud had smothered it. She sighed and reached for her Adidas jacket. She needed a walk.

22

AVA WOKE AT EIGHT AND IMMEDIATELY CHECKED HER email. Maria and Mimi had both written again.

Ava, you can't be so casual about Maria's mother, Mimi wrote. This is an enormous event for Maria. She needs support, and she needs it from no one else but you. If you aren't prepared to meet the woman, then I think you need to let Maria know and you need to tell her why. And I have to say that if she means what I think she means to you, you do need to do this.

Ava closed the message and sighed, thinking over what Mimi had written. Then she clicked on an email from Maria. I hope everything is going well. I didn't hear back from you yesterday. Did you receive my email about my mother visiting?

Ava wrote, I'm getting caught up and just read your message. If you are happy about your mother visiting, then I'm happy for you. Will I get to meet her? Miss you. Ava.

Ava was startled when she returned to her inbox and saw an email from Michael Lee. She hesitated before finally opening it. When you have the time, call me, or better still could you arrange to come to Hong Kong? There are some things I need to discuss with you. It was signed, Warmest regards, Michael.

Now what the hell is this about? she thought, and then remembered the remark her father had made in his message about wanting to talk to her about Michael. She wrote to her father, Why do you need to talk to me about Michael? And then for good measure, she added, And how did you ever get Mummy and Bruce to play nice? And why are you staying an extra week in Toronto?

She closed the computer and looked over at the boxes on the floor. She knew she was going to spend the day going through more of them, so she didn't need to dress up, but she was rankled by Helen's remark about not looking professional. She put on her black Brooks Brothers shirt and cotton slacks, fixed her hair with the ivory chignon pin, and even put on a little makeup.

She went downstairs to have breakfast in the hotel's restaurant. From where she sat she had a view of the lobby, and at around ten o'clock a view of Helen Byrne pushing a baggage trolley through the front doors.

Ava went to meet her. "You're early," she said to Helen's back.

Helen spun around, her hair wet, water dripping down her face. "I have some shopping to do, so I thought I'd take advantage of coming into town. But there's all this goddamn rain."

"I'm glad to see you, and actually I have your money."

They rode the elevator together, Helen rubbing at her hair with the sleeve of her denim shirt. When they walked into the room, Helen left Ava with the boxes and headed directly to the bathroom. She came out with a towel wrapped around her head. "Eight more boxes," she said. "The taxi didn't want to take them, so I had to pay extra."

Ava handed her the bundle of cash that she had withdrawn from an ATM the night before. Helen counted the bills, her lips moving as she did so.

"I meant to ask you," Ava said. "Around the time that Maurice died, maybe shortly thereafter, Nancy received a lump-sum payment of one hundred thousand U.S. dollars. It was sent to her from a bank in Kowloon, Hong Kong. Did she mention anything to you about this?"

"Not that I can remember."

"It was a large amount. From what I can see in those files, Maurice didn't have any money. When you said he left her comfortable, I assumed they had money in the bank."

"They lived hand-to-mouth most of the time."

"But you said he left her comfortable."

"I figured it was insurance."

"And she never said?"

"No."

"How much of it was left when she died?"

"About half."

"Did Nancy leave any records? Bank statements, that kind of thing?"

"No, she wasn't much for clutter."

"Okay, I guess that's that," Ava said. "Just one thing more: I've prepared a bill of sale I'd like you to sign."

Helen looked dubious. "Ms. Byrne, I don't want ownership of these records ever to come into question. I typed this up last night. All it says is that you have sold me these twelve boxes of Maurice O'Toole memorabilia."

"Memorabilia. That's a fancy word."

"Can you think of a better one?"

"Maurice's shit."

"You can add that in brackets if you want."

Helen looked at Ava, her eyes roaming up and down the length of her body. "You're a sharp little thing, aren't you."

"Not always," Ava said.

"Whatever. Give me a pen," she said.

She signed the document and Ava saw her to the door. She then turned to the boxes, which were still sitting on the trolley. She unloaded them, rolled the trolley into the hallway, and got ready to spend the day with Maurice O'Toole.

The first two boxes were no different than those she had dug through the night before. Still she opened every file and looked at every piece of paper, setting aside the Fauvist art references. When she finished, she checked her notebook. Between Sørensen's and O'Toole's records and Torrence's assessments, she had now accounted for every apparent forgery, which according to her numbers the Wongs had paid $73 million for. There had been twenty paintings on those Wuhan walls. Five were genuine. She now had a paper trail that led directly to O'Toole and Sørensen and the fifteen that weren't. And not one of those documents had brought her any closer to Glen Hughes.

The next box was depressingly barren: no Fauvists and no evidence of anything other than Maurice O'Toole's inability to sell his own artwork for more than a few hundred euros. She shoved it aside and started in on the next box.

The name *Manet* leapt out at her from one of the tabs. She plucked the file and sat on the pure white couch. She felt a shiver of anticipation as she opened it, and then a full-blown smile spread across her face.

The photo of the painting showed a man facing a firing squad. Underneath O'Toole had written: *The Execution of the Emperor Maximilian, dated 1867, completed June 1997.* She leafed through the accompanying paperwork, looking for the letter requesting the piece. She couldn't find one but there was an invoice made out from Maurice O'Toole to the Hughes Art Gallery, Church Street, London, and a copy of a DHL shipping slip dated June 17, with the gallery's address. The invoice had one word on it: *Manet.*

Ava went back to the box and extracted the bank statements file. She found the month the shipment had been made and looked for a deposit. There wasn't any. She turned to the next month and there it was: ten thousand pounds sterling, converted into euros. The deposit slip was attached. O'Toole had written *Hughes Gallery* on it. He had also copied the cheque and stapled it to the slip. The cheque had two signatures on it, Edwin Hughes and Glen Hughes, and in the bottom left-hand corner someone had written the O'Toole invoice number.

She put everything together in one file and returned to the boxes.

In the next box she found the name *Modigliani.* The painting was titled *Self-Portrait, 1919.* The paper trail was identical to that of the Manet, right down to the copy of a cheque with two signatures.

In next box she found another Modigliani, *Portrait of Jacques Lipchitz, 1916.* O'Toole hadn't kept the shipping slip, but everything else was there.

She checked the tabs in the final two boxes and found nothing of any interest. It didn't matter — she had what she needed.

Ava sat on the couch holding the three file folders on her lap like Christmas gifts. Somewhere, somehow, these paintings had been sold to people who weren't named Wong and didn't live in Wuhan.

She went online to look for the paintings. A quick search for the Manet and the Modigliani self-portrait drew blanks. But the Lipchitz portrait had sold at auction for seven million pounds two months after O'Toole shipped it to London. The consignee wasn't named, and neither was the purchaser. The auction house was Harrington's.

She reached for her phone to call Frederick Locke.

23

IT WAS LATE AFTERNOON WHEN AVA'S FLIGHT LANDED at Heathrow, which planted her in the midst of rush hour traffic. What should have been a half-hour drive to the Harrington's offices in Westminster turned into an hour-and-a-half commute. The only consolation she took was that it would give Frederick Locke more time to do his research.

The phone conversation she'd had with Locke from her Dublin hotel room that morning had not gone entirely well, and she blamed herself for that. Her two-month layoff had taken a toll. She wasn't as sharp as she normally was, first with Edwin Hughes and now with Locke.

Locke's initial reaction to her discovery of the Manet and the two Modigliani paintings had taken her aback. His attention immediately, solely, and obsessively focused on the Modigliani Lipchitz portrait that Harrington's had sold. She had heard panic in his voice, and when he said he would have to call in his boss to join their discussion, she knew she had gone off track.

"You can't do that," she said.

"I have no choice. If we sold —"

"Frederick, stop. Listen to me. There is no hard proof of anything. I have suspicions, nothing more than that. Let's not alarm anyone until we're certain of the facts, and until you and I have had a chance to talk and decide how best to handle this. There are more people involved in this than Harrington's. My client, for one. Now, I'm going to be in London sometime late this afternoon. I'll bring what I have with me for you to review. Until then, this is strictly between me and you."

When he didn't answer, she pushed, "If you won't promise that you'll handle it this way, I'll do it on my own. That will take Harrington's out of the loop. I think you'll agree that it would better serve your purposes to be very much part of the decision-making process. I mean, you don't want to pick up the *Daily Telegraph* two weeks from now and read about how your firm sold a forgery, do you? What would that say about your competence in performing due diligence?"

"You make a point," he said, sounding uncertain.

"What does that mean?"

"I promise."

"You promise what, exactly?"

"This will remain between you and me."

"Until we — and I stress the *we* — decide how to handle it. Agreed?"

"Agreed."

"Okay, so write down these names and dates," she said, and dictated the titles of the Manet and Modigliani paintings and the earliest date they could have appeared on the market. "I want to know who bought them, for how much, and where those paintings are now."

"I'll do what I can."

"I'm sure you will. I'll call you when I land."

She had phoned again as soon as she stepped into the taxi at Heathrow. "I'm in London."

"I'm still trying to locate the third painting," Locke said.

"My driver says we're going to be sitting in traffic for a while."

"I'm not going anywhere, believe me."

"See you when I get there."

Harrington's was on New Bond Street, almost directly across from Sotheby's auction house. A security guard looked suspiciously at her carry-on. But when she gave him her name, he handed her a badge and pointed to a bank of elevators. "Fifth floor. Mr. Locke is expecting you."

When she exited the elevator, a man with a name tag that read LOCKE was standing in front of her. She had half-expected to see another Brian Torrence — tall, gangly, a bit dishevelled; instead she found herself staring up at a mountain of a man. He was easily six foot four, broad without being fat, and had short brown hair and a bushy beard. "Ava Lee, I presume," he said.

"That's me. And you are Frederick Locke."

He nodded. "I've reserved one of our small boardrooms. Shall we go?"

It was past six o'clock. She followed him past rows of empty offices furnished with pedestrian metal desks and chairs. The boardroom housed a round wooden table with matching chairs. Ava looked out the window, which faced Sotheby's. "Keeping the competition close?" she said.

Locke didn't answer. Instead he sat down, three file folders in front of him. "This is rather serious," he began.

"That's why I'm here."

He tapped the top file. "I've managed to locate the three paintings you identified. The Modigliani self-portrait was sold to a private collector for six and a half million pounds."

"Do you have a name?"

"In a minute," he said, raising his hand. "The Manet was sold to another private collector for five million pounds, and the Lipchitz portrait, as you found out, was sold through our house for seven million pounds."

"Can I have the names?"

"Please, Ms. Lee," he said, the easygoing banter of their initial phone calls gone.

"Ava."

"Ava, if your suspicions are correct, then my firm has several problems. One of them is financial, another calls into question our reputation, and the third — in reference to the two paintings we didn't sell — has tremendous ethical implications."

"By ethical do you mean should we tell the people who bought forgeries that they bought forgeries?"

"Something like that, although not quite so simply stated."

"I have some ethical issues myself," she said.

"How so?"

"I have a client who was swindled out of seventy-three million dollars. My primary obligation is to retrieve that money."

"I'm sure that if your assertions are true you'll have everything you need to pursue legal action against the people who did this."

"Glen Hughes, and maybe Edwin Hughes."

"You seem convinced."

"My problem is that my client won't want to take legal action against either Hughes, not until all other options have been exhausted. Even then he may choose — for reasons of his own — to maintain his privacy."

"That seems strange to me."

"You attitude would seem strange to him. He's Chinese, as you know, and there's a cultural divide that isn't easily explained. There's also a gap between the way business is conducted in China and the way it's conducted here. My client would just as soon shake your hand as sign a contract. The difference to him is negligible in terms of his expectation of being delivered what you promise. And if you fail to deliver, then he expects you to compensate him — without bringing lawyers into it."

"I'm not sure I completely understand."

"And I'm not sure how much more I can say."

Locke began to pluck at his beard. "I give you the information you want — and then what?"

"I sit down with Hughes and persuade him to make restitution."

"But your client has no connection to these three paintings."

"The Hughes brothers — either of them, both of them — don't care about being sued by some Chinese businessman with cultural pretensions, particularly when their tracks were so cleverly covered. As you and Brian Torrence know, they or one of them officially sold the Fauvist paintings to a dealer in Hong Kong named Kwong, or to his business, Great Wall Antiques and Fine Art. Kwong is dead. The business is closed, the records destroyed."

"And what about these three paintings?"

"The Hughes brothers may not be so willing to be sued by the owners of these three paintings, or by Harrington's. It's one thing to mock a man from Wuhan but it's another to screw around with — well, with whom? Who bought the paintings? Tell me, and then I'll tell you how much leverage I think we have and I'll tell you how I'll proceed."

"You haven't proved the paintings are forgeries," he said.

"Fair enough," she said, opening her Shanghai Tang computer bag.

She passed him one file. "That's the Manet. There's a photo of it, titled and double-dated. There's an invoice made out to the Hughes Art Gallery with *Manet* on it. The painting was shipped by DHL; there's a copy of the delivery slip made out to the Hughes Gallery address. Finally, there's a copy of a cancelled cheque made out to Maurice O'Toole and signed by both Edwin and Glen Hughes. You'll see on the memo line that the invoice number is referenced."

He went through the documentation with great care. Then he looked up at her, shook his head, and went through it again.

"What O'Toole did was very clever," he said, looking out the window. "There were three known versions, variations of *The Execution of the Emperor Maximilian*, all dated around the same time, before this fourth one came on the market. We heard rumblings about it but it never came to auction. A Manet enthusiast in Scotland purchased it from an unknown source, who now appears to have been the Hughes brothers."

"He did due diligence?"

"Buying from the Hughes brothers would have been

considered due diligence enough, although if he went to other authorities, they could have been fooled."

"Who bought it?"

"The Earl of Moncrieff."

"He sounds impressive."

Locke looked down at her bag. "Can I see the other two files?"

She took the Manet file back and passed him the one for the Modigliani self-portrait. He took as much time going through that paperwork. Ava admired his thoroughness.

"Again, clever. There are many self-portraits, and this one seems plausible. It was sold into a private collection in London. The owner is Harold Holmes."

"The media tycoon?"

"That's him."

"Now here's your part in this," Ava said, sliding the Lipchitz portrait file towards him.

"In 1916 Modigliani did a portrait of Jacques and Berthe Lipchitz. O'Toole painted Jacques alone. There's no reason to think that Modigliani might not have done the same," Locke said.

"But it was sold at auction, through your firm. Surely the provenance was examined inside and out."

"According to our records, it was."

"Who looked at it?"

"Not me, if that's what you're insinuating. I was too junior to look at something like this."

"Then who?"

He looked uncomfortable. "I think, for now, that has to be remain internal to Harrington's."

"Then who was the buyer?"

"Jonathan Reiner."

"I've heard of him too."

"Not surprising. He's one of the five wealthiest men in the U.K."

Ava had written the names in her notebook as Locke reluctantly gave them to her. "Moncrieff — tell me about him."

"Considers himself to be a true patron of the arts, and he has the money to indulge his interest. He lends many of his paintings to Scottish museums and galleries, and he sponsors young Scottish artists."

"So all in all, the Hughes brothers have messed with some big boys."

"Couldn't have been much bigger, unless they were selling to the Queen and the National Gallery."

She held out her hand for the Lipchitz file.

"Can I keep this for a day or two?" Locke asked.

"Afraid not."

"I'll make some copies, then."

"Not yet," Ava said.

"I thought we had an understanding."

"Frederick, I trust you enough to have come here with these files, but until I resolve my differences with the Hughes brothers I prefer to keep these documents under my control. Things happen, you know. One of your assistants sees something, questions are asked or little comments are made, and then your boss is asking what's going on and you don't want to lie to him. And so on and so on. So for both our sakes, I'll hang on to them for now."

"You said we'd agree together how to proceed," he insisted, his face reddening.

"And we will, once I'm finished with the Hughes brothers."

"What if they refuse to co-operate with you? What if they won't give you what you want?"

"Then I'll be back here with my tail between my legs, files in hand, and we'll chat. Either way, successful or not, the files are coming back here."

"I'm not going to convince you otherwise, am I."

"No."

"So now what?"

"Do you have addresses for the three buyers?"

"Yes, they're in here."

"Can I have them, please?"

He hesitated.

"Frederick, I can find them easily enough. All I want you to do is save me some time."

He took a slip of paper out of each of his files and passed them to her.

"Now I need to use a computer, a printer, and a photocopier."

24

IT TOOK HER CLOSE TO TWO HOURS TO PREPARE THE
packages for Edwin and Glen Hughes. Locke hung about
nearby, acutely interested but too polite to pry. Ava bundled
the files together and put a big rubber band around them
before jamming them into her bag. It was past eight o'clock
and she was hungry. She thought for a second about asking
Locke to join her for dinner, then immediately threw the
idea aside.

She called the Fletcher and enquired about a room. They
were only too happy to welcome her back, she was told. She
felt as if she had hardly left.

"I'm staying at the Fletcher Hotel in Kensington," she
told Locke.

"Do you want a ride? My car is nearby."

"The tube will do fine. I've bothered you enough today."

"*Bothered* is hardly the word I would use," he said.
"Emotionally ravaged is more like it."

"I'm sorry. I know this must have been upsetting."

"The consequences are just beginning to sink in. It's one
thing to discuss forgeries in the abstract. It's quite another

to have them staring you in the face when you know all the participants and are imagining how everyone is going to react. I'm not going to sleep well, I can tell you that."

"If it's of any comfort, this should be over soon," Ava said.

"How soon?" he asked.

"Hopefully I'll see Edwin Hughes tomorrow, and if that goes as planned I'll be onto Glen Hughes right after."

"Can you call me?"

"When it's completely finished, not before."

"And you'll bring the files here?"

"I promise," Ava said. "And you won't discuss this with anyone, not even your shadow, until then?"

"I promise."

Ava extended her hand. Locke took it and shook it vigorously. His eyes bored into hers, looking for doubt. She stared back and then smiled. She trusted this one.

"I'll walk you down," Locke said.

When they reached the street, he hesitated at the door. Ava looked around and saw a sign for the underground. "There's my transportation," she said, and walked towards the tube station before he could speak.

She took the train to Kensington High Street. It was past eight o'clock when she got there, and when she walked up the steps, she saw that for once it wasn't raining. She went to Marks & Spencer and bought a tuna sandwich — confirming first that the tuna was albacore, not skipjack or yellowfin — and a bottle of white burgundy.

An hour later she was sitting in T-shirt and panties at her computer, the half-empty bottle of wine next to her, reading about the Earl of Moncrieff. She had already googled Holmes and Reiner, and the Earl was just as formidable.

She could only imagine how horrific it would be to have all three gunning for you. She hoped the Hughes brothers had as much imagination as she did.

She opened her email. Maria was elated at Ava's reaction to the possibility of her mother's visit. Ava blinked, surprised that her girlfriend had read so much into what she had thought was guarded support. She sat back in her chair. *Maybe Mimi is right*, she thought. *Maybe it's time to make a commitment.*

Her father had also written to her. The first part of his message made her smile. A détente had been reached between Bruce and Jennie Lee because he had bribed his wife. He had given her a choice: maintain the hostility and he would catch the first plane back to Hong Kong as soon as they landed in Toronto, or make things work and he would spend an extra week in Richmond Hill.

His response to her question about why he needed to talk to her about Michael wasn't so clear. Michael has some financial problems that he's trying to work through. I'm not sure it's going well. I'll talk to him when I get back to Toronto tomorrow. I don't want to say anything more than that until I know all the details.

She checked the time. It was still the middle of the night in Hong Kong. Normally she didn't email Uncle, but she didn't want to wait up to call him. So she wrote, Call Wong May Ling. Finalize a financial arrangement. I think I've finally found some information about who did this, information that we can use to get some of the Wongs' money back. I'll call you in the morning, my time.

Ava climbed onto the bed with the files she intended to take to Edwin Hughes in the morning. She went through each of them in detail, making sure that the spelling and grammar were accurate in the letters she had prepared. It seemed trivial, but she wanted nothing to detract from the professionalism she intended to impart. This time she was going to be prepared. This time Edwin Hughes wasn't going to shuffle her out the door.

She turned on the television and found herself watching an old episode of *Prime Suspect*. She had seen all of the shows when they came out, and then had bought the DVDs. She made Mimi watch them with her, though she was too embarrassed to admit that she identified with Helen Mirren's character. It wasn't Jane Tennison's persistence, smarts, indifference to chauvinism, or toughness that appealed to Ava's sense of herself; it was the fact that no matter how many people were around, Tennison was essentially alone — and she was okay with being alone.

Ava fell asleep on top of the bed, the television still on. She woke at four, cold and needing to pee. She turned off the TV, went to the bathroom, and then crawled under the duvet.

When she opened the bedroom drapes the next morning at seven, she blinked in surprise. The sun was shining, and the people outside were wearing dresses and short sleeves. She quickly made instant coffee, downed it, brushed her teeth and hair, put on her running gear, and headed downstairs.

The weather was glorious, the smell of flowers wafting across the High Street from Kensington Gardens. She did three full laps through the Gardens and Hyde Park, the longest run she'd had in months. As she jogged back to the hotel, her thoughts turned to Edwin Hughes. She remembered him sitting behind his desk, his brown leather wingtips resting on the Sørensen paperwork as if it was so much garbage. She remembered him calling for the girl in the red dress — Lisa was her name — to tell her the meeting with Ms. Lee was over, and would she kindly escort her from the premises.

By the time Ava got back to the hotel, she was wired. She put on the blue-and-white pinstriped Brooks Brothers shirt, her black linen slacks, and her alligator heels. She pulled her hair back as tightly as she could, fastening it in place with the ivory chignon pin. She completed the look with a light touch of red lipstick, some mascara, and her Annick Goutal perfume. She slipped on her Cartier Tank Française watch and her gold crucifix, stood back, and looked at herself in the mirror. Dressed for battle again, but this time with more purpose.

It was nine thirty, four thirty in the afternoon in Hong Kong. She phoned Uncle.

"I was waiting," he said.

"I'm sorry. I was getting organized for my meeting."

"Your email pleased me."

"I think we have a pathway to some kind of resolution."

"How much can you get back?"

"I don't know yet, but they have money, these people."

"Who are they?"

"Two brothers: their names are Edwin and Glen Hughes. One of them may have had nothing to do with this at all; I'm just not one hundred percent sure yet. I'll know in a while."

Ava heard his dog yapping in the background and then the voice of his housekeeper, Lourdes, telling it to be quiet.

He was still at his apartment. "I have been back and forth on the phone with May Ling all day."

"And?"

"We have an agreement," he said.

She thought his tone sounded strange — flat, tentative. Not many things excited Uncle, but money usually did. And this could be a lot of money.

"Was she pleased with the developments?" she asked.

"More than pleased, I would say. She wanted to call you, of course, and I told her you were completely out of reach," Uncle said. "Pleased or not, though, she still negotiated very hard."

"What did we end up with?"

"Twenty percent."

It was a substantial discount from their usual fee of thirty percent, but given the amount of money involved, it was still a healthy commission. "Good . . . Why doesn't that seem to please you?"

"As I said, we talked all morning. She is a smart woman, May Ling. Once she knew we had a chance to recover the money, she knew we would not walk away so easily. As much as she wants to appease her husband, the business-woman — the Wuhan woman in her — could not keep from haggling."

"I understand," Ava said.

"That is when Wong Changxing got involved."

Ava froze. "How?" she said.

"He was evidently listening to my negotiations with May. When she kept pushing for fifteen percent, he interrupted and told her that twenty percent was fine."

"She told me she'd keep him away from this," Ava said.

"It was probably unrealistic of us to believe her," Uncle said. "They are close, those two. They spend every minute of most days together. She would have found it hard not to share, especially when she knows how much it means to him."

"This is a problem for me, Uncle," Ava said slowly.

"When we were in Wuhan, I agreed with you. Now I do not. After my talk with May I called Changxing directly. He apologized for stepping into the middle of the negotiations. He said he overheard May talking to me earlier in the day, and he persuaded her to tell him what was going on. He seemed calm, not like he was when we were in Wuhan. He wants his money back, he said, nothing more than that. He said he was so emotional in Wuhan because we were the first people they had told about the treachery. He got carried away."

"And you believe him?"

"I do," Uncle said.

Ava had never told Uncle she didn't trust his judgement. She wasn't sure she ever could. "If you are certain," she said.

"I am."

25

BY THE TIME SHE REACHED CHURCH STREET, THE WONGS
were gone from her mind. *Let Uncle handle them*, she
thought.

She got to the gallery at quarter to ten, so she walked
across the street and stood in the entrance to a bakery,
which gave her a clear view of the gallery's front door. At
five to ten Lisa arrived, the short red dress replaced by a
twin in black. *She is a magnificent-looking woman*, Ava
thought.

She waited for Edwin Hughes. At quarter past she
thought about calling the gallery to see if he was there
already, and then thought better of it. *Be patient*, she
thought.

At ten thirty Hughes drove past in an old-model Jaguar.
He found a parking spot on her side of the street, about
twenty metres past the bakery. She watched him get out
of the car, cross the street, and walk into the gallery. He
was wearing a navy-blue suit with broad white pinstripes. *It
takes a confident man to wear a suit like that*, Ava thought as
she watched Hughes walk with long, easy strides, his back

straight, his six-foot frame giving off an aura of dominance.

She gave him ten minutes to get settled and then crossed the street, the file folders pressed against her hip.

A bell tinkled when she opened the door. She hadn't noticed it the last time — just another sign of how inattentive she had been. The bell brought Lisa out from the back, a smile on her face that instantaneously disappeared when she saw Ava.

"I don't think he'll want to speak to you," she said, drawing near.

"Not his choice, I'm afraid," Ava said.

"Ms. Lee, isn't it?"

"Yes."

"I can't permit you to go back there."

"Lisa, isn't it?"

"Yes."

"Lisa, this doesn't involve you. I need to speak to Mr. Hughes and I'm going to do exactly that. Please don't interfere."

"This place is filled with cameras and alarms," Lisa said in rush. "I can have security here in five minutes."

"If that's the case, then let Mr. Hughes call for security if he doesn't want to talk to me. Same result, yes? I'll get thrown out. But you can stay out of it."

"You're serious, aren't you."

"Very, and equally determined."

Lisa looked down at Ava. "Go. He's in his office in the back."

The office door was open. Hughes had the same brown wingtips planted on the desk but was turned sideways, talking on the phone. Ava stood quietly until he felt her presence. He kept talking. She walked into the office and sat in the chair across from his desk.

He turned, looked at her, and then did a double take. "I'll call you back," he said and hung up the phone. His feet dropped to the ground with a thud. "Now what the hell do you want?" he said.

"We're going to have a talk, and this time you're going to listen."

"We are going to have no such thing. I want you to leave the premises."

"What are you afraid of?"

"Absolutely nothing. I just find you annoying in the extreme. You came here before with frivolous charges concerning my brother and tried to implicate me in the matter. I didn't like it then, and I'm not about to sit and let you make a repeat."

Ava shrugged. "All right, then we'll change the subject. How about we talk about the fake Manet you sold to the Earl of Moncrieff?"

He didn't move. His eyes never left her, and she watched them morph from confusion to doubt and then detected the first signs of panic. "Or how about the Modigliani you sold to Harold Holmes?" she continued. "Or the one that Jonathan Reiner bought at a Harrington auction. Tell me, what did you do? Pay off the evaluator at Harrington's?"

"That's nonsense," he sputtered.

"You mean about the evaluator?" Ava said.

"That and the rest of your fantasy," he said. "I'm going to call security. This conversation is over."

She threw her files onto his desk. "I found Maurice O'Toole's records," she said. "He was meticulous. Invoices, photos, dates, shipping slips, cancelled cheques. I have them all. I think you'll find them neatly arranged."

He stared at the files with the look of a man who has just been told his wife is having an affair with their teen-age son's best friend, and here were the photos, graphic and unmistakable, to prove it.

"This time I'm not leaving the office," Ava said.

He reached for the documents, read them once, twice, three times, his face draining of colour. People's reactions to shock interested Ava. It is easy to keep up a pretence for a short while, but eventually the brain takes over, and as it absorbs the horrible reality it begins to relay messages to a mouth that gapes, to glands that bleed sweat, to skin that sags, and in Hughes' case, an eyelid that twitched.

He closed the files and looked at her. "Interesting mate-rial," he said coolly.

"I thought so."

"I am slightly perplexed, though. I thought your interest and your client's interest lay in some supposed Fauvist art forgeries. Isn't this a bit of a diversion?"

"They are linked."

"I fail to see any connection."

"Your and your brother's marks are all over these frauds. I need to know if the same is true for the Fauvists."

"Good God, girl, we've been through this. I had nothing, absolutely nothing, to do with that crazy Fauvist scheme. That was Glen and Glen alone."

"The truth?"

"Absolutely," he said eagerly.

"Is it the reason you and he split?"

"Yes, among others, but it was the primary reason."

"I want you to tell me everything you know about it."

"And then what? You'll make these disappear?" he said, waving at the files. "Or am I going to have to pay you to make that happen?"

"We'll talk later about what you need to make happen. In the meantime, talk to me about your brother and the Fauvists."

"Why should I do that?" he persisted.

"These other three paintings don't have to be an issue unless you choose to make them one," she said.

His phone rang. "Lisa's extension," he said to Ava.

"Talk to her."

He picked up the phone, listened, and then said quickly, "No, everything is just fine. Ms. Lee will be here for a while longer. If we need anything, I'll ring through." He hung up the phone and looked at Ava. "I did hear you correctly before Lisa phoned? You're prepared to forget about these paintings?"

"If I get your co-operation, we can work something out," Ava said, pulling her notebook from her bag. "But I need you to start by telling me about your business and how you got into this forgery game."

"You're prepared to forget about these paintings?" he said.

Ava admired his stubbornness. "My sole interest is in recovering the funds that my clients lost buying that Fauvist art. I'm going to do whatever I have to do to make that happen. If what you tell me helps, then yes, I am prepared to forget about these paintings."

"How far back do you want me to go?"

"Start at the beginning."

He drew a deep breath. "The gallery was started by my

grandfather nearly a century ago, and it's been the family business ever since. Both Glen and I were afforded first-class fine arts educations — there was never any doubt about what we would be doing with our lives. I joined the firm right out of university; Glen apprenticed first at Sotheby's. My father died suddenly about five years after Glen came on board. That was when we ran into troubles. The inheritance taxes in this country are criminal, and my father had done virtually no estate planning. We were faced with a crippling tax bill. To pay up would have meant liquidating the business. That's when Glen came up with the idea of having Maurice O'Toole do the Manet. I have to tell you — not that it may matter to you — we agonized over the decision. Glen said we should have Maurice do it and, if we didn't think it passed muster, we would forget the whole idea."

"It was good enough to fool the Earl, yes?"

"It's bloody good enough to fool just about anyone who isn't trying to determine if it's a fake. I mean, the colours, the brushstrokes, the canvas, the nails — Maurice was a marvel."

"And you authenticated it?"

"Yes, we did. Mind you, we did call in several colleagues, who — for a hefty fee — also swore it was genuine. They were mainly taking our word for it, of course, and they gave the painting only what you could call a rough once-over."

"And it worked so well you repeated the exercise?"

"Twice more, that's all," he said, and then quickly added, "I don't mean to minimize the money involved."

"Why twice?"

"Those were our retirement funds — about six million each. This business looks attractive enough from the outside, but it's bloody hard work, and expensive work, because appearances have to be maintained. Then there's the matter of buying and selling. You know the adage 'Buy low, sell high'?"

"Even the Chinese understand that."

"I thought the Chinese invented it," he said, a smile tugging at his lips.

"They invented most things — why not that too?" Ava said.

"Well, in our business there is no intrinsic value in anything. A painting is only worth what someone is willing to pay for it. Today Jackson Pollock is a hot commodity, tomorrow he could be a throwaway. Okay, maybe not to that extreme, but you see, here we don't deal in Jackson Pollock; the core of the business is your run-of-the-mill painter. More risk, less reward. So cash is always tight, and the value of the business — and our net worth — is hanging on the walls. We decided to cash in twice, put the money aside, and then get on with running the business as our father had done."

"Except Glen didn't stop?"

"No, he didn't. But I did. I wasn't proud of what we had done. I rationalized it, of course, but I was never proud, and I never — I swear to you — never even thought about doing it again."

"When did you find out that Glen was still at it?"

"Five years ago."

"When Maurice O'Toole died?"

He looked surprised. "Yes, precisely. Nancy came to see me here at the gallery. Maurice was broke when he died; she had nothing. She said she knew we'd been making all kinds of money from the Derains, the Dufys, and the like. She was looking for a lump-sum payment, a kind of death benefit, from our Liechtenstein account. I told her I didn't know what she was talking about. She brought with her the same kind of paperwork you showed me today. It took me aback, I don't mind telling you, finding out that Glen had still been working with Maurice and that he had a bank account in Liechtenstein. I told her she needed to talk to Glen."

"She must have, because he sent her a hundred thousand dollars from a bank account in Kowloon," Ava said.

"Kowloon too? My brother does get around." Edwin Hughes took off his jacket and stood to hang it on a coat rack next to the Derain Tower Bridge painting. "I told you this one was real, didn't I?" he said.

"You did."

"Would you like a tea or coffee? Water?" he asked as he sat down again.

"I'm fine. Can we get back to your brother?"

He sighed. "We had it out, of course. He told me he needed the money. He was already twice divorced and was working on a third, and between the ex-wives and the kiddies and an expensive lifestyle, he had burned through the Modigliani money and a lot more on top of that. He swore to me then that he'd stop, and I believed him."

"You weren't worried about him, about the scheme being exposed?"

Hughes grimaced. "We were already joined at the hip, so to speak, through our previous transgressions. Although neither of us discussed it directly, we knew it. And then there was the matter of your Hong Kong clients."

"What does that mean?"

He grimaced again. "These are Glen's words, not mine. I'm not a lover of all mankind, but neither am I a racist. Glen tends to wander to the right on most issues. He said — and again, these are his words — that he had found a 'dead ignorant' dealer in Hong Kong who was selling the stuff to an 'even more ignorant' collector somewhere in China. He said he could have sent them crayon sketches done by a six-year-old and passed them off as a rare find, and they'd believe him. He said there wasn't a chance in hell the collector would figure things out, and if he did he would have the dealer in Hong Kong to blame. Glen said he and the collector never met, never even communicated."

"That's true."

"And then he promised me he'd stop, but of course he didn't."

"How did you find that out?" Ava asked.

"Helga Sørensen," Hughes said.

Thank God for smart wives, Ava thought. "What happened?"

"The dealer in Hong Kong died, and Glen decided he'd made enough money and it was time to get out while he still could. He told me later he had thought about hooking up with someone else in Hong Kong, but the fellow there had been the perfect middleman. He didn't want to trust anyone else."

"How did he meet Kwong — that was the dealer's name — in the first place?"

"Believe it or not, Kwong took out an ad in the *Arts Journal* looking for Fauvist paintings. Glen contacted him and the two of them went at it."

"So Glen decides to pack it in when Kwong dies?"

"Exactly. And Helga's upset because it's become their best source of income. She evidently wrote to Glen a few times but he never answered her. So she wrote to the gallery saying that if we didn't want more Fauvists then Jan could paint something else. When I opened the letter, I felt absolutely betrayed."

"And you confronted your brother?"

"I did. I decided to terminate our business relationship and, if you must know, our personal relationship. We haven't spoken in two years."

"How did you divide things?"

"We didn't. I had scheduled a meeting with our family solicitor to negotiate a settlement over this business, when I became ill. I was hospitalized for about a week while they muddled around with my heart. The day I came home, Glen had a letter delivered to me. It said that he had signed over his shares in the business to me, that they were essentially worthless anyway, and that he had long since outgrown the Hughes Gallery," he said, looking pained. "I thought it was cowardly of him to do things that way, and I thought he was denigrating all the good work my father had done and that he and I had done together."

Ava felt a twinge of sympathy for Edwin Hughes, paralleled by a growing dislike for his brother. She said, "You know, I wouldn't mind having a coffee now. I take it black."

Hughes stood. "I'll get it and a tea for myself. I could use a break."

Ava waited, checking her watch. *It's taking him a long time*, she was thinking, just as he appeared at the door with two delicate china cups balanced on exquisite saucers.

"Sorry, the water took forever to boil," he said.

They sipped their drinks quietly, Ava's eyes drawn almost magnetically to the Derain. "My father bought it in the 1950s for what was a considerable sum then," he said. "It's worth much more now, but for years Derain's value languished. It would please my father no end to find his judgement finally validated by the market. It's the finest piece the family owns. What a coincidence, eh?"

Ava nodded and then said, "Talk to me about your brother. What kind of man is he?"

"It's difficult to be objective."

"Then don't be."

"No, I should try," he said. He leaned back, placed his hands behind his neck, and put his feet on the desk.

"First of all, he is an absolutely great appraiser. He knows his stuff, he really does, and has a fine eye for what's going to be hot. That's what's upsetting to me. If he'd stuck to our knitting, this business could have done well. Instead he went after money, and when he got the money, he lost interest in our venture," he said. "I mentioned the wives. Well, there were also the houses, the yacht, the wine collection, the useless wealthy friends. I wasn't paying too much attention. I mean, I saw what was going on; I just didn't stop to think about how he could afford it."

"He was stealing," Ava said.

Hughes nodded. "The money changed him in many other ways as well. Glen was always a bit cocky but he disguised his hubris with a smart sense of humour. Having the money allowed him to let loose the extremes in his character. Plainly said, he didn't need to be polite anymore, so he wasn't. He became vain, boastful, and over-the-top arrogant."

"He doesn't sound very likeable."

"I have grown to detest him."

"When did he move to New York?"

"The week I came out of the hospital. He didn't visit me there, or at home. He contacted me by letter, saying that London had become provincial and that New York was where the action was."

"And how has he done in New York?"

Hughes pursed his lips. "I hear things, of course. It seems he's doing famously. I'm not sure how much of it I actually believe, though. Glen has always been able to impart that aura of success."

"Maybe he's gone back to selling forgeries. Maybe he's found some dumb Russian instead of a dumb Chinese."

"Who knows? And except for you, who really cares?" Hughes said. "I'm more concerned about the three paintings in these files on my desk. Where are we going with this?"

Ava leafed through her notebook. "Before we discuss that, I'm curious about the painting you sold through Harrington's. It had to be authenticated by them, didn't it? Wasn't that a worry for you?"

"We paid Sam Rice fifty thousand pounds to sign off on it."

"He worked for Harrington's?"

"Still does. He runs the whole bloody place now."

That's a twist, Ava thought.

Hughes patted the files. "So, what are your plans for these?"

"I'm going to go after your brother," Ava said.

"For the Fauvist scheme?"

"Yes, of course."

Hughes said, "O'Toole's files should help you in that regard. I'm assuming Maurice kept as careful a record of them as he did of these. The Sørensen paperwork, I have to tell you, was a bit sketchy."

"I'm not going to use the O'Toole files other than as a way of keeping score."

"I don't understand."

"All they prove is that your brother hired O'Toole to paint them. They dead-end with Kwong. Your brother could take the same position with me that you did: 'The Chinese can sue.'"

"And why wouldn't they?"

"I had this same conversation yesterday with a consultant I'm using," Ava said. "In a nutshell, my client doesn't want to look foolish. He would never expose himself to the kind of public ridicule a lawsuit of this nature would invite. Glen referred to him as, what, ignorant? Why would he want the rest of the world to think the same?"

Hughes looked down at the files on his desk. Ava reached into her bag and pulled out an additional one. "There are four letters in here, addressed to the Earl of Moncrieff, Harold Holmes, and Jonathan Reiner, and to Frederick Locke at Harrington's. The letters explain in detail how they came to be in possession of forged paintings. Accompanying each letter will be a complete file, just like those you have in front of you," Ava said. "Here, you can read the letters if you want."

She was pleased with them. Each addressed the single painting that related to the letter's recipient. They were short and to the point — no hint of hysteria, nothing overstated, just a chronological statement of the facts with appendices noted and a line that said the original invoices, photos, etc. were available for viewing if necessary. The letter was signed by Ava. In a postscript she added that she had come across the painting in question as part of a broader investigation. She was passing along the information in the interests of art scholarship and wasn't seeking any compensation or acknowledgement.

The colour that had re-emerged in Hughes' face as he was talking to Ava visibly began to drain. His right eye began to flicker again.

"This would destroy me," he said.

"That is the intent."

"You said —"

"The question is, how is your brother going to react to the same threat?"

"He would go mad."

"I don't want mad. I want fear. Fear of complete destruction of his professional reputation, of public disgrace, of having to defend himself against three powerful, angry, rich, vindictive men. And I'd like to think he couldn't sleep at night for worrying about going to prison."

Whatever comfort Edwin Hughes was feeling about the direction of their conversation seemed to vanish at the mention of the word *prison*. Ava could see his body tense. He swallowed, and then took two deep breaths.

"I think — actually no, I'm certain — you would achieve that reaction. I am, I think, in some ways braver than my brother, and you've certainly had that effect — and more — on me," he said slowly.

"Good. That's what I was hoping to hear."

"So that's the plan, is it? To use the threat of exposing

these three paintings to get him to pay back for the Fauvist works?"

"It's the leverage I have at hand," she said.

"And if it works?"

"Those letters go back into my bag."

"What else can I do to help?" he said.

Ava smiled. "I want you to start by writing down everything you told me today — everything, every detail about the Fauvists. Do it on gallery stationery. Take your time; be thorough. Implicate your brother in every imaginable way you can. Be specific about Nancy O'Toole and Helga Sørensen. Mention the Liechtenstein account. Describe his relationship with Kwong — but leave out any remarks about ignorant Chinese."

"You don't want anything about the three earlier forgeries?"

"Of course I do. That will be your second document: a complete and frank confession. And don't bother with the rationalizations — no one will care. And I'd like you to make mention of our meeting and that you've reviewed my paperwork and judge it to be genuine, and that I have my bases covered."

He shuddered. "Yes, you do."

"When you're finished, date both of the documents and have them witnessed. Lisa will do."

"Is that all?"

"No, I want all the information you have on your brother: addresses, phone numbers, email, and so on. What you don't have, get."

"And then?"

"Contact him. Phone is best."

Hughes looked worried. "We haven't spoken in two years. I'm not sure he would even take my call."

"That's your problem. You need to talk to him."

"To say what?"

"He's about to hit a bump in the road."

"You actually want me to tell him about you?"

"Yes. I want you to set up a meeting between me and him."

"You want me to talk about the paintings?"

"Yes, but I don't want you to mention the Fauvists. Let's keep the focus strictly on the other three. Tell him that I've unearthed Maurice O'Toole's files and that I have a suspicion, borne out by some documentation, that the Hughes Gallery was involved in financing and selling forgeries. Tell him that for a million dollars I'll go away, and that you've already agreed to pay half."

"What if he doesn't want to pay?"

"You need to convince him. Tell him that if he saw the documentation I have, he would agree immediately that a million dollars is getting off cheap. And if you think it would be effective, describe the letters I've drafted to the Earl and the others."

"What if he wants to see the documentation?"

"Then he has to see me with it. I won't let it out of my possession, out of my sight."

"He can be stubborn."

"Mr. Hughes, you're approaching this from the wrong direction. You have an opportunity here to do something quite remarkable. You should be relishing it, not nitpicking the challenges. Your brother is going to be paying a very heavy price for his stupidity. He owes my client more than seventy million dollars, and one way or another, I'm going to collect it. Whatever hurt he caused you and this business is nothing compared to the hurt he's going to be feeling. So whatever you have to say, say it."

"I understand that," he said deliberately. "I also understand only too well the other implications if he doesn't co-operate. I just need to talk this through a bit." He paused. "What if, on the other hand, he is immediately agreeable? What if he says he'll pay the half-million and he doesn't need to see you or the paperwork?"

"Slim chance. But if it does happen, bluff. Tell him I'm quite insistent on doing the transaction in person."

She could see he wasn't convinced. "Are you scared?" she asked, pointing to the files.

"You know I am."

"Then impart your concerns to your brother. That's all you really have to do."

She stood up and he flinched. *What does he think I'm going to do?* she thought. She picked up the files, secured them with the rubber band, and held them in her lap. "I know I don't have to say this, but I don't like to take things for granted. These files aren't my only copy. My colleague in Hong Kong has a set, and he's also aware of you and your brother and what role you've played in this situation. So if anyone got any ideas about trying to take me out of the equation, it wouldn't make any difference. In fact, it would probably make things worse. I think that's a message that might be worth passing along to your brother as well."

"You didn't have to say that."

"I've said it anyway."

"You're leaving?"

"You have some work to do," she said. "I'll be back in four hours. Is that enough time?"

"Yes, it is."

"It will be about ten o'clock in New York by then, so you can call your brother as well."

"He's a late sleeper."

"Get him out of bed."

26

AVA WALKED DOWN CHURCH STREET BACK TO THE
hotel. She phoned Uncle from her room. It was dinnertime
in Hong Kong, so she wasn't surprised to hear the clatter
of dishes in the background when he answered his phone.

"*Wei.*"

"I've just left Edwin Hughes. It went well, I think. Now I
need to get to the other brother, Glen," she said.

"Is he in London?"

"New York."

"How soon will you leave?"

"After Edwin gives me what I want, so I can't leave until
maybe late today, more likely tomorrow morning." She
heard voices. "Are you with someone?"

"I'm at the noodle shop near Kowloon Station, Andy's
place. Sonny is with me."

"Say hello to Andy for me," she said, and heard Uncle
relay her greeting.

"Ava, these brothers," Uncle said, "how much money do
they still have? How much do you think you can recover?"

She didn't answer him immediately. The same question

had occurred to her after Edwin's rant about his brother's lifestyle. "I don't have a clue," she finally said, "but I'll call you the instant I know."

She hung up and was thinking about going downstairs for lunch, when her cellphone rang. May Ling. She let it go to voicemail. A moment later it rang again. Irritated, she picked it up, ready to silence it until the afternoon, when she saw a London number appear on the screen.

"Ava Lee."

"Frederick here. I'm just calling to see how things are going."

"I believe I told you I'd phone when I had something to report."

"I'm anxious," he said. "I was up half the night worrying about all this. The more I think about it, the more I realize how difficult this could be for my firm."

"Then stop thinking about it."

"Easily said."

"Leave the office, go to a movie, find a distraction," Ava said.

"How are things going?" he asked again.

She sighed. "Quite well, actually. With any luck, you and I should be able to sit down in a day or two with all the facts at our fingertips and make an informed decision."

"I'm counting on that."

So is Edwin Hughes, she thought, and hung up.

Ava took the elevator to the lobby and had lunch in the hotel's Stable Bar. She then headed outdoors, where the sun was still visible through a bank of clouds that grew darker towards the horizon. She decided to take a walk around the Gardens, and was on her third circuit when her phone rang. The incoming number was for the Hughes Gallery. *That was quick*, she thought.

"This is Ava Lee," she said.

"I've finished my paperwork. You can come by and pick it up anytime," Hughes said.

"Have you spoken to your brother?"

"Yes, not more than ten minutes ago. I think you'll find him co-operative."

She checked her watch. It was just past one o'clock. "I'm on my way now," Ava said. She was near the bridge that spanned the Serpentine, so she reversed course and headed back to the High Street. She called her travel agent in Toronto as she walked.

"Gail, it's Ava. I need to fly to New York. Can you see if there's a late-afternoon flight out of Heathrow, something that could get me there sometime early this evening? I won't be near my computer for a while, so call me when you have the information. I'm not sure what part of the city I'll be going to, so let's hold off on a hotel until I know for certain."

As Ava approached the gallery she saw Lisa waiting by the front door, looking embarrassed. Ava wondered if she'd read the papers she'd been asked to witness. "Mr. Hughes is in the back," she said softly, as if it were a secret. *She's been told something*, Ava thought.

Ava walked to the offices in the back and found Hughes standing by a photocopier just outside his office, feeding it notepaper with handwriting on it. "That was prompt," he said when he saw her.

"I was just around the corner."

He turned his back to her as he finished making the copies. He sorted the papers into three neat stacks and stapled each stack together. "One for me, one for you, and I thought you'd want one for Glen, so I took the liberty," he said, handing her two sets.

"Do you mind if I sit to read?"

"Let's go into the office."

There were nine pages of notes, double-spaced, six of them devoted to the earlier forgeries and the remaining three recounting his knowledge of the Fauvist scam, including his meeting with Nancy O'Toole, the letter from Helga Sørensen, and his brother's admission to him of his guilt. It was a straightforward account, unemotional and not the least bit self-serving. She respected him for his directness.

Ava pulled out her Moleskine notebook and checked the notes she had made that morning against the documents Hughes had drafted. "Mr. Hughes," she said, "on a separate piece of paper I'd like you to make a list of the so-called art experts who authenticated the Manet and the Modiglianis."

"Is that necessary?"

"Yes, I want that information."

He hesitated. "What bearing does it have on this? I've already given you a full confession."

"It will give me additional leverage with your brother," she said, not at all sure it would but figuring it never hurt to have extra ammunition.

"All right," he said.

"I also don't see any of the information I asked for about your brother."

"That's done, but I've separated it from these documents."

"Good. Now, do you have a fax machine?"

"Next to the photocopier."

"I'd like to send a copy of your notes to Hong Kong."

"Go ahead," he said.

Ava put Uncle's name on a cover sheet and wrote, *Here is an accurate description of how the Wongs were cheated. I'm leaving for New York in a few hours. I'll be in touch.* She dialled his Hong Kong fax number and fed the papers through the machine.

Her cellphone rang as the transmission started. Her travel agent told her there was a five-o'clock flight to JFK that got in at eight forty-five. Ava figured that by the time she'd cleared Customs and found her way into Manhattan it would be at least ten o'clock. She hoped Glen Hughes didn't mind working nights. "Hang on a second," Ava said to Gail, and walked back to Edwin Hughes' office. "Where does your brother live?" she asked.

"On 65th Street near Lexington Avenue, on the Upper East Side," he said.

She repeated this to Gail.

"There's a Mandarin Oriental Hotel at Columbus Circle and 60th Street," Gail said. "It's on the southwest corner of Central Park. You can have a room with a park view if you don't mind paying a thousand dollars a night."

"Book the flight and the room," Ava said.

"I'm finished with the list," Hughes said, as she hung up the phone.

She read the document quickly. The only name she recognized was Sam Rice, only because Hughes had mentioned him specifically.

"And here is the information on my brother."

"Only one address. Is that his house or his office?"

"Both, evidently. He told me he has his office on the ground floor and the living quarters are upstairs."

"A townhouse?"

"That's what he told me."

"Is he living alone?"

"Yes, wife number three vacated several months ago."

Ava thought Hughes looked curiously relaxed. *This is the man*, she thought, *whom Edwin Hughes said he detested.* "So, you say you spoke to your brother and he's going to be co-operative?"

"I did, and he said he would be."

"He took your call so easily?"

"I used Lisa's mobile. He probably thought it was some old girlfriend trying to reach him."

"Was it strained, your conversation?"

"What does that matter?" Hughes asked. "You got what you wanted."

"How hard did you have to push?"

He laughed and then slowly shook his head. "My brother has a remarkably fine-tuned instinct for survival. He can identify danger from miles away, and I only had to start talking about you and Maurice O'Toole before he had the situation sussed out. He thought the half-million was cheap. He said he'd pay it. He may posture a bit, protest, negotiate, whine, threaten — he has a whole range of theatrics he can call on — but in the end he said he'll pay. His only concern, actually, was about my ability to pay my share. I almost thought he was going to offer to fund that too."

"Did you go into the letters I've drafted for the Earl and the others?"

"I didn't have to. Glen understood the implications of this going public far quicker than I did."

"So he's expecting me?"

"Of course. I told him I thought you'd be there in a day or two, and that you'd contact him directly."

This has gone well, Ava thought. *Maybe too well.*

Edwin Hughes fussed with the papers on his desk. Ava tried to think of anything she might have missed. When she was satisfied she had covered everything, she stood up, put his notes in her bag, and said, "Thanks for this."

He walked out from behind the desk. "I'll walk with you to the door."

She hadn't been physically close to him before, and now that she was, she could smell a distinct body odour. Hughes hadn't showered or used deodorant that morning, or else he had been sweating up a storm. On his breath she also picked up the unmistakeable scent of whisky. Fear and booze were a bad combination.

He was walking beside her when he reached out to touch her elbow. Ava recoiled. He realized at once that he had overstepped his boundaries, pulled his hand back, and jammed it into his jacket pocket. "Ms. Lee, I have something I'd like to ask you," he said.

"I can't promise I'll answer."

"My brother, Glen — you are going to hurt him, aren't you?"

She wasn't quite sure what he meant and looked at him sideways. Hughes' face betrayed nothing. "Does he care about his money?" she asked.

"Passionately."

"Then I am going to hurt him."

27

SHE CALLED GLEN HUGHES FROM THE DELTA BUSINESS- class lounge at Heathrow, although she wasn't expecting to reach him. So when she heard "This is Glen Hughes," she was taken aback, and stumbled before saying, "This is Ava Lee."

"I didn't expect to hear from you quite so soon," he said.

There wasn't a hint of tension in his voice. If anything, he seemed disinterested, bored. *Maybe that's the impression he's trying to give me*, Ava thought. His accent was more refined than Edwin's, the pace of his words slower, languid.

Ava was sitting at the bar, a glass of wine and a small plate of smoked salmon finger sandwiches in front of her. "I didn't see any point in wasting time," she said.

"Indeed not."

"I'm at Heathrow. I'm scheduled to get into New York tonight around nine o'clock. Is it possible we could meet tonight?"

"There's absolutely no chance of that. I have a function at the Whitney."

"I don't mind working late."

"Ms. Lee, I'm quite sure you have my address."

"I do."

"Well, in that case, I'll see you here tomorrow morning any time after eleven," he said and hung up. Ava shook her head. It wasn't often that she was so deftly dismissed.

She heard the call to board, quickly downed the last of her wine, and gathered her bags to head for the plane.

The business-class cabin was almost full. Ava settled into her seat and waved at the flight attendant, who was already getting impatient with demanding passengers. "I don't want anything to eat," she told her. "After we take off, just bring me two glasses of your best white wine."

As soon as they were in the air, Ava put on her earphones and settled back to watch Martin Scorsese's *The Departed*, a remake of one of the best Hong Kong films ever made, *Infernal Affairs*. Ava wasn't sure that Scorsese would be able to capture the complexity of the original, and was disappointed to see that he hadn't. The American version added an unconvincing love triangle and ended in the most predictable way: the bad guy got shot. In the Chinese version, the bad guy, played by Andy Lau, had been left to deal with inner demons that eventually drove him to madness. *Maybe*, Ava thought, *the difference between the* gweilo *and the Chinese approach to the same story can be found in the film's titles.* The name of the original Cantonese version, translated literally, was "non-stop path," a reference to Avici, the lowest level of hell in Buddhism. That's where the Lau character ended up, in a never-ending cycle of torment.

Ava turned off the entertainment system and pulled out her notebook. She had made only rough calculations of what Glen Hughes had actually pocketed; now she wanted to fix a final number. It turned out to be $73,450,000. She wondered how much of it he would be good for. He would start off with denial, of course, as they all did. Then that would give way to accepting minimal responsibility, before finally capitulating. That's when the negotiations would really start.

Ava wasn't in the instalment payment business. She and Uncle would take one shot at getting everything they could for the client, collect their commission, and then move on. She had been lucky on her last few jobs: the culprits had been identified early on and the money was still recoverable. The Hughes scam went back ten years, and from everything Edwin had said, Glen Hughes had burned through a lot of the funds in that time.

JFK was a zoo when they landed. Ava waited in line at Customs for more than an hour, her patience wearing thin. But the taxi line was mercifully short and the traffic to Manhattan light; at close to eleven o'clock Ava arrived at the Mandarin Oriental Hotel. She hadn't slept much on the plane, which was unusual for her, and with the time difference it felt like four a.m. She was hungry, but her need to sleep overwhelmed her need for food, and by eleven thirty she was showered and tucked into bed.

She slept a dreamless sleep and woke at nine. It was the longest uninterrupted rest she'd had in weeks. She immediately went to the window and opened the drapes. Central Park gleamed at her, bursting into green under a warm spring sun.

She boiled water in the kettle at the bar and made a Starbucks VIA instant coffee. Then she settled in at the desk and booted her computer. An email message from

Mimi confirmed that she and Derek were actively looking for a house in Leaside, an affluent Toronto neighbourhood. She also wrote that Maria had been really happy with Ava's reaction to her mother's visit. I don't know what you're looking for in a woman, she added, but you seem to have one who is smart, gorgeous, and loves you to death. When I first met her I thought she was perfect for you. Now I'm more convinced than ever. Ava reread the part about Maria, and for the first time since she had left Toronto she found herself really missing her.

She went back to her inbox and saw she had received another message from Michael Lee. She opened it with caution. I hope your current job is going well, he wrote. I just want to remind you to give me a call as soon as it ends. Ava wondered if he knew what she did for a living. She had assumed that this was something her father didn't know in any detail. Now she wasn't quite so sure.

She closed Michael's message and saw that she had one from Frederick Locke. How are things proceeding? Please let me know, and try to keep me updated on a more regular basis, could you? Frankly, this entire crisis is wearing on my nerves. I'm having trouble sleeping and my concentration is shot. I can't stop thinking about all the possible ramifications of our discovery, he wrote.

Our discovery? Ava thought. She wrote to him, Please stay calm. Everything is under control.

She logged out of her email account and took a shower. When she came out of the bathroom, she took her time dressing. She chose her pink Brooks Brothers shirt and the black linen slacks, completing the outfit with her black leather Cole Haan pumps. She had about an hour to get to

Glen Hughes' residence, enough time, she figured, to take a detour around Central Park.

Ava packed her bag with her notebook and some of the files. She was still left with the three bound with a rubber band, which she carried in her hand.

From the hotel on 60th Street she headed north on 8th Avenue, with Central Park to her right. She had been in, through, and around the park many times. Its southern perimeter was marked by 59th Street, and 110th Street was to its north, a distance of about four kilometres. From west to east the park spanned less than a kilometre. She calculated her route from the Mandarin to Hughes' place on East 65th to be about eight kilometres, which meant she had to maintain a brisk pace. After ten minutes she knew it wasn't going to work. Her shoes weren't built for speed, and the sun was so bright that she was already sweating.

At West 85th she turned into the park and crossed the Great Lawn towards Fifth Avenue. As she exited onto Fifth she saw a sign for the Guggenheim Museum to the north, and another for the Metropolitan Museum of Art to the south. Ava headed over to Lexington Avenue and walked south, past signs pointing to the Whitney Museum of American Art and then the Frick Collection. Glen Hughes had evidently planted himself in the middle of the high-class art world.

She got to 65th Street with ten minutes to spare. Hughes lived in the middle of a row of eight townhouses, each three storeys high. Ava couldn't even begin to guess what they would cost — three million? six million? One housed a psychiatrist's office. Two were lawyers' offices. A brass plaque that read GLEN HUGHES, ART CONSULTANT was screwed into the wall to the right of Hughes' bright red door.

There was no knocker and no buzzer. Ava rapped on the door and waited. No answer. She rapped again. No answer. She was trying to extract her cellphone from her bag when the door was flung open.

Glen Hughes towered over her. He was at least six foot four, long and lean like his brother, but his blow-dried dark blond hair hung down over his ears. He was wearing blue silk pyjamas, and Ava wondered if she had woken him until she saw the cup in his hand. "Ms. Lee, right on time," he said, and then stood aside to let her pass. "Go through to the first door on the left," he directed.

The hallway had dark oak floors, pearl-white walls, and a ceiling that was a facsimile of the Sistine Chapel's. Ava couldn't help but stare, her mouth slightly ajar.

"It's striking, isn't it? I wish I could say it was my idea, but the previous occupant was a rabid Roman Catholic," Hughes said.

She turned left into what was obviously his office. It had the same dark oak floor but was covered with a rich, glorious Persian rug. Rows of paintings hung three and four high. There was an antique desk, and behind it was a floor-to-ceiling bookcase, every inch filled. In front of the desk were two delicate wooden chairs, their seats upholstered in white silk.

Ava couldn't remember ever entering a room that was quite so opulent, so beautifully put together, and the words tumbled from her mouth before she could think. "This is stunning."

"Why, thank you. We do try to represent our values and tastes in everything we do," he said.

He was behind her, and when she turned, his face was not more than a foot from hers. She saw the long, pointed nose, the chin that ended sharply, the thin red lips. But it was his eyes that held her attention. Helga had said it looked as if he had one large eye, and at that close proximity Ava had the same sensation. The eyes were blue like his brother's, but not so open, not in the least curious. *Dead — that's the right word*, Ava thought.

She sat without being asked and he moved to the chair behind the desk. "Would you like something to drink?" he asked as he settled in.

"No, I'm fine."

He smiled at her. "So here we have the vicious little Ms. Lee."

"That isn't a word I would choose to describe myself."

"And what word would you choose?"

"I'm an accountant."

"I know you are."

He's awfully casual, she thought, and remembered Edwin Hughes' description of his brother as cocky. His reference to her as an accountant, his whole manner, was a bit unsettling. Had she told Edwin she was an accountant? She couldn't remember.

"You quite panicked my brother, you know, putting ideas about prison — not to mention disgrace and bankruptcy — into his head."

"This is a serious business."

"A man selling newspapers on a street corner thinks he's involved in a serious business. Isn't it all a matter of perspective?"

Ava sat back in the chair and tried to engage Glen

Hughes' eyes, but they were wandering, almost blissfully, from painting to painting. She said, "Edwin told you about the information I have?"

"About the three paintings Maurice O'Toole did for us? About your threat to write to Harold Holmes and the rest? About the million dollars you intend to extort from us?"

Ava felt her stomach turn. "I beg your pardon?"

"It's an entire crock," Hughes boomed.

"Mr. Hughes, I have proof positive that you and your brother commissioned and sold three fake paintings to some of the most prestigious collectors in the United Kingdom."

"I know that, but that's not why you're here, is it, Ms. Lee? You have no interest in a million dollars."

"What are you trying to say?" she asked.

"You're here about the Fauvist pieces I sold to that ignorant amateur in Hong Kong. What was his name? Kwan? Wang? Wing?"

So Edwin told him absolutely everything, she thought. "Kwong," she said.

"Yes, Mr. Kwong. That's why you're here."

He stared triumphantly at her. *A man full of himself, a man who loves to hear himself talk,* she thought.

"I know all about what you're up to," he said, as if he had just scored a debating point.

"And what is that?"

"You want me to repay the money that some fool in China paid Kwong for that art."

Ava closed her eyes. "Yes, that's why I'm here," she said.

"And my understanding is that you intend to use O'Toole's rather excellent Manet and Modiglianis as your bargaining chips. Pay in China, save our skins in the U.K. and here. That's the general idea, yes?"

"Yes," she said, wondering what Edwin hadn't told him.

He had been holding the cup in his hand, letting it hover in midair, a prop. Now he placed it gently on the saucer. Ava noticed a tiny dribble of saliva at the corner of his mouth. *He's more agitated than he's letting on*, she thought.

"Before we go down that rather complicated path I would like to see the proof you supposedly have. Edwin did go on about it, but he has less experience with this kind of thing and is prone to overreact. You have no objections, I assume?"

Ava removed the rubber band from the files she'd been carrying. She found the file with records of the Modigliani that had been purchased by Harold Holmes, and passed it to Hughes.

"I need to go to the toilet," he said. "Do you mind if I take this with me?"

"It's only a copy," she said.

"I wasn't going to flush it," he said with amusement.

He didn't look at her as he walked past, but when he brushed by she could smell perfume.

Ava opened her bag and took out the letters she had drafted to the Earl of Moncrieff, Holmes, and Reiner. She put them on Hughes' desk, turned so that he could read them.

He is a presence, she thought, *a man who can fill a room*. Without him the room took on a different character: more serene, more exquisite. She admired the dark oak bookcase, which soared at least fourteen feet to the ceiling. Her eyes skimmed over the book titles — art tomes, all of them. Then she turned and looked at the walls, which were covered in paintings. Many of them were abstract, though scattered among them was an occasional object, a landscape, a portrait. She remembered Edwin Hughes saying that his brother had an eye for what would be hot. The paintings seemed to fairly represent that notion.

Glen Hughes re-entered the room with a burst of energy that put Ava on immediate guard. He saw her flinch and smiled. He swept past her and sat behind his desk, putting his feet, encased in Calvin Klein slippers, up on it. He held the file aloft before tossing it back to her. "Unfortunately for me, Maurice seems to have been as careful with his record-keeping as he was with his painting," he said.

She hadn't expected complete capitulation. "I left those letters on your desk," she said slowly. "Those will be sent to the gentlemen mentioned if we can't reach an agreement."

"If I don't concede to your extortion, you mean?"

"If you wish to put it like that."

Hughes had long, slender fingers. His nails were manicured and lacquered. He put his index finger on the letters and slid them back to her. "I don't need to read these. I am quite sure, as Edwin said, that they would result in our destruction," he said casually.

"So where does that leave us?" Ava asked.

"Trying to make an arrangement," Hughes said.

"I believe you have something in mind already," Ava said.

"First of all, I'd like to know just how much money you think we're talking about."

"Seventy-three million."

Hughes ran his fingers through his hair, only to have it flop immediately back into place. "That seems to be about right," he said.

Is he playing with me? she thought. "Okay, then write me a certified cheque or send me a wire."

He laughed. "Ms. Lee, I have not even close to that amount of money."

Ava went quiet again. "I can't give you a monthly instalment plan," she finally said. "You have this townhouse, other assets."

"Yes, we can talk about those."

"And you have Liechtenstein."

She expected the mention of Liechtenstein to at least give him pause, but without missing a beat he said, "I'll give you Liechtenstein — all of it — if you'll take it sight unseen and walk out that front door."

"Mr. Hughes, I suspect you have some kind of plan. I mean, between the time your brother told you about my interest in the Fauvist forgeries and now, you've managed to come up with a proposal that you think will work. But instead of telling me what it is, you'd rather play this silly game."

He turned towards her, his eyes looking in her direction without actually seeing her. "My brother didn't tell me about the Fauvists. I figured that out myself. A Chinese woman poking around in Maurice O'Toole's papers — what kind of sense does that make? This wasn't some random search; this wasn't a coincidence. And believe me, when I questioned Edwin, he did more sputtering than an old Vauxhall. It wasn't too hard to reach the conclusion that the Hong Kong business had come unglued. I have done only one large piece of business in my entire life with someone Chinese, so it didn't take any great intelligence to realize that your interest was in the

Fauvists. Then when I got your name from Edwin, I did some research. There you were, Ms. Lee, an accountant aligned with a firm in Hong Kong that specializes in collecting odd debts for Asian clients."

"You have me, and now I also know how smart you are," Ava said. "So what's your plan?"

He didn't acknowledge her jibe. "That depends completely on what your priorities are."

"I want my clients to be repaid."

"And it depends on how practical you are."

"I want the money repaid — that is exactly how practical I am."

"Do you care how?"

"I won't know that until I hear what you have in mind."

"I have hardly any cash," he said in a rush.

"So you've said."

"I think if I maxed out all my credit cards and my lines of credit, borrowed from friends, I might be able to come up with three or four million, no more than that."

"Ex-wives are a horrible thing," Ava said.

"I own this townhouse, of course, and I think it's now worth close to five million, but there's a mortgage, and in this economy who knows how long it would take to sell."

He's playing with me, Ava thought, and decided to wait. *Sooner or later he'll tell me what he has in mind.*

"You have nothing to say?" he said.

"This seems to be your meeting. I'm just a spectator."

"If you want seventy-odd million, and if you want it sooner rather than later, then the resolution to both our problems is behind you on my walls."

She looked up. "You'll give us paintings?"

"Yes, and not just any paintings," he said, standing up. "Come with me; I'll show you something."

He came to her side and extended a hand towards her. Ava ignored it as she got to her feet.

Hughes walked to the back of the room, Ava trailing. He stopped and pointed up. "That is a Picasso. To the left there, two over, a Gauguin. They would fetch you at least seventy million at auction. I'll give them to you, today if you want, though I think it would be wise to let me manage their sale or consignment to auction."

"Are they real?"

"Of course not," Hughes said.

28

AVA LEFT HUGHES' TOWNHOUSE AT TWELVE THIRTY, walked over to Fifth Avenue, turned right, and began the long walk around Central Park. It was close to two thirty when she arrived at the Mandarin Oriental, no more certain about what she was going to do than when she had left Glen Hughes.

In her ten years with Uncle she thought she had seen and heard just about everything. None of it came close to what Hughes was proposing. On the surface it was audacious, risky, and undoubtedly criminal. Yet, as Hughes explained to her how the process would work, how his checks and balances would come into play, how the Wongs would be insulated from any fallout if it all went south, she had come to admit that it was workable. It was still criminal, but it was workable. Ava hadn't refused his offer.

"First things first," she had told him. "I need to confirm that the Liechtenstein account is as barren as you claim. I need you to instruct Georges Brun to make available to me everything connected to the account." He agreed, and offered to do it by conference call there and then. She took him up on it, listening as he called Brun to confirm a current balance of just over a hundred thousand dollars and to bemoan his bad run of luck.

She asked for his bank account information, PINs, and passwords. He gave the details to her and then sat next to her at his computer as she accessed the account and found minimal cash holdings. She then asked to see the deed to the house and his mortgage agreement. He had paid just over four million for it two years before and had mortgaged half.

"Those other paintings," she said, motioning to the walls, "how many of them are real?"

"Most."

"What are they worth?"

"In ten years, maybe millions. Right now, they're investments in young artists."

She did a rough calculation. If she took all his cash and sold the house she might net four million, but there was no guarantee, given the state of the housing market. "How did you burn through so much money?" she asked.

"I have three ex-wives. They all took a big chunk since, like you, I prefer a one-time payment rather than a monthly bloodletting. And then, of course, I have led quite a comfortable life."

"Your brother mentioned some other assets, like a yacht."

"You're welcome to it, but you'll have to pay some marina costs to get access to it, and then there's the bank loan against it."

"Stocks and bonds?"

"Dribs and drabs."

"I'd still like to see the accounts."

Ten minutes later she had found another few hundred thousand.

He sensed her frustration. "You do know, I hope, that what I propose is very practical and very doable. If your clients truly want their money back, this is the quickest and most direct way to make it happen."

"You mentioned auction — that isn't a dangerous route to take?"

"Not if you manage it properly, go to the right auction house."

"Harrington's, of course" she said.

He nodded.

"With Sam Rice authenticating whatever you want him to sign off on."

His lips went taut and his eyes became more focused on Ava. "That isn't a name we should be throwing about."

"How many do you propose selling through Harrington's?"

"I'd sell them both through Harrington's, but only one — the Picasso — at auction. I believe they already have a private buyer lined up for the Gauguin. Not many Gauguins come onto the open market, so there's a waiting list for his work."

"So you've already talked this over with Sam Rice?"

He looked annoyed. "Naturally."

"What commission would they take?"

"At auction, probably twenty percent; on a private bro-kered sale it would be around ten percent."

She stared at the wall. "Are the paintings that well done?"

"They are superb."

"Who did them?"

"That doesn't matter, does it? It wasn't Maurice O'Toole, of course. This chap may actually be better than Maurice.

They're hard to find, people with this kind of talent. I found this one just eight months ago."

"I'm surprised, given your financial situation, that you haven't sold them by now."

A painful grimace crept onto his face. "I haven't had them that long. I was getting ready to send the Picasso to market, but then you unfortunately dropped into my life."

"So why go through Harrington's? Why not broker your own private sale, pocket the money, and pay us off?"

"We need the aura of respectability and integrity, the cloak of academic professionalism that Harrington's provides. And then there's Sam himself. If Sam Rice puts his reputation behind a piece of art, not many people in my business would challenge him."

Questions kept popping into her head but there was no structure to them. She needed time to think, to put things into some kind of rational context. "I need time," she said.

"I'll be here," he said.

"I'll call before I come back, but expect it to be sooner rather than later. We can't let this thing linger."

She had turned off her cellphone while she walked, not wanting any disruption of her thought process. She turned it on while she was riding the elevator back to her room; her heart sank when she saw that May Ling Wong had called three times, twice in the past hour. It was two a.m. in Wuhan. Uncle had called as well, Ava guessing because May Ling and maybe even Changxing were all over him. And finally Frederick Locke had phoned, his voicemail message sounding nervous and guilty.

Sam Rice, Ava thought instantly. Frederick Locke had talked to Rice, Rice had called Glen Hughes, and Hughes had thrown her some bullshit story about tracking her down through Hong Kong. That was why Hughes was so prepared. He and Rice had had time to concoct their scheme.

Locke was the only one she wanted to talk to, and she didn't waste any time when he answered his phone.

"You told Sam Rice about me, about the three paintings, about the Fauvists, about the Hughes brothers — you told Sam Rice absolutely fucking everything," she said.

He didn't respond right away, and she found herself getting angrier. "We had a deal, you weasel. You promised me this would stay between me and you. Now you've compromised my position."

"Ava, I couldn't help it. When I checked to see who had authenticated the Modigliani, it was Sam. I nearly shit myself. He's The Man here. He's more than my boss — he *is* Harrington's. I had to tell him what was going on. I thought he would get upset and tell me that our findings were crap, but he didn't. He just sort of rolled his eyes and said no one's perfect and that it was possible he'd made a mistake."

"And then he called Glen Hughes."

"If you say he did, then he did. I have to tell you, for me this redefines being between a rock and a hard place."

She began to calm down. It wasn't going to do her any good to get Locke more bent out of shape. "Frederick, I'm not going to do anything about this, okay? Let's just take a deep breath and take a step back. I've met with Hughes and I'm still negotiating. There may be a way out of this that suits everyone, but in the meantime, keep your mouth shut. Don't talk to Rice about it. And sure as hell don't tell anyone else."

"I'm not going in to the office tomorrow."

"That's a positive start."

"The forgeries — what are you going to do?"

"Frederick, I told you in London that I would talk to you before I did anything. That's still our agreement."

"Ava, there's no way I can talk to you about them, or what to do about them, without involving Sam Rice."

"Can we please first get to a point where we have something concrete to discuss? I can't have you running off half-cocked to Sam Rice with every morsel of information I give you," Ava said, knowing that she had given Locke the last piece of information he would get from her until the case was completely resolved.

"Yes, I understand," he said.

"Then sit tight and keep quiet. I'll get back to you as soon as there's something to report."

"I'll do the best I can."

"Thank you," she said, closing her phone.

She sat slumped over the desk in her room, feeling like a punching bag. Things seemed to be completely out of control. Locke was talking to Rice. Rice was talking to Hughes. The two of them were organizing a repayment plan that was full of risk, and it was illegal. May Ling Wong was making her crazy, and God knows what she was saying to Uncle. Being on the cruise ship with her mother and Bruce was starting to look like the good old days.

She needed to unwind. The walk hadn't done it, and a run was just as unlikely to help. She called the hotel spa and asked how much they charged for a massage. For $625 she could get an hour-and-fifty-minute treatment that would have cost her maybe $30 in Bangkok, double that in Hong

Kong. "When can you take me?"

"Now," the woman said.

"I'm on my way."

It began with a footbath and moved to a warm body scrub, with two Thai women working her from head to toe. When it was time for the massage, one asked, "How hard?"

"As hard as you can make it, unless I scream," Ava said.

They almost did make her yelp, but somewhere between the work on her hamstrings and her bum muscles, Ava began to think more clearly.

When the women had her sit up so they could do a simultaneous head and foot massage, she had already made up her mind about what to do and was beginning to relax. "Tell me, do you do both heads?" she asked the woman working on hers.

"What do you mean?"

"When I was in China, in Yantai, I drove past a massage parlour every day. There was a big sign that said 'head massage' in English, Chinese, and Korean. But underneath the main sign were a whole bunch of other letters in Korean. When I asked my guide what it meant, he said the parlour claimed to specialize in massaging Korean 'little heads,'" she said, pointing to her groin.

The women giggled and nodded. She gave each of them a hundred-dollar tip after the session.

Ava phoned Glen Hughes from her room. He answered just as it was going to voicemail. He was as suave as ever, but this time with a tinge of eagerness sneaking into his voice. "Ms. Lee, I was hoping you'd call back today."

"There's a restaurant called Asiate on the thirty-fifth floor of the Mandarin Oriental Hotel on Columbus Circle. Can you meet me there for dinner tonight at seven?" she asked.

"Gladly."

Ava called downstairs, made the reservation, and turned on her computer. Hughes hadn't been exaggerating about Sam Rice. The Harrington's website, naturally enough, made him out to be the world's greatest authority on twentieth-century painting. Other sites weren't quite so effusive but were certainly respectful. Ava recognized the names of some of the museums and galleries that used him as a consultant. It seemed that Hughes was right — a Sam Rice authentication went a very long way.

She searched for his photo online. He had a round, moonlike face with a small, pert nose and close-set eyes. His lips were large, out of proportion to his other features. He was bald, with only a fringe of grey hair running around his head like a train track. He and the elegant Glen Hughes weren't exactly a physical match.

Ava logged on to an art site to look at Gauguin and Picasso values. The numbers startled her. Gauguin paintings had fetched prices north of thirty million; Picassos had sold in the eighty- and ninety-million-dollar range. *What a hell of a business*, she thought.

29

AT A QUARTER TO SEVEN AVA WALKED INTO ASIATE. IT was still light outside, and she managed to get a table that looked directly onto Central Park through floor-to-ceiling glass. The park was alive with activity, boarders and in-line skaters vying for space with joggers, walkers, and nannies and mothers pushing baby carriages. *I'll take a run in the morning,* she thought, and tried to remember the last time she'd run in three great parks on one job.

The restaurant positioned itself as pan-Asian. Ava generally wasn't a fan of fusion cuisine, but she had eaten here before and the fish had been tremendous.

Her cellphone rang and she moved to answer it, only to have a waiter appear almost immediately at her table. "No cellphones are permitted in the restaurant," he said.

She checked the incoming number to make sure it wasn't Glen Hughes. It was Uncle. She turned off the phone and slipped it back into her bag.

"Thank you," the waiter said, and then asked if she wanted something to drink. She ordered a sparkling water to tide her over until Hughes got there.

He showed up exactly on time, the blue silk pyjamas replaced by a black linen shirt, beige cotton slacks with cuffs, and a pair of gorgeous brown leather shoes. He and Edwin, she guessed, had their shoes made at the same place. As he walked across the room towards her, she saw several heads turn in his direction. He was the kind of man who looked like someone you should know.

"Nice view," he said as he sat down. "I've never been here before." Then he looked at her glass. "Water?"

"I was waiting for you before ordering anything else."

"I'm a wine drinker."

"Me too. White, preferably, and tonight white certainly, because I'm going to order fish."

"I can drink white with anything."

She picked up the wine menu.

"No, let me look after choosing the wine," he said. He read the list intently. Ava would have just turned to the white burgundies and ordered something moderately priced. Hughes turned his selection process into a production. The waiter came back to the table and waited while Hughes turned the pages back and forth.

"I fancy a Riesling. Are you okay with that?" he finally said.

"That's fine."

"They have a Trimbach Clos Sainte Hune that looks interesting. It's three hundred dollars, but I'm in a bit of a mood for celebrating," he said, and then grinned at Ava. "We are here to celebrate, I assume?"

"I'd love to try the Riesling," she said.

When the waiter left, Hughes poured himself a glass of water and sat back in his chair. "I was awfully glad you called. The other options, as I saw them, weren't the least appealing."

"I looked up Sam Rice on the Internet. He does have credentials."

"As I said."

"I also looked up Gauguin and Picasso prices, and unless I'm totally wrong, the two of them should sell for closer to a hundred million dollars."

"We do have commissions to look after."

"Even then there's going to be some money left over."

"Sam and I need some additional retirement funds."

"I'm prepared to concede you that as long as I get everything else I want," she said.

Hughes' grin turned into a very large smile. His teeth were capped, perfectly straight and white as paper, with just the right amount of gum showing. "I'm so happy to hear you say that."

"You don't know what I want yet."

The waiter interrupted and the wine ritual ensued, with Hughes an active participant. When their drinks were finally poured, the waiter asked if they'd like to order. Ava didn't hesitate, ordering foie gras and black sea bass with oyster mushrooms. Hughes dithered around again before settling on Hawaiian blue prawns and wagyu beef tenderloin.

"Cheers," he said, lifting his glass.

"*Salut.*"

"Can we talk business now?" he asked, setting down his glass.

"Sure. Look, I spent the afternoon reviewing what happened this morning, and I do agree with you: my clients' only chance of retrieving a substantial part of their money is through the sale of those two paintings. And I think that between you and Sam Rice there's enough credibility to make it happen."

"Thank you for including me with Sam."

"But —"

"Ah, the big but."

"Not so big, and there are three of them."

"I'm listening."

"First of all, and most important to me, it is absolutely essential that only four people in the world know about these paintings — me, you, Sam Rice, and the artist. And I want your complete assurance that you have the artist under control."

"He will not say a word. He has a bit of a reputation himself, and it's growing. He won't do anything to endanger it."

"Are you sure?"

"Absolutely convinced."

"Next, this morning you talked about consigning the paintings in your name to Harrington's and then having them pay the Wongs from the proceeds. I don't want to do that. I want the proceeds to be deposited into your Liechtenstein account and then have them transferred to whatever bank account I designate."

"I thought you would have trusted Harrington's more than me."

"It isn't a matter of trust. I need to insulate my clients from any potential fallout. This makes them three times removed and puts that Liechtenstein account into play as another barrier. Besides, if you do anything funny, we know where to find you."

"That sounds sinister."

"Not everyone on my side plays as nicely as I do."

"Noted," he said, shifting uncomfortably in his seat.

"And last, there's the matter of timing and attention. Bluntly speaking, I don't want to wait for an auction and I don't want the risk attached to the publicity an auction might generate. So sell both of the paintings privately. Take a discount on the Picasso if you have to, but just get Harrington's to sell it as fast as they can."

"We would save on commissions," he said.

"All the better — that can accommodate the discount."

"Is that it? Have we covered the buts?"

Ava sipped her wine. It was lighter than what she was used to and it was going down very easily. She had no doubt they would go through the first bottle in no time. "Yes, though I still want to talk about timing."

"Sam is waiting up for me in London to find out if we have an arrangement. Since we do, he'll instruct some people from his New York office to come by the house in the morning. They'll crate the two paintings and ship them to England by courier, accompanied by all the appropriate paperwork and provenance. It will be up to Sam to judge the best time for him to officially put his seal of approval on them and to start contacting potential buyers."

"What is a normal timeline for authentication?"

"Could be weeks, months even. No two situations are the same. In this case the provenance is quite straightforward and Sam has my written professional opinion that the paintings are wonderfully genuine, so in theory he could do it in a day. Though he won't."

"Best guess?"

"A month."

"I don't want it to take that long."

"What do you have in mind?"

"A week."

Hughes sighed. "I'm concerned about the optics. These are two important paintings, and Sam can't seem to be in a rush. He'll likely have more than one buyer for them and he'll want to play the buyers against one another, get the highest price we can. Besides, the longer it takes, the better it will look."

"Why don't the two of you come up with a story saying you contacted him about them several months ago. That's feasible, no?"

"Yes, it is possible."

"You could say it was then that you sent him the detailed photos, copies of the provenance, and whatever else, short of his having actual physical possession of the paintings. Couldn't that shorten his timeline?"

"Are you always this creative?" he asked as their food arrived.

They ate silently, the wine, as she had predicted, extending to a second bottle. Ava hoped Hughes was concentrating on ways to meet her deadline. Her thoughts turned to Uncle. There was no way she could tell him how she intended to reclaim the money. As he got older he was becoming more and more cautious, and he might not approve of her involving them and the Wongs — however far removed — in a fraud, even if to correct the first fraud. So Ava would have to go it alone on this one. In all their years together, she had never barefaced lied to him, although she had once in a while withheld information. She hoped he wouldn't push her too hard to find out exactly how she had come up with the money. Uncle had often said that he trusted her judgement when it came to making big decisions. This was a time when she'd run with that trust.

"How is your fish?" Glen Hughes asked, spiking her thoughts.

"As good as last time," she said, and noticed that he had made quick work of his wagyu. When he was done, he waited for her to finish, his impatience beginning to show. She suspected he was anxious to call Sam Rice.

"You can leave anytime," she said.

"We're finished?"

"I am."

"You don't want anything in writing? You seemed keen enough to get my brother to put his foibles on paper."

"Between Maurice O'Toole and Edwin I have everything I need to ensure your continuing co-operation."

"Our agreement?"

"The last thing I want on paper."

"So that's it?"

"No, not quite," Ava said, dipping into her bag. "We'll need to keep in touch. My cellphone number and email address are on that card. Let me know how your conversation goes with Sam Rice, and keep me up to date on the timeline. Don't be surprised if I contact you now and then as well. When the paintings are eventually sold and the money is in your possession, I'll give you details of the bank account where I want it sent."

"You're leaving New York?"

"That's the plan, unless you think there's a need for me to be here."

"No, I'll handle things."

"I'm counting on it," Ava said.

Hughes called for the bill. With the tip, Ava figured it would be close to a thousand dollars. Adding in her spa treatment and two nights at the hotel, she had put more than $3,500 into the Mandarin Oriental's till. *Thank God for expense accounts*, she thought.

They walked out of the restaurant together as heads swivelled in their direction. "We are a striking couple," Hughes said.

"You're the attraction," Ava said. "I'm just the sideshow."

30

AVA WAITED UNTIL NINE THIRTY BEFORE CALLING
Uncle. By then she figured he'd be eating breakfast with his
cronies at one of the many restaurants that surrounded his
apartment in Kowloon, and would be unable to question
her in any great detail. Her objective was simple: tell him
what he and the Wongs wanted to hear, go to bed, and get
a morning flight out of New York for Toronto. After that it
was up to Sam Rice and Glen Hughes.

So Ava was surprised when Lourdes answered his cellphone. "He isn't well, Ava," she said. "He woke with a fever
and went back to bed."

"Have him call me when he gets up. Tell him it's important."

She groaned — she had been primed.

The wine was now having an effect on her. She lay on
the bed fully clothed and turned on the television. She had
gotten no more than five minutes into a reality show before
she fell asleep.

She woke up suddenly, the duvet wrapped clumsily
around her, with an urgent need to pee. She stumbled to the

bathroom with no real sense of time or place. It wasn't until she came back into the bedroom and saw the clock that Ava realized she had slept in her clothes for eight and a half hours.

She checked her cellphone. No calls. *What's going on with Uncle?* she thought.

She took off her shirt and slacks and climbed back into bed in her underwear and bra. The duvet was still warm. She dozed, her mind flitting back and forth between the deal she'd struck with Glen Hughes and all the things that could go wrong. After half an hour she hauled herself out of bed and called Hong Kong.

Lourdes again answered Uncle's phone. "He had food poisoning, I think. He's spent all day between the bathroom and the bed. He's just putting on some clothes to go out for dinner, so he must feel a little better. Hold on."

"*Wei*," the familiar voice said a few minutes later.

"Food poisoning?"

"I ate some raw oysters last night. Not so good."

"Take better care of yourself."

"I try," Uncle said, his voice sounding weak. "Lourdes said you called earlier."

"It's about the Wong matter," Ava said. "It's resolved."

She had been in his apartment many times. In her mind's eye she could see him leaning back in his old armchair, his feet not quite touching the ground, a small table to his right layered with newspapers and racing forms, the phone held to his ear. "Resolved?"

Ava realized the word was far too vague. "I got the money," she said.

"How much of it?" he asked. There was anticipation, some pleasure in his voice.

"I think I have all of it — seventy million or so. I won't know until we finalize all the liquidations of assets and the transfers, but I think I'm close."

She heard him breathe deeply and knew he was already calculating their commission and planning his phone call to the Wongs. She had listened to him make such calls before. Low-key, slow-paced, building towards a climax, the good news hinted at, then delivered only when the massive scale of the task had been explained. Uncle made every successful job sound as if they had performed a miracle. He could have been an actor. And then she thought, *Maybe he is.*

"Ava, this is remarkable," he said.

"Hughes was co-operative. The leverage we had through the other paintings scared him. We could have destroyed his reputation, set the animals loose on him, and probably have caused him to go to prison, or worse."

"I am surprised he still has the money," Uncle said. "Usually this type of person squanders much of it."

"Lucky — we were lucky," Ava said carefully. "It isn't all in one place, though, and liquidating some assets and arranging the transfers will be a challenge. But I've already started the process, and in a week or two — maybe two, to be on the safe side — everything should be done."

"Are you certain about the amounts?"

"Yes, within ten percent or so."

"And you have control of the assets?"

"Yes," she said, biting her lower lip.

"And the timing?"

She knew he was going to call Changxing Wong as soon as they hung up and that he was identifying the boundaries of what he could say. Knowing how cautious he was, she was sure he would fudge the amount she had given him even more: the ten percent would turn into twenty, maybe even thirty. He would also play with the timelines, and her two weeks would become three weeks or a month.

"Two weeks should see it done."

He hesitated and she braced herself for more questions. Instead he asked, "Ava, would you like to call May Ling yourself and give her the news?"

"No," she said, more quickly than she should have.

"They are too important for you to carry a grudge, and May Ling thinks very highly of you. She could be an important ally in the years ahead. I have told you, you need to build more bridges. It is all well and good while I am still active, but when I step aside, Ava, you need to have your own alliances — friends, *guanxi*."

He said it slowly, carefully, and she knew he was speaking from love.

"Uncle, when you step aside, I step aside with you."

"You are too young —"

"Some things have nothing to do with age."

"Ava, you know my religion is Tao."

"Yes, I know."

"May Ling is Taoist as well, and when we spoke of you, she said to me that the second she looked into your eyes she felt *qi*, life force, flow between you."

"I'm not sure what that means, and right now I don't have any interest in finding out."

Uncle sighed. "I will phone Changxing tonight," he said. "They have both been calling me, wondering about your progress. Regardless of your skepticism, they were tremendously impressed by the way you managed Edwin Hughes. Of course, they do not fully understand that *gwei-los* do not have our sense of family. No Chinese of any character would do that to his brother."

He had passed along her fax from Edwin Hughes' office to the Wongs, she realized. It was unusual, and she felt unsettled. *How close is Uncle getting to them?* she thought. "Uncle, you gave them copies of the paperwork I sent you?"

"Yes," he said.

Ava swallowed hard. "Well, when you speak with him tonight — with them — please ask that May Ling not call me. I am very serious about that."

"I still think you are misjudging her," Uncle said. "But I will tell her."

It was just past seven o'clock in New York. Ava looked outside, hoping to see the sun, and there it was, its rays emanating like a personal invitation. She made herself instant coffee, downed it quickly, put on her running gear, and headed downstairs.

She did a complete lap of the park, slowing down when she got to East 65th Street, thoughts of dropping in on Glen Hughes entering her mind. She decided against it and finished her run back to the hotel.

By nine Ava had called Gail and asked her to book a one-o'clock Air Canada flight back home to Pearson Airport. She emailed Mimi and her mother to let them know she was arriving that day, and that she'd call later. She wrote to Maria, I'm arriving this afternoon around 2:15 p.m. from New York on Air Canada. If you can meet me at the airport, that's great. If you can't, call me later at the apartment. Love, Ava.

She sat at the desk with her notebook. She laid out the gist of her agreement with Glen Hughes and then started making a list of loose ends, calls she had to make, promises that needed to be kept. There was a hotel in Dublin with twelve boxes in storage. Edwin Hughes and Helga Sørensen both deserved a call to calm their nerves. Then she thought of Nina, and just as quickly pushed the thought aside. If Ava was going to maintain her relationship with Maria, Nina would have to become a distant memory.

Back home, back to Toronto, she thought. It had been one hell of a week. And it wasn't over; it wouldn't be over until the money had found its way through Harrington's to Liechtenstein to Uncle's account in Hong Kong. *Don't start taking things for granted. Don't be a jinx*, she told herself. *There are still so many things that could go wrong.*

She called Glen Hughes, her mind still swimming in a pool of anxiety.

"Glen, it's Ava Lee," she said.

"My dear Ms. Lee, how nice to hear from you. I have to tell you, before you say anything, that was a wonderful dinner last night. I will be going back there again — under different circumstances, I hope."

"I thought the meal was fine as well."

"I also have to say that a friend of mine — a client, actually — was in the restaurant and saw us together. He's insanely jealous. He called me this morning to find out who you are. He thought I was dating some Hong Kong starlet."

"Tell him thank you."

"You're calling for an update, no doubt."

"Exactly."

"We're bang on schedule. In about an hour, the Harrington's team will be here to collect the paintings and send them to London. I spoke with our friend there last night, and he likes the idea of going private, even at a discount. He thinks it will be an efficient exercise. As for your time constraints, well, he thinks the deal can be concluded within ten days."

"Mr. Hughes, I am impressed."

"Coming from you, I assume that's a compliment."

"It is."

"I appreciate it."

"But let's not get ahead of ourselves. If we can stay focused for ten more days the compliments will mean something more," Ava said.

"Let me assure you, I am focused."

"I'm leaving New York this afternoon, but you can email me or reach me at the phone number I gave you if the need arises."

"Oh, I'll call if it's necessary," Hughes said. "And actually, you might hear from our friend in London as well. I passed your number on to him. He said he was having a bit of an issue with one of his employees and might need to enlist your aid."

"Frederick Locke?"

"He didn't give me a name."

It has to be Locke, Ava thought. *What is he up to now?*

"Does your friend want me to call him?" she asked.

"No, he says he'll call you if he needs you."

"Fair enough."

"Ah, the Harrington van just pulled up in front of the house. I'm going to go and look after the boys," Hughes said. "Safe journey."

Ava packed her carry-on, placing the files in the bottom

of the bag, the Steinum sweaters on top, and everything else jammed in between.

It was a half-hour cab ride to LaGuardia, and she was checked in and through security in fifteen minutes. Ava sat at the departures gate and watched CNN on an overhead television. She thought about turning on her laptop, but she was already in shutdown mode. She had just leaned her head back and closed her eyes when her cellphone rang. She was reaching for the phone to turn it off when she noticed the U.K. area code.

"Ave Lee," she said.

"Ms. Lee, this is Sam Rice calling."

His voice was a deep growl, made all the more distinctive by an accent she couldn't quite place. "Mr. Rice, how are you?"

"I've been bloody better."

"What's the problem?"

"Your cohort, Frederick Locke, is the problem."

"What exactly is he doing?"

"He's acting like an old lady over those paintings you unearthed. You know he came to me about them shortly after you met?"

"Yes, Frederick told me. I was surprised, actually. I thought he and I had an understanding that nothing would be said or done until I had a chance to work things out on my end."

"Well, the fool couldn't contain himself," Rice barked. "He came to me, and now he's been dithering about whether or not you're going to plunge the firm into some kind of crisis."

"You know that's not going to happen."

"I know, but Locke doesn't."

"I'll call him."

"No, it's gone past a phone call. He came to me in the first place because he doesn't want sole responsibility for making a decision that has so many far-reaching implications."

"Does he know about your involvement with the Modigliani?"

"Of course he does, and that's one of the problems, though not in the way you might think."

"I don't understand."

"Locke believes I was taken in by the painting, that I made an error in professional judgement — nothing more than that. He's concerned that if the painting is revealed as a forgery, then my reputation will take a serious hit, and of course the firm's along with it."

"So he wants to bury the fact of the forgeries?"

"He and I have had some long and tedious discussions about the ethics of this situation, about the pros and cons of going public. The bloody fool thought we should let the owners know about the forgeries. He thought we could keep it contained among the parties involved. I got rid of that fantasy in no time. I told him it would explode and that none of us had any idea of the direction it would take, how it would end. I even told him we would have to prepare to have every transaction this firm has made over the past ten years or so examined and re-examined. And God knows how many other mistakes would be found. And even if none were found, God knows how many clients would lose trust in us."

"So what does Locke want to do?" she asked.

"He has now agreed that for the good of the firm, my reputation, and the peace of mind of our clients, the best course of action is to ignore the fact that the forgeries exist. I call it our strategy of blissful ignorance."

"And Locke thinks I'm the only person who can upset that," she said.

"Precisely, which is why I need you to come to London as soon as possible."

"And what am I going to do in London?"

"Internally, we have kept this strictly between Frederick and myself. I want to keep it that way. So you'll meet with just the two of us and you'll give both of us complete assurance that you have no interest in pursuing this matter further."

"That sounds a little loose, don't you think? Will Locke be satisfied with my word?" she asked.

"He's most keen to have you actually meet me and for me to be the one to persuade you to stand down. He's handing you off, of course — transferring any and all responsibility for the decision to trust you to me."

"Still, what's my promise worth?"

"Well, you could offer to give up your files."

And give up all my leverage? she thought. "No, not until all the financial matters are settled."

"Then what do you suggest?"

"Draw up a written agreement, some kind of non-disclosure contract that binds all parties to secrecy."

"That's a bit of smoke and mirrors, isn't it?"

"Look, make reference to the paintings in it. Say something like, while the parties have questions about their authenticity, they have agreed on balance that the paintings could be genuine and that they have agreed not to pursue the matter any further. You and I can sign it. Leave him out of it. That should cover his ass, calm him down."

"Okay, I can see where you're going with this. I'll work on something, and I won't tell him. I'll spring it on both of you in the meeting and I'll make more of it than it actually is."

"And I'll spin it back," Ava said. "I actually made some promises to Edwin Hughes and the Sørensens that I'd keep them out of this if they co-operated. I'll make it clear that I'm just as anxious to keep this quiet as you are."

"Well, Ms. Lee, it appears we have a plan."

"But I don't have a flight," Ava said. "Let me work on getting to London. I'll be there either late tonight or early tomorrow morning. Either way, I can be at your offices by eleven. Does that work?"

"That sounds fine. And Ms. Lee, thanks for doing this. I know it's a bit extreme bringing you all the way back here just to help settle Locke, but we can't afford to have any flies in our ointment."

"Careful is good," Ava said. "And that raises some questions in my mind about the Picasso and the Gauguin. How are you going to handle them? Surely Locke is going to be atwitter for a while."

"No one here knows about them yet, and I'm going to keep it that way. They'll be sold through my private client list, a list that I guard with my life. My CFO will personally handle the accounting. At year-end the sale and the commissions will show up on the books as a surprise burst of profit. I've done it before and no one will be shocked by it."

"Frederick Locke?"

"Not a whisper to him."

31

AVA THOUGHT SHE'D CHANGE HER SCHEDULE AND FLY directly to London, but Gail dissuaded her from that idea. "There isn't a single direct route from LaGuardia right now," she said. The best she could do was a one-stopper through Detroit or Philadelphia. "You might as well come back to Toronto and catch one of the overnight Air Canada flights," she said.

Ava's flight to Toronto landed on time, and she phoned Maria from the limo. Her job at the Colombian consulate, as an assistant trade commissioner, came with reasonably flexible hours. She got Maria's office voicemail, hung up, and dialled her cellphone, only to get voicemail again. She left a message, saying her plans had changed and that she was off to London at eight o'clock that evening. She'd email when she knew when she was coming home.

Ava walked into her apartment feeling both welcomed and relieved by the familiar surroundings. She realized that with the cruise factored in, it had been more than two weeks since she'd been home. She unpacked her bags and sniffed at her running shoes. The smell wasn't noticeable but she would still soak them. She laid the Steinum sweaters on her bed and stood back to look at them. It was her experience that some clothes didn't travel well. Something that looked absolutely fabulous in a bar on a Thai beach could seem absurd in Toronto. A *barong* looked great in Manila, not so hot in New York. To her delight, the Steinums, if anything, seemed even more beautiful than when she had bought them. Mimi would look wonderful in hers. So would Maria: her light copper skin and wild mop of curly black hair went well with bright colours.

She packed a fresh set of clothes: a midnight-blue shirt with an Italian collar she had bought during her previous trip to London, a white Brooks Brothers button-down shirt, a clean pair of black Brooks Brothers slacks, and a light tan pencil skirt that came just above the knee. She threw in a pair of brown stilettos. She debated whether she needed to bring the files with her, and decided against it. They would just be dead weight.

After a quick shower she put on a T-shirt and a clean tracksuit consisting of dark blue Adidas pants and jacket. It was five o'clock and she realized she was going to run into rush hour. Dinner would have to wait until she got to the airport.

"Don Valley Parkway or Gardiner Expressway?" the cab driver asked.

"Your call. They're both going to be slow," she said.

They were crawling along the Gardiner when Maria called her back. "I'm so mad. I had a meeting I couldn't get out of," she said.

"That's okay; this should be a quick trip. I may even get home tomorrow night."

"I've missed you so much."

"Me too."

Their conversation stalled. Neither of them was entirely comfortable with sharing endearments over the phone. "Look, I'll email as soon as I figure out my schedule." Ava said.

"I've already told the office I'm taking a few days off. When you get back, I'm going to stick by you till you can't stand it anymore."

"Do you still have a key to my place?" Ava asked, knowing she did, and also knowing that Maria would never think of using it without Ava's express permission.

"Yes."

"After work, go over there. I bought two sweaters. They're on the bed. One is for Mimi, the other is for you. You have first pick."

"I'm leaving in five minutes."

Pearson Airport was jammed but most of the crowds were for U.S. departures. The international departures area was a peaceful island by comparison. She checked in and then hit the lounge for a couple of glasses of white wine. She figured if she had two more on the flight, she'd sleep most of the way to London.

They boarded and took off exactly on schedule. Within fifteen minutes of liftoff Ava had a glass of wine and was nestled in her seat watching *Extras*. Her intention was to watch one episode while she sipped her wine and relaxed enough to sleep, but Ricky Gervais and Stephen Merchant were so funny, and the series premise so clever, that she had to force herself to turn off the entertainment system after three episodes. She dozed off, and woke only when the flight attendant told passengers to prepare for landing.

They disembarked at Heathrow at nine a.m. Ava hustled through Immigration and went to the ladies' loo. She brushed her teeth, washed her face, and fixed her hair with the ivory chignon pin. Then she went into a cubicle to change into her midnight-blue shirt, tan skirt, and brown stilettos. Then she stood at the mirror to apply a light touch of red lipstick and black mascara. By nine thirty she was in a taxi line and by nine forty-five was inching her way into London.

Sam Rice had impressed her the day before. He saw no reason to discuss their involvement, no reason to make excuses for his actions. He knew they had a problem and he was eager to address it and put it behind him. She liked a no-nonsense approach, and she was sure that when she got to Harrington's, Rice would be well organized.

She reached New Bond Street at ten past eleven. The last time she had been to Harrington's it was after office hours, and she had been greeted by a security guard. This time she found herself talking to a beautiful young black woman with short, stylish hair. Ava signed in, was given a visitor's badge, and was told that Mr. Rice was waiting for her in the boardroom on the third floor.

When the elevator doors opened, Frederick Locke was waiting for her. He looked sheepish, and Ava saw no reason to let him off the hook. "I hope you're here to apologize. Do you even understand what it is to make a promise?"

"I'm sorry."

"That doesn't mean anything to me."

"You have no idea how tortured I was feeling. I mean, I was having nightmares, Ava, about how this would affect the firm. I had to tell Sam. And he's been great, really great."

"I talked to him yesterday."

"I know, and I couldn't have been more pleased."

"Frederick, we all want the same thing here, but we're not going to get it if we can't trust each other."

"Ava, I'm so sorry. This will never happen again."

"Where is Mr. Rice?"

"In the boardroom."

"Let's go see him."

Ava was guided through the high-rent district of Harrington's: big offices filled with antique furnishings and collectible paintings on the walls. The boardroom was large; in the centre was a massive oak table surrounded by matching chairs. The only modern piece in the room was a credenza pushed against the wall. On it was a tray with a coffee urn, cups, saucers, and bottles of water.

Sam Rice stood to meet her. He was extraordinarily pale, his skin almost translucent, which made his full red lips and ice-blue eyes stand out. He was large and soft, about six foot two and close to three hundred pounds.

"Ms. Lee."

"Mr. Rice."

"Sam."

"Ava."

"Thanks so much for coming at such short notice."

"This is important," Ava said.

"For all of us."

"Are you Scottish, Sam?" she asked.

"Welsh."

"Ah. I love your accent."

"There was a time when it was a handicap. The auction, the art business in the U.K. was run by an old boys' club who all went to the same public schools and the same university and spoke with one accent. It's only in recent times that they've made room for us provincials."

Ava sat down in a chair directly across from Rice. Locke looped around the table and sat next to his boss. "Coffee, tea, water?" Rice asked.

"I'm fine."

He saw her looking at the table. "It was Oliver Cromwell's. It was the family dining table, and some of the chairs were his as well. The table has been in our firm for more than a hundred years."

"And how many times over those hundred years has the company dealt with an issue like this?"

Frederick Locke glanced at his boss, and Ava saw that he was as curious as she was to know the answer. "More often than I care to recount," Rice said. "This isn't an exact science, you know, and sadly, things do slip through the cracks. We like to keep our secrets well buried. My predecessors always believed that sustaining the credibility of the firm was our primary goal. Without trust, we have nothing. So if from time to time they needed to shade the truth for the sake of the greater good, they were prepared to do that."

"And you learned your lessons from them?"

Rice smiled. "I guess that's as good a lead-in to the subject at hand as we can expect. Ava, would you like to start?"

She liked the way he had sidestepped her question and passed the meeting over to her. "As you both know by now, I was hired by a client in China to investigate a potential scam involving some Fauvist paintings," Ava began. "In the course of my research I came across possible irregularities involving some other paintings not directly connected to my client. I have since resolved the Fauvist issue to my client's satisfaction, and the other paintings now hold zero interest for them or me."

"For the record, what does that mean exactly?"

"As far as we're concerned, they don't exist. I understand that you can't take the exact same position, at least with one of them, since you sold it at auction. So I'm curious — for the record — as to how you want to proceed."

Rice looked at Locke as if to say, *See? Nothing to worry about.*

"The painting you refer to, the one that was sold through Harrington's for a client — we have reviewed the provenance and our original evaluation, and on balance we think it would be irresponsible to cast any shadow of doubt upon it," Rice said.

"So we seem to be on exactly the same page," Ava said.

The door behind Ava opened. She turned and saw a young woman with a slip of paper in her hand. Rice looked annoyed. "What is it, Melissa?" he said.

The woman seemed distressed. "Excuse me, Mr. Rice, but something has come up and Mr. Tomlinson thought you should be informed."

"Can't it wait?"

"He thought not."

"Well, what is it then?"

"Excuse me," the woman said to Ava as she reached past her to hand the note to Rice.

He read it and then looked up. Ava saw shock in his eyes. "Does he have any more details?" he asked.

"No, sir."

Rice stared at Ava and she felt a shiver. *Does this have something to do with me? The Wongs?* she wondered. No one knew she was at Harrington's.

"There has been an incident at the Hughes Art Gallery in Kensington," Rice said.

"An incident?"

"Something serious enough to involve the police. They have the gallery cordoned off."

Ava froze.

"How does Tomlinson know this?" Locke asked.

"He lives in the neighbourhood. He went past the gallery on his way to work and saw that the police were there. He called from his mobile," Melissa said.

"That's all he knows?" Locke pressed.

"Melissa, is Tomlinson still there?" Rice asked.

"Yes, sir."

"Do you have his mobile number handy?"

"I wrote it on the bottom of the paper," she said, pointing to the slip in Rice's hand.

"I'll call him from outside. I'll be right back," Rice said as he moved quickly towards the door.

When he was gone, Locke said quietly, "What can this mean?"

Ava didn't know if he was talking to her or himself, and in either case she wasn't going to respond. She had too many questions in her own head.

"I want to go to the gallery," she said to Locke. "Can you drive me?"

"You don't want to wait for Sam? It could be something minor."

Ava got to her feet. "If you won't drive me then I'll just catch a taxi downstairs."

"I think we should wait for Sam," Locke said.

She turned and left the boardroom. As she was walking to the elevator she saw Sam Rice standing at a desk, a phone to his ear. The look on his face told her more than she wanted to know. "Ava, wait!" he yelled.

She didn't stop. The elevator doors opened as soon as she got there and she stepped in. As the doors closed she saw Sam Rice running towards her. He moved quickly for a big man, but not quickly enough.

Ava was starting to give the taxi driver the gallery address when she caught herself. The street would probably be closed to traffic. She directed him instead to the Fletcher Hotel.

Sitting in the back of the taxi she tried to calm herself down. *I don't know,* she told herself, *what happened on Church Street.* But the dull throb in the pit of her stomach wouldn't go away.

Her cellphone rang. Harrington's. "Ava, we're on our way. Sam and I are getting into his car as I speak," Frederick Locke said.

"See you there," Ava said, turning off the phone and throwing it into the bottom of her purse.

As the cab pulled into the Fletcher Hotel, she looked up Church Street and saw police barriers and what looked like the blinking lights of police cars and ambulances. She went into the hotel and almost threw her bag at the concierge. "I'm Ms. Lee. Tag my bag and store it for me. I'll be back."

She walked slowly towards the gallery, trying to let the scene develop gradually in her mind rather than erupt before her. She was accustomed to the yellow tapes used to seal off crime scenes, the wooden barriers to keep onlookers — two and three deep around the outer perimeter — back. She tried to find a gap in the crowd, and at the north end she saw an opening and wormed her way to the front.

Three ambulances were parked outside the gallery. *Waiting*, Ava thought. Uniformed police stood in a small circle next to their cars; others in plain clothes huddled by the gallery's door. Beyond the ambulances Ava saw two television trucks, and to her right, cameramen stood with reporters holding microphones.

"Do you know what's happened?" Ava asked the woman next to her.

"Bit of a shoot-up, I gather. Robbery attempt maybe."

One of the television crews moved towards Ava as the cameraman tried to find a good angle for his shot.

"Excuse me," Ava said to the reporter. "Do you know what happened here? I'm acquainted with the people who work at the gallery."

"A shooting. Actually, shootings."

"How many?"

"Three."

Ava paled, the throb in her stomach now beginning to pound. "You wouldn't have any names, would you?"

"Nothing official," the reporter said. "You say you know the people at the gallery?"

"Yes, two of them. Edwin Hughes and his assistant, Lisa."

The reporter checked her clipboard. "We came up with those names ourselves, but they haven't been confirmed." She moved off, following the cameraman, who had found a position that gave him a clear shot of the doorway.

It's strangely quiet, Ava thought. The uniformed police were standing like sentries, staring back at the onlookers, while the plainclothes officers whispered back and forth and occasionally walked in and out of the building. When they moved, Ava saw a gurney, flanked by two ambulance attendants and a policeman, rolling out of the gallery. There was a white body bag on it. The crowd gasped, and Ava heard several women moan. The man next to her said, "God love us."

They pushed the gurney to the last ambulance in the row, and another gurney began its progress from the gallery, with an identical white zippered body bag. Ava stared at the bags, almost willing herself to see through them. *The bodies are small*, she thought. *Female probably.*

A third gurney came through the door. A pair of brown leather wingtips lay beside the body bag.

Ava gagged. The man next to her said, "Go easy, there."

She breathed deeply through her nose. Then she started to move away, back towards the bakery door where only a few days before she had lain in wait for Edwin Hughes.

It took ten minutes to clear space for the ambulances. As they drove away, the crowd began to disperse. Ava walked towards the crime scene, her eye on the television reporter, who was in deep discussion with one of the plainclothes police officers. She watched them talk, the reporter making notes and then calling over the cameraman to film her report, the HUGHES GALLERY sign prominent in the background as she spoke into the camera.

The reporter did three takes before she was satisfied. The cameraman went off to get more exterior shots and the reporter walked to her car, which had been parked behind the ambulances. Ava caught up to her as she skirted the barrier.

"Did you get the names?" Ava asked.

It took the woman a second to recognize her, and then she looked around to see if anyone else was listening. "The two you mentioned, plus a third, a woman named Bonnie Knox. They think she was a customer."

"How did they die?"

"I'm not sure I should say anything more."

"Please, this is important to me," Ava said.

The reporter lowered her voice. "They think it was some kind of gangland thing. The three of them were shot in the back of the head, and were probably on their knees when it was done."

"But why the women, the customer?"

"Innocent bystanders, they think — a robbery gone bad. Hughes must have tried to resist and the women got caught up in the mess," she said. "It'll be all over the news in the next hour or two and the police will make some kind of statement before the afternoon is out. Until then, keep this between us, eh?"

Ava nodded and began walking slowly back to the hotel. She met Sam Rice and Frederick Locke on the way. "I couldn't find a bloody parking spot," Rice said, breathless. "I've been circling for ages."

"You didn't miss anything," Ava said quietly.

"What happened?" Locke asked.

"You can hear about it on the news in an hour or two, I'm told."

"Is Edwin all right?" Rice said.

She looked away. "No, he's not, and there's nothing we

can do to help. Now I need to be alone for a while, and you should go back to the office."

"Ava —"

"No, Sam, I can't talk to you or anyone else right now. I'll call you later and we can continue the discussion we were having this morning. Although I suspect it might be irrelevant now."

She half walked and half ran to the hotel. "Do you have a room available?" she asked the front-desk clerk.

"Of course, Ms. Lee, and welcome back to the Fletcher Hotel."

32

AVA LAY IN THE DARK WITH THE DRAPES TIGHTLY drawn, the digital clock by the bed unplugged. Her mind was jumping from one scenario to another; her feelings oscillated from confusion to rage to grief in an instant. Underlying it all was the sickening realization that she had been betrayed.

She didn't know how long she had been in bed before she finally found the energy to get up. She opened the drapes to a sunny day, the Gardens lit up like — what, a Fauvist painting?

She turned on the television and flipped channels, looking for news of the shootings, but there was nothing. Leaving the TV on, Ava went into the bathroom. She stripped and climbed into the shower, the water as hot as she could bear. For ten minutes she let it pelt her, more punishing than cleansing. Feeling no less lost, she wrapped herself in the hotel's terrycloth bathrobe, a towel around her head, and went back into the bedroom.

She crawled back into bed. Even in the robe she felt cold, and she pulled the duvet up to her chin. She was listening to a quiz show when she heard the host's voice interrupted by a reporter's and the words "multiple shootings." Ava sat up.

The presenter sat at a desk with three photos displayed behind him. She recognized Edwin Hughes and Lisa. The third picture was of Bonnie Knox, a woman in her early thirties, the mother of two young children. The news report cut to the scene outside the art gallery. The reporter she had talked to was conducting an interview with one of the plainclothes officers. He was subdued, confirming only that three people had been shot dead. There were no suspects and no apparent motive, although they were treating it as a robbery. The reporter pushed the officer to confirm that the three victims had been killed execution-style. "We have no firm motive and we can't speculate," the policeman repeated.

Ava turned off the television. It was time to call Hong Kong.

She punched in Uncle's number. Her call went directly to voicemail. She checked the time. It was midnight in Hong Kong. She left him a message: "This is Ava. Please call me back."

She hung up the phone and sat quietly. *One more call*, she thought.

May Ling Wong answered the phone with a tentative "*Wei?*"

"This is Ava. I'm in London."

The phone went deathly silent.

"Why did you do it?" Ava asked quietly. She could hear May Ling breathing. "Why?" she demanded.

"I am so sorry," May Ling said softly. "But it was necessary."

"Necessary? You killed the wrong man. Edwin had nothing to do with the Fauvists. He helped us."

"He led you to Glen Hughes. We thought it wisest to eliminate the connection."

"And the women — what about the two women?"

"The women weren't part of this," May Ling said carefully. "I was distressed when I heard about them. But you know how these things are; you send someone to do a job and something unexpected always happens. The men involved thought it best that there be no witnesses. It's sad, but it couldn't be helped."

"One of them was just a customer. She had two young children. You've made orphans out of them."

"I'm sorry."

"Sorry? You should never have gone near Edwin Hughes. I had him neutralized. He was never going to divulge what he knew."

"We discussed this —"

"Who is *we*?" Ava interrupted.

There was a pause, and Ava felt her spirits sink even lower. "Changxing and me," May said.

Ava wasn't sure she believed that. "And the two of you decided that Edwin Hughes had to die?"

"It was necessary."

"How about Glen Hughes? Are your people tracking him? When does he die?"

"Not yet."

"But he will?"

"Maybe not," May said slowly.

You bitch, Ava thought. *You sneaky bitch.* "You made me a promise," she said, and then regretted the words.

"And I made it in good faith. But my husband found out about our arrangement. He has had no peace — you saw him in Wuhan. This will help ease his pain."

"You should never have done what you did."

"I will talk to my husband about the other man. Maybe there's a way —"

"No," Ava said.

"But if we get our money back he may —"

"No!" Ava yelled.

The line went silent. Then Ava heard a sigh. *She's calculating*, Ava thought. *She wants to ask me about the money but she doesn't want to do it directly. She doesn't want to push me even further off course.*

"Have you spoken to Uncle?" May Ling said.

It was the first time Uncle had been mentioned, and it caught Ava off guard. "No, I haven't."

"He wasn't pleased with us. He wasn't as angry as you are, but he wasn't pleased."

"When did he know?"

"Hours ago."

"How did he find out?"

"Changxing called him."

And Uncle didn't phone me, Ava thought.

"He wasn't pleased," May insisted.

"I have to go now," Ava said.

"Wait —"

Ava shut the phone, threw it on the bed, and then sat by the window, watching the people below strolling, laughing, talking on cellphones, going about their normal business. That's all she had been doing — going about her normal business. That was the job. Find the bad guy, get the money.

And do it all with a minimum of fuss. And always, always, always keeping the client out of the process. She should have known from the start that the Wongs weren't going to be passive. They were too rich, too powerful, too used to getting their own way. She'd been naive to think that she could work with May Ling alone when she and Changxing were like one person. Ava guessed that he had known about every conversation she had with May from the outset. And then the two of them had somehow co-opted Uncle, persuading him to pass on information that he normally kept between Ava and himself.

What's done is done, she told herself. *No more wallowing. Think about now.* Ava looked at her reflection in the window and thought about May that first night in Wuhan, sitting on the bed, crying over her husband's pain. "Fuck you, Auntie May," she said to her reflection.

33

SHE PHONED SAM RICE FIRST. "AVA, I'M GLAD YOU called. I was beginning to worry about you."

"I'm okay, considering. You did hear the news reports about Edwin and the two women?"

"Of course. How tragic, how unbelievably tragic."

Ava detected no sign of strain in his voice. "They were shot," she said.

"I know. I called a friend of a friend who works at New Scotland Yard and he filled me in on the details. It was a robbery, evidently. Several paintings were missing from the walls."

"Have you spoken to Glen?"

"Yes, twice. The first time when I came back from the gallery, and the second when I finished my chat with the chap at Scotland Yard. He's devastated, obviously."

"I was going to call him."

"I would wait if I were you. He's trying to reach Edwin's family right now and plans to be in England tomorrow. Assuming we have the other thing well in hand, he can concentrate on rebuilding that relationship."

"You intend to go ahead with the sale of the Picasso and the Gauguin?"

"Why, of course."

"On the same schedule?"

"Why not?"

Ava looked out the window, trying to figure out what to say next. How could they not see the connection between the deaths and the paintings? She had expected alarm, panic, fear. *Ignorance is sometimes a good thing*, she thought. "Can you move even faster?"

"We had an understanding —"

"I know. The thing is, this Edwin Hughes affair has upset me more than I can say. I'd like to put this job behind me."

"Anything is possible, at a cost," he said slowly. "I have specific buyers in mind for both paintings, but I was going to dangle them in front of a few other people and try to start a bidding war. If I go directly to the most likely purchasers and if I want them to respond quickly, I'll lose some of that edge. Our final sale price will be lower. How much, I don't know, but definitely lower."

"I'm prepared to live with that."

"But are we?" Rice said.

"I'm sorry, I don't understand."

"You want to net about seventy million dollars. I've calculated that after commissions and expenses, I can return that to you and still have about ten million for Glen and me. If I follow your directions now, we might gross only eighty or ninety million. Let's say it's eighty. Now, if you take your seventy, that leaves me with virtually nothing after commissions. As I see it, I'm the one creating the value and I'm the one taking the risk. Without me, there is no sale."

"As a brokered sale, Harrington's gets ten percent?"

"Yes, and that's not negotiable."

She calculated. "Are you sure you can get eighty million if you flip the paintings as quickly as possible?"

"Yes, I can get eighty."

"Okay, Harrington's gets ten percent and I'll guarantee you and Glen five million each, regardless of the final selling price. I'll still want the money to go to Liechtenstein until I give instructions for where my portion is to be sent."

"And your clients will be okay with that?"

Ava thought about May Ling and Changxing high up in their castle in Wuhan, ready to unleash another killer. "My clients are my concern. I'll handle them," she said.

"When you say 'sell them quickly,' what kind of time frame do you have in mind?"

"Twenty-four hours."

"Good God."

"Is it possible?"

He paused and then said slowly, "It is, but we're now most definitely in the eighty-million range."

"I told you, I can live with that."

"Then I'll make my calls. I have one client on standby in Japan and the other is in Germany. I'll press them to close. If I can get them to do it, I'll let you know. I won't call you directly, though. You'll receive an email and probably a voicemail from my wife. Her name is Roxanne. And Ava, I think we should make it a matter of practice in future to conduct all this business between her and you."

"Then I'll look to hear from Roxanne."

"That still leaves the other three paintings, especially the Modigliani that Locke is fretting about."

"That paper you wanted me to sign this morning — show it to Locke and send it over to my hotel, will you? I'll sign it and have it sent directly back. That should mollify Frederick. Tell him that as well as protecting Harrington's, we decided under the circumstances to keep Edwin's reputation intact. That's one more piece of security for Locke."

"I thought the very same thing. I think Locke will be completely onside with this."

"Locke is your problem now," Ava said. "I just want to finish this job. I'm ready to go home."

34

AVA HUNG UP FROM SPEAKING WITH SAM RICE FEEL-
ing that she had reassumed some measure of control. *Now
I need to talk to Uncle*, she thought.

She tried his line and it again went directly to voicemail.
She had a long list of phone numbers of people associated
with him, and the first and most obvious choice was Sonny.

"*Wei*," Sonny answered on the second ring, the sound of
traffic audible in the background.

"It's Ava. I need to talk to Uncle. Do you know where
he is?"

"He's inside."

"I don't have a magic phone, Sonny. What do you mean
by inside?"

"Massage."

"This late?"

"He's been sick. He slept most of the day and is better
now. He thought that a *guasha* treatment would help."

Ava had experienced a *guasha* treatment once: a hot por-
celain spoon was dipped in hot oil and used to scrape the
back until it was almost raw. It was supposed to leach out

impurities. All it did was leave her back red and sore for a week. "When will he be done?"

"Maybe ten minutes."

"Have him call me as soon as he's out."

"Okay."

"Sonny, this is very important."

"I'll tell him."

She turned on her computer and logged on to a site that listed all the U.K. newspapers. The Hughes Gallery killings were front-page news: a robbery gone wrong; three bodies found in the back office, hands tied, a bullet in the back of each head. The office had been ransacked and two paintings were missing. There were no known suspects, although several people in the area saw a tall blond man leaving the gallery around the time of the shootings.

Her cellphone rang.

"Why didn't you phone me to tell me about the shootings?" she said before he could speak.

"I was ill," Uncle said. "Not thinking very clearly, and I knew we would have an intense conversation."

"Uncle, what happened?"

"What we feared when we first met the Wongs in Wuhan. Wong Changxing wanted revenge more than he wanted his money back. The wife, though, really wants the money. That's why Glen Hughes is still alive."

"But they killed the wrong man."

"No, that was deliberate."

"Why?"

"Despite your information, Changxing believed that Edwin and Glen had to be in it together. They were brothers, after all, brothers in the same business, brothers who had worked together before. And even if they weren't in it together, he thought killing Edwin would send a very clear message to Glen that he was next. They want their money, of course, and they won't do anything until they have it. In the meantime, I'm sure Wong likes thinking about the terror he has brought to Glen Hughes."

"They told you all this?"

"Wong called me so he could gloat. He was very pleased with himself, and he thought that I would be pleased too. Remember, I am from Wuhan. I know how they think, I know how they act," Uncle said. "In Hubei province, killing or seriously injuring a person who owes you money is considered to be stupid. If they are dead, how can they pay? So you always pick someone close to them as a way of delivering a message that cannot be ignored. That is the way it was when I was a young man. That is the way it still is with some people. He thought I would appreciate the fact that some of the old ways survive."

Ava thought of Glen Hughes, oblivious to the subtleties of messages from Wuhan.

"May said you weren't pleased with them," she said.

"I knew what it would mean to you."

"They lied to me."

"They did."

"I gave my word to Edwin Hughes that if he helped, he would be safe."

"They knew that. I told them."

"So they made a liar out of me as well."

"I know," Uncle said.

Ava struggled to keep her emotions in check. "They played me for a fool."

"You are never a fool."

"So what am I supposed to do now?"

"Let us finish the contract, collect our money, and move on."

"I wish it were that easy for me," she said.

"There are times when you have to —"

"And there are times," Ava interrupted, "when I can't roll over and close my eyes and pretend nothing happened."

"What are you saying?"

"I may not want to finish the job."

He paused. "I thought it was done," Uncle said, "that the money is secured, that we are waiting for some transactions to conclude."

"The money isn't secure at all. With one phone call I can make it disappear."

Ava waited for Uncle to reply. *Please, don't disappointment me*, she thought.

"That is your decision. You do what you think is best."

"And you'll support me?"

"That is a question you know you never have to ask," he said quietly.

She felt her face flush. His reprimand stung. "I'm sorry, Uncle, I meant no disrespect. This job has affected my emotions."

"I prefer it when you are thinking with your head."

"My head is still working," she said. "And what it's telling me is that we need to go back to the Wongs and remind them who they're doing business with."

"You have something in mind, don't you."

"Uncle," she said, avoiding his question, "are you prepared to walk away from our commission?"

"Money I never had is money I cannot lose."

"I may make enemies of the Wongs."

"Ava, for what it is worth, I do not think that is possible. Changxing sees things in me that even I do not see in myself anymore. He will do what he can to avoid conflict with me."

"It is May Ling who is my worry."

"You have too much malice for her. She is formidable, that is true, but when I separate her in my mind from her husband, all I see is a practical woman whose love for her husband has pushed her to do things she would not have done by her own choosing."

Ava thought of the woman who had sat on her bed in Wuhan, of the strange conversation they'd had, of the tears. And then she thought of Edwin, Lisa, Bonnie Knox.

"Uncle, I have to save Glen Hughes' life."

"What do you want me to do?"

"We need to renegotiate our agreement with the Wongs."

"That would be difficult for me to do over the phone. I believe I would have to go to Wuhan."

Ava drew a deep breath. "I don't want you to do that," she said quietly. "I want to do it."

"You do not know the man," he said.

"No, but I know the woman, and I think she can persuade the man."

"You are so sure of that?"

"I am."

The line went quiet and she heard Sonny yelling in the background. She realized they were still on the street outside the massage parlour. "A drunk just bumped into the car. Sonny is sending him on his way," Uncle said.

"I'll talk to the woman," Ava said.

"Yes, I think that might be best."

"Thank you."

He sighed. "We men pretend we control things."

"Uncle, if you don't want me to do this —"

"No, you have assessed the situation properly. May Ling is the one who can be reasoned with. If there is any chance to renegotiate the agreement, then it has to be between you and her."

"I'm going to call her now."

"Let me know when she succumbs."

35

AVA WENT TO THE WINDOW AND LOOKED OUT ON Kensington Gardens. She thought of Wuhan, of the cranes that formed its skyline, of air so foul that streetlights filtered through construction debris. She thought of May Ling and Changxing sitting on the top floor of their eight-storey mansion with the entire world living below, looking up at them.

Westerners couldn't understand power as it was exerted in China. As men like Changxing accumulated wealth and contacts and influence, they correspondingly became increasingly immune to the everyday nuisances of life, and from the laws and constraints that applied to most citizens. As long as they were careful not to flaunt their status, stayed within the broad guidelines of the law, and didn't cause any public embarrassment or become a threat to their political and military allies, there was hardly anything they couldn't do, and there was virtually no one who would risk raising a hand against them. It gave men such as Changxing an overblown sense of security, a sense of invulnerability to the vagaries of the outside world. It had taken an Englishman to prick the bubble he lived in, the bubble that Ava had been hired to patch. Now all she wanted to do was take that small tear and turn it into a gaping hole.

She picked up her phone.

"*Wei*," May Ling said.

"Auntie, it's Ava."

The line went silent. "I did not expect to hear from you so soon," May Ling said finally.

"I spoke to Uncle."

"What did he say?"

"Auntie, he said I should do what I think is right."

"I've asked you not to call me Auntie."

"I can't call you anything else."

"Why?"

"You know or you don't know — what does it matter? The thing is, we need to renegotiate our agreement."

"We finalized it with Uncle."

"Auntie, the ground has shifted. This is now between you and me."

"My husband —"

"Fuck your husband."

She could hear May Ling breathing deeply. "Shall I have Changxing call Uncle?" she asked coldly.

"Yes, do that, Auntie. Have the two men talk. And then say goodbye to your money and watch Wong Changxing become the biggest fool the new China has ever seen."

The line was quiet. "Why are you doing this?" May Ling whispered.

"You lied to me."

"And no one has done that to you before?"

"You took the lives of three innocent people."

"I've explained that."

"Auntie, your explanation does not excuse the fact that you betrayed me."

"Don't call me Auntie anymore," May Ling snapped, and then went quiet, composing herself. "Tell me," she said calmly, "what is it that you want?"

Ava looked up Church Street and thought she could see the barriers that surrounded the Hughes Art Gallery. "I want our fee to be its regular thirty percent."

"Uncle and I agreed on twenty."

"It's now thirty, which is what it should have been in the first place."

"And if I agree, are there more demands?"

"Yes."

"So why should I agree?"

"Because the demands are joined. It isn't one or the other."

"What else do you want?"

"Glen Hughes lives. He lives for as long as his health allows. He lives, and all his family and his friends live. No one who is close to Glen Hughes has an accident."

"If that isn't possible?"

"Then, Auntie, from our side, three things happen. The money — all of it — disappears. More important, perhaps, is that the world will find out that Wong Changxing bought fifteen fake paintings and paid seventy-three million dollars for them in a pathetic attempt to be something he's not. And finally I will somehow, in some way, link — at least in the public's mind — the death of those three people to the two of you."

"Does Uncle know what your position is?"

"Call him and ask."

"I may."

"Call him on another line. I'll wait."

May Ling paused. "Thirty percent?"

"And Glen Hughes lives."

"I need to talk to Changxing —"

"No, you don't," Ava snapped. "You and I alone will agree on how this business is to be concluded. The men may be told, but not consulted."

"Or?"

"As I said, there will be no money and I will do everything I can to shame and humiliate your husband. Maybe no one in China will ever know what happened, but the rest of the world will. And I can guarantee that by the time I'm finished there will be so many rumours about the killings in Kensington that not a country in the world will give either of you a visa."

May Ling went quiet. "Thirty percent," she whispered, "and Hughes lives?"

"Yes."

"That's all?"

"Yes."

"And we get the seventy-three million?"

"No, I think by the time I've paid certain expenses, I'll recover about sixty million. Subtracting our commission, that will leave you about forty million."

"You would sacrifice twenty million in commission for Glen Hughes' life?"

"And you would forgo forty million and risk your husband's reputation, everything he's built, for the life of a man you've never met?"

"I see the logic in your position," May Ling said carefully. "But I don't know if my husband will."

Ava thought of Glen Hughes. He was already on his way to England to comfort his brother's widow because of what he thought was a robbery gone wrong. "Tell Changxing that letting Hughes live is a greater and more prolonged torture. He'll be a man living in perpetual terror, waiting for the gun that will take his life just as his brother's was taken. In some ways, letting him live is a greater punishment than killing him."

"There is a sense of justice in that."

"Shall I tell Uncle?"

"Yes, you can tell him," May Ling said. "I will make my husband understand."

"I hope so, Auntie, because I am a vengeful woman."

"That is another quality," May Ling said softly, "that we seem to share."

36

THE FIRST AIR CANADA FLIGHT OUT OF HEATHROW TO Toronto was at eleven a.m. Ava was checked in by nine thirty and sitting in the lounge and online ten minutes later. There was an email message from Roxanne Rice, saying the two paintings had sold for eighty-four million. The money would be in the Liechtenstein account within forty-eight hours. The Wongs would net just over forty million after Harrington's commissions and expenses, the five million each for Hughes and Rice, and the thirty percent she and Uncle had earned as their commission. Ava sent Roxanne her thanks and asked her to pass along best wishes to her husband. She then emailed her flight schedule to Maria, Mimi, and her mother and told them she would contact them when she reached her condo in Yorkville.

It was mid-evening in Hong Kong. *Uncle should be at dinner*, she thought. She had called him the night before to update him on her talk with May Ling Wong. He hadn't been surprised by her apparent success but was now as anxious as she was to put this case behind them. She knew he would be pleased that the money would be available so quickly. His cellphone rang once and went directly to voicemail. *That's strange*, she thought, and dialled his home number.

"*Wei*," he answered.

"You're at home this time of night?" she said.

"My stomach keeps acting up. I went to see a doctor this afternoon and had acupuncture. Now I am drinking nothing but warm water and eating only congee for two days."

"I worry about you."

"Please do not. I am not falling apart — not yet, anyway."

"I'm at Heathrow, heading home. I was just told that our money will be available within the next two or three days."

"Excellent. I will call Changxing."

"I wonder if he'll make any mention of the changes in our agreement."

"He has already. He called me earlier today," Uncle said and made a small noise that sounded to Ava like a laugh. "That wife of his told him she thought they should increase our commission to the regular rate. She said you had done some remarkable work and that she had perhaps been disrespectful, haggling with me the way she did. He told me he had felt that way all along, and he instructed his wife to follow her instincts and pay us thirty percent. He made it sound as if he was giving me a gift."

"I see."

"He also said he had been thinking about Glen Hughes."

"And?"

"He thinks Hughes must be going crazy with fear. 'He is living in hell,' he said. He has decided to leave him there."

"May Ling is a clever woman."

"Yes, she is," Uncle said slowly. "She could be an important contact in years to come. Anyone with her kind of *guangxi* should not so easily be set aside."

"Uncle —"

"I know you do not want to hear that and I will not mention it again, but that does not make it any less true," he said.

Before she could answer, the announcement came that her flight was ready to board. "I have to go, Uncle."

"Safe journey," he said.

Eight hours later Ava was walking through the arrivals hall at Pearson Airport, heading towards the limousine service. Then she heard her name. She turned to see Mimi, her mother, Maria, and Marcus Lee all waving at her.

Mimi and her mother were standing together; Marcus was to his wife's left and Maria several metres to Mimi's right. It was an awkward grouping, given that her mother never liked to concede looks to any other woman; tall, blonde, beautiful Mimi was an overpowering presence. Maria was wearing the Steinum sweater. Shy as always, she gave Ava a small smile, a tiny wave.

Ava went directly to Maria. They kissed discreetly, and then Maria said, "Mimi introduced me to your parents."

"As what?"

"Your friend."

Ava turned and walked over to her parents and Mimi, Maria trailing behind.

"Welcome home," Mimi said, holding out her arms. The two women hugged.

Ava looked at Jennie Lee. "Mummy, you've met Maria."

"Yes," Jennie said. "I told her that I've never seen a girl who looked so good in bright colours."

Ava smiled. "Even though I wasn't expecting any of you, I'm really happy to see you. But now I really want to get home. How will we handle transportation?"

"I have Mummy's car," Marcus Lee said.

"Maria and I came together in a limo. It's waiting outside," said Mimi.

Ava looked at her parents. "If you don't mind, I'll ride with the girls. Maybe we can meet later for dinner."

Marcus Lee looked uncomfortable, and Ava wondered if she had offended him. "Daddy, it's just more practical."

"Can we talk privately for a moment?" he said.

Ava looked at her mother and saw concern etched on her face. "Of course," she said.

They moved to the side, leaving the other three women.

"Michael called me this morning," Marcus said. "We talked in detail about his problems. I think he needs your help."

"Daddy, I've just met him, and then only for two minutes."

"He's your brother."

"Until a few days ago he was only a name."

She saw the pain in her father's eyes and felt her cheeks flush in shame.

"He wanted me to help him. I can't. It's beyond my capacity. He needs you."

"What do you think I do?" she asked.

"I don't live in a bubble in Hong Kong. I know who Uncle is, and was. And things are said about you — some of them alarming, some of them more complimentary. Michael is my oldest child. When I die, he will become the head of this family. I need you to respect that. Right now he's at risk and he's put most of his assets at risk. I don't want to watch my oldest child lose his future."

"What do you want me to do?"

"Help him."

"How?"

"Call him and he'll explain."

"But you know what happened?"

"I know enough to understand that he needs your help."

"I'll call him," she said quietly.

Marcus leaned down and kissed his daughter on the forehead. "It's always been my dream to bring my children together. I regret that it's under these circumstances."

"It's a family and a structure that you created," she said.

"I haven't always been wise."

The three women were standing where Ava had left them. Jennie looked pointedly at Ava as she walked back towards them. She saw in her mother's eyes that Marcus had confided in her. Jennie mouthed, *Momentai?* and Ava knew that her mother stood with him.

Ava gave a slight nod and mouthed, *Momentai.*

"I was serious about dinner tonight," Ava said to Jennie.

Her mother glanced at Maria and Mimi. "I think I'd rather have your father to myself tonight, and I think your friends would like to have you to themselves as well. Now off you go with them. We can talk later."

When Marcus rejoined them, Jennie reached for his hand. "The girls need to leave for the city," she said. "We should go home."

Ava watched as they walked towards the escalator that would take them to the parking garage, her mother still holding on to his hand. His head was turned in her direction, talking. Her eyes never left his face. She couldn't remember a time when they had seemed closer.

"Time to go home, girls," Ava said, leading them towards the exit.

The three women got into the back of the limousine, Ava in the middle, Maria with her arm looped through hers, and Mimi's chin resting on Ava's shoulder, a wide grin on her face.

"You haven't stopped smiling since I've arrived," Ava said. She felt Mimi nudge her gently in the ribs. "You're really going to live in Leaside?"

"Yes."

"With all those young professionals and their nannies?"

"That's the plan — including the nanny."

"You're pregnant?" Ava blurted.

"Absolutely."

"I hope Derek's asked you to marry him," she said.

"He has."

"Geez, what have I started?"

"Everything," Mimi said, punching Ava's arm.

ACKNOWLEDGEMENTS

This is the second book in the Ava Lee series, a fact that amazes me. What began with a name and a glimmer of an idea has turned into something with a very large life of its own. None of this happened, of course, without the active support of many people. And in my case, many of those people are women.

My thanks to Kristine Wookey, who championed Ava from the start and without whose support none of this might have happened.

To my agent, Carolyn Forde, and agent Bruce Westwood.

To Paddy Torsney, Farah Mohammed, and Nicole Valiant, the "Godmothers," who read every manuscript and who continue to beat the drum.

To Sarah MacLachlan and her team at House of Anansi Press.

To my dedicated and talented editor, the great Janie Yoon.

And to Ian Ross, Executive Director of the Burlington Art Centre and friend. His insight into art fraud and forgeries was invaluable.

Read on for an excerpt from
Ian Hamilton's next Ava Lee novel

THE
RED POLE
OF
MACAU

Coming Winter 2014
in trade paperback
from Picador

www.picadorusa.com
www.twitter.com/picadorusa • www.facebook.com/picadorusa
picadorbookroom.tumblr.com

AVA LEE WOKE TO THE SENSATION OF LIPS KISSING her forehead. She opened her eyes to semi-darkness and saw her girlfriend, Maria, hovering over her, her face in shadow. Ava extended her arms, but Maria shook her head and passed over the phone. "He says his name is Michael and that he's your brother," she said.

"I didn't hear it ring," Ava said. "And he's my half-brother, from my father's first wife. The one I told you I met in Hong Kong."

"I think he first phoned half an hour ago. I didn't answer it then. He's called back every ten minutes since."

Ava glanced sideways at the bedside clock. It was just past eight a.m., eight in the evening in Hong Kong, where she assumed the call originated. She reached under her pillow, pulled out a black Giordano T-shirt, and slipped it over her head. Then she held out her hand for the phone. "I'll talk to him out here," she said, rolling out of bed and walking to the kitchen. "Michael?"

"Yes."

"This is an early call."

"I'm sorry. I spoke to Dad last night," he said, his voice strained. "He said he met you at the Toronto airport and explained that we are having some problems here. He said you were going to call me."

"I was, later today."

"I have to go out in about half an hour and I won't be available for the rest of the evening. I didn't want to wait until tomorrow for us to talk."

"Daddy said there was an issue in Hong Kong. He didn't say any more than that, and he didn't tell me it was so urgent."

He sighed. "I'm sorry."

Ava sat at her kitchen table and looked down onto Yorkville Avenue. Her condo was situated in the very heart of Toronto, and the Yorkville district was one of the city's trendiest, but at eight on a weekday morning the streets were devoid of shoppers and restaurant-goers. Farther away she could see that Avenue Road, a main north–south artery, was jammed with commuter traffic. "What's going on?" she asked.

"We're in a bit of a mess."

"Who is *we*?"

"My partner, Simon To, and me."

"Explain what you mean by a mess."

The line went silent. All Ava could hear was deep breathing, as if he was trying to gather together his thoughts and his emotions. "We own a franchise operation: some convenience stores and high-end noodle shops. We were looking at putting one of each into a large new retail mall in Macau, either renting the space or buying it. We were midway through negotiations when the developers asked if we'd like to up the ante, if we'd like to invest in the entire project. It's something we'd always thought about, accumulating some real estate. Simon didn't see how we could go wrong putting money into Macau. So we did."

"How much money?"

"A hundred and fifty million."

"U.S. dollars?" Ava said, shocked.

"No, Hong Kong."

"So about twenty million U.S.?"

"Yes."

That's still a lot of money, she thought, *but in Macau it won't buy much land.* "So you took a minority share?"

"Yes. As I said, it's a large project."

"So what's gone wrong?"

"The development has run into all kinds of delays and we've been trying to pull our money out. They won't let us. In fact, we're getting leaned on to put in more."

"And you don't want to?"

"We can't, and our bank is all over us about the hundred and fifty million."

"The real estate developer is from Hong Kong?"

"No, he's Macanese."

"You obviously have a contract."

"We do."

"Have you spoken to lawyers?"

"Do you have any idea how time-consuming and money-eating a process it is for a Hong Kong company to pursue one based in Macau?" he said, a trace of impatience in his voice.

Maybe you should have considered that before you did the deal, she thought. "So what do you think I can do?" she asked.

"Communications between them and us have been getting more difficult by the day. My partner can't talk to them without losing his temper, and every conversation I have with these people just seems to make things worse. We need a fresh set of eyes and ears. We need a new perspective."

"Michael, what did Daddy tell you I did for a living?" Ava asked.

"He said you were a problem-solver."

"All I do is collect bad debts."

"If things keep going the way they are, I'm afraid this could become one," he said, his voice heavy.

"You don't mean that," she said.

"No, not really. We just need to find a way to negotiate ourselves out of this situation."

"And you think I can do that?"

"Dad says if anyone can, it's you."

"It isn't my usual line of work."

"I don't care, and we'd pay a fee."

"I couldn't charge one," she said.

"Ava, please, whatever it takes to get you here, I'll do it. We're at an impasse."

How strange is this? Ava thought. She had met Michael Lee exactly once, and then for only a few minutes in a Hong Kong restaurant, and now he was inviting, almost begging her into his life.

Ava was the younger daughter in their father Marcus Lee's second family. He had married three times, and in the tradition of wealthy Chinese men, supported and loved each of his families. His first wife had given him four sons, of whom Michael was the eldest. It was understood that Marcus's business and the bulk of his wealth would ultimately reside with the first family, and that Michael would become head of the entire clan if anything happened to Marcus.

Ava's mother, Jennie, had given Marcus two daughters and a volatile relationship. It had become so fractious that Marcus eventually moved them to Vancouver, a city Jennie Lee couldn't abide. She lasted two years there before taking Ava and her sister, Marian, to Toronto, where the girls were raised and educated. Marcus had taken a third wife shortly after shipping Jennie and the girls to Canada. She had given him two more children, a girl and a boy, and they now lived in Australia.

Jennie Lee had never worked. Marcus bought them a house and cars, paid the bills, and looked after the girls' educations. He still talked to Jennie every day, and he visited Canada every year for a two-week stay. This year had been unusual. He had joined Jennie, Ava, Marian, and Marian's husband and two daughters on a two-week cruise through the southern Caribbean, and then returned to Toronto to stay for another week with Jennie. He was still at her house, in the suburb of Richmond Hill to the north.

Ava's mother had never been jealous about the first family. She knew that the first wife and her family would always be pre-eminent. All she asked was that Marcus be fair in his treatment of her and the girls. And he always had been. He talked to Jennie about his four sons from the first marriage, so she knew about them and had made their names known to Ava and Marian. But none of them had ever met until the week before.

The thing that Ava didn't know was how open Marcus Lee was about her and Marian with the rest of his extended family. She would have assumed that Michael knew they existed, but it was still a surprise when he approached her in the Hong Kong restaurant and said he recognized her from pictures their father had shown him. He had known exactly who she was, and he seemed eager to start a relationship.

Ava found it unsettling. It was one thing to understand and accept the complicated layers of Marcus Lee's life and to know where you fit among them. It was another to confront the physical reality of someone who until then had been just a name, just a shadow.

"Michael, I got home only yesterday. I've been on the road for more than a week. Is there anything I can do from here?" she said.

He hesitated.

"There must be a contract."

"Yes."

"Email it to me and I'll look at it right away."

"It's all very basic stuff. I don't see how that can help."

"Michael, let me be the judge of that. After I've gone through it we can talk."

"Okay," he said, still reluctant.

"And by the way, how much does Daddy actually know about your problem?"

"Why do you ask?"

"I expect I'll be talking to him today. I don't want to be indiscreet."

"He knows about the size of it but I haven't discussed all the details."

"Then neither will I."

"Thank you."

"Look, I promise I'll read the contract as soon as I get it, and then we can talk," she said.

"I'll email it right away and I'll call when I get back from this function. It will be around midnight."

Ava closed the phone. The sun was glistening off the windows of the condos across the street, taking, she imagined, the chill out of the spring air. It was her favourite time of year in Canada: the world coming to life, full of promise. The last thing she felt like doing was getting on another plane for Hong Kong. After scurrying around Wuhan in China, London, Denmark, Dublin, New York, and then London again, chasing money and forged art, she felt she deserved more than one day in Toronto.

She thought about going back to bed, but Michael's problem was now bouncing around in her head. She turned on her laptop and scanned her email. As she did, a message arrived from Michael with the heading Contract. She opened the message and the attachment and scrolled down. Michael was right; it was a standard agreement.

They had partnered with a company called the Ma Shing Realty Corporation, which had secured a reasonably large plot of land on the Cotai Strip of Macau, the so-called Las Vegas of the East with casinos such as the Venetian and Wynn. The plan was to build a shopping centre to service the casino customers. Michael and Simon would be given space for a convenience store and a noodle shop and thirty percent ownership of the complex in return for their investment.

On balance, Ava thought it looked like a well thought-out deal. Macau was booming, its sixteen casinos generating more income than Las Vegas's hundred or more. She knew Chinese gamblers. Their money would be pumped into the tables, not hotel rooms, big-name boutiques, or expensive restaurants. Convenience stores and noodle shops were more their style, so the concept seemed sound. She checked the timeline. Ground should have been broken more than a year ago. Michael and Simon should already be occupying their spaces.

She went over the contract a second time, examining the wording, which was quite loose. There were no penalties if Ma Shing did not meet specified dates. There was also no exit provision for Michael. It didn't say that his money was locked in, but there was no clause in the contract to trigger taking it out.

If her father hadn't asked her to help and if Michael hadn't been her brother, she probably would have told him that his best option was to be patient and wait for the centre to get built. But they both seemed so distressed that Ava wondered if something else was in play.

And then a thought occurred to her: *Whose money is really at risk here?* She reached for the phone to call Richmond Hill and then paused. Her father had been vague the day before, saying only that Michael had a problem. What more was he likely to say? *Well, all I can do is ask,* she thought, as she punched in the number.

Her mother answered on the fourth ring.

"You're up so early?" Ava asked.

"Daddy has gone for a walk. I made him coffee and toast before he left."

"I wanted to talk to him about Michael."

Jennie Lee sighed. "Such a mess."

"Has Daddy told you what's going on?" Ava asked, realizing that maybe she didn't have to talk to him.

"I'm not sure that —"

"Michael just called me and then he sent me some information."

"So you should have everything you need."

"Except I can't make much sense of it."

"You need to speak to your father."

"I can't imagine that he'll tell me any more than he did yesterday."

"And that's not enough?"

"No. For one thing, I want to know if he's involved in this investment."

She could hear her mother inhaling and wondered if she was holding a cigarette to her lips or airing out some tension. "He's not involved — at least, not directly."

Ava felt a door opening and barged through. "Michael said he borrowed the money they put into it. Did Daddy secure the loan?"

"No, but he might as well have."

"What do you mean?"

"I don't know how much I should tell you."

"You should tell me absolutely everything if you want me to help."

"That's what I told your father, but he's a little embarrassed about the situation."

"Why?"

"He doesn't think Michael and his partner did proper due diligence. He said that, on his own, Michael is quite conservative and not much of a risk taker. His partner, Simon To, is another story. He's aggressive, rude, and at times too greedy. Your father thinks that Simon talked or pushed Michael into this thing."

"If the shopping centre gets built, it isn't that bad a deal," Ava said.

"But they don't have time to wait."

"What do you mean?"

"Your father said they've breached a loan covenant at the bank. The bank is demanding its money back. If they don't come up with it, the bank will put them out of business."

"Businesses go under all the time. If Daddy didn't secure the loan then they have no recourse with him."

"You don't understand," Jennie Lee said slowly. "They used Daddy's bank to get their loan. Even though he hasn't guaranteed anything, he expects the bank to start squeezing his business very soon. At the very least he thinks they will restrict his working line of credit. They could even refuse to renew the line of credit, and it's scheduled for a review in three months."

"He can find another bank."

"Yes, he probably can, but that doesn't address the depth of obligation he feels towards Michael," Jennie said, and paused. "Ava, there's no way that Marcus Lee will stand back and let his son's business go under. It would bring so much shame upon the entire family. He's spent his life building a reputation, and he couldn't bear to see it sullied. He'd sell everything he owns and give it to Michael rather than let him fail in such a public way."

Ava was taken aback by the passion and certainty in her mother's voice. She also noticed a tinge of anger. Michael Lee had no fans in Richmond Hill. "You do know that we're talking about twenty million U.S. dollars?" Ava asked.

"Enough money to ruin your father," Jennie said.

"And his ability to support the family?" Ava said.

"I don't want to think about that. Your father will do what he thinks is best. It won't change how I feel about him."

Ava thought about her mother and about the two aunties and half-siblings she had never met. "I guess I'm going to Hong Kong," she said quietly. "Even though I'm not sure there's anything I can do."

"You'll figure something out when you get there."

"Let's hope."

"Ava?"

"Yes, Mummy?"

"I am very proud of you."

Ava paused, not sure how to respond. "Look, tell Daddy I called and that I spoke to Michael and I'm heading over there."

"Will you phone him before you leave?"

Ava felt a presence behind her, and turned to see Maria standing naked in the doorway of the bedroom.

"No, Mummy, there isn't any need."

"But if he calls you, you won't tell him —"

"I won't say anything about what we discussed."

"I love you."

"Love you too," Ava said, and closed her phone.

"And I love you as well," Maria said.

Ava stared at her and smiled. "Isn't it time you got dressed for work?"

"You're leaving?"

"Yes, I'm going to Hong Kong. It's family business that I can't avoid."

"What time?" she said, her disappointment rippling across the room.

"Tonight."

Maria shook her head of thick, curly black hair. "Then I'm going back to bed," she said. "Join me."

READ MORE FROM THE AVA LEE SERIES BY IAN HAMILTON

"One of my favorite new mystery series, perfect escapism."
—Sarah Weinman, *National Post*

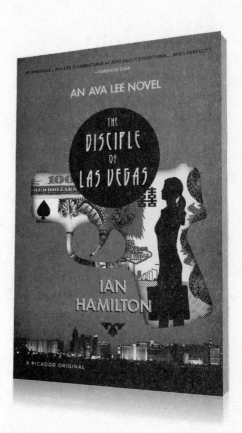

"Slick, fast-moving escapism reminiscent of Ian Fleming, with more to come in what shapes up as a high-energy, high-concept series." —*Booklist*

"A fascinating story of a hunt for stolen millions. And the hunter, Ava Lee, is a compelling heroine: tough, smart, and resourceful."
—Meg Gardiner, author of *The Nightmare Thief*

ISBN 978-1-250-03193-8
E-ISBN 978-1-250-03194-5

Buy the book:
www.picadorusa.com/thediscipleoflasvegas